Charmian Clift was born i⬚⬚⬚⬚⬚⬚⬚⬚⬚⬚⬚⬚⬚⬚⬚⬚⬚⬚⬚⬚⬚⬚.
When she was eight she filled an exercise book with poems and illustrations, but it was not until she was about twenty that she realised that she wanted to be a writer.

In 1946 she joined the staff of the Melbourne *Argus*, where she met the war correspondent George Johnston; they were married the following year. In 1948 the couple's collaborative novel, *High Valley*, won the *Sydney Morning Herald* prize, and they continued to collaborate after moving to London in 1951. In 1954 the family settled in Greece where, over the next ten years, Charmian Clift wrote the two travel books *Mermaid Singing* and *Peel Me a Lotus* and her two novels, *Walk to the Paradise Gardens* and *Honour's Mimic*.

After returning to Sydney in late 1964 Clift began writing a weekly newspaper column which quickly gained a wide and devoted readership. These essays have been collected in the anthologies *Images in Aspic*, *The World of Charmian Clift*, *Trouble in Lotus Land* and *Being Alone With Oneself*.

Charmian Clift died in 1969.

Also by Charmian Clift

Mermaid Singing
Peel Me a Lotus
Walk to the Paradise Gardens
Images in Aspic
The World of Charmian Clift
Trouble in Lotus Land
Being Alone With Oneself

By Charmian Clift and George Johnston

High Valley
The Sponge Divers

IMPRINT

Honour's Mimic

CHARMIAN CLIFT

Angus&Robertson
An imprint of HarperCollins*Publishers*

AN ANGUS & ROBERTSON BOOK
An imprint of HarperCollinsPublishers

First published in 1964 by Hutchinson & Co. Ltd
Republished in 1989 by William Collins Pty Ltd
This edition published in 1992 by
CollinsAngus&Robertson Publishers Pty Limited (ACN 009 913 517)
A division of HarperCollinsPublishers (Australia) Pty Limited
25-31 Ryde Road, Pymble NSW 2073, Australia

HarperCollinsPublishers (New Zealand) Limited
31 View Road, Glenfield, Auckland 10, New Zealand

HarperCollinsPublishers Limited
77-85 Fulham Palace Road, London W6 8JB, United Kingdom

National Library of Australia
Cataloguing-in-Publication data:

Clift, Charmian, 1923–1969

   Honour's Mimic

   ISBN 0 207 17560 8

   I. Title

A823.3

Cover illustration by Louise Tuckwell
Printed in Australia by Griffin Press

5 4 3 2 1
95 94 93 92

For Magda

. . . compared to this,
All honour's mimic, all wealth alchemy.

JOHN DONNE

AUTHOR'S NOTE

This story is fiction. The characters do not exist, nor did the incident occur, excepting in my imagination, although the book was occasioned by the actual face of a sponge diver which has haunted me for eight years.

1

Milly had been crying again.

She cried often in those wild late-winter days. Furtively in her bedroom after Demetrius had gone off to the sponge warehouse, and Aliki—observant, inquisitive, indefatigably garrulous—had dusted the handsome reproduction furniture and smoothed with envious hands the gold brocade expanse of the matrimonial bed; more openly in the new aseptic bathroom (which at least had a lock); and occasionally (and passionately) in the lovely alien garden, where banana-trees tossed ragged banners across the glowing citrus fruit and beyond a crepitant bamboo thicket a grove of young figs were already putting out leaves like tiny, green, hopeful hands.

She cried when storms purpled the gaunt shoulders of the mountains and came smoking down the valley. She cried when the house—so badly built—swayed in a gale, and lumps of plaster, obscenely white and hairy, jumped out at her from the walls. She cried when Aliki's second-cousin, Tasso the postman, delivered the loving parental letters and the bundles of glossy magazines—*The Queen, Vogue, The Field, Town and Country—to keep you in touch, dear.* She cried when the brand-new plumbing failed mysteriously to function (Aliki said it was the sea rushing up the pipes), when the gas bottle ran out in the middle of cooking (she could never calculate the time it ought to last), when she was dressing to receive a call from, or to make a call on, the innumerable black-garbed female relatives, when her brain went blank and she could not remember the simplest words of the language, like meat and tomorrow and thank you very much, and whenever, passing one of the ornate gilded mirrors that she and Demetrius had chosen in London, she looked into her cowed and blotted eyes and frantically sought to find her so recent vernal beauty.

'Milly love, don't worry about it so. It's the most natural thing in the world that you should cry buckets. I did both times. Just let go and have a really good howl and get it over.'

In the window-seat her sister-in-law, Kathy Bassett, soothed automatically, reluctant to withdraw her attention from the mountain she had been contemplating. It hung over the narrow valley like a petrified wave, still streaked with the churned yellow of an old turbulence and bearing on its crest the wreckage of a town which it appeared to be about to fling contemptuously into the valley below. The window-glass was flawed and by moving her head Kathy could make the mountain leap to the height of the Himalayas, shimmer down to a hillock, subside altogether into nothing but a plain. There had been a storm in the morning which left the valley steaming, but the air was washed into sublimity, and for the reaching out of her hand she felt that she might stroke the moving flank of the mountain or pluck from its precariousness one of the twelve little white chapels that glittered among the high ruins like celestial droppings. She could see the separate blue cubes of the village below it, and the trail scribbled lazily down the rock-face. The sound of bells came clearly, the agitated whickering of animals, the keening cry of a herdsman, and once an intermittent descending pinpricking of sharp light that she guessed to be a milk-can being carried down to the port on some shepherd's head.

For the first time in many months Kathy surprised in herself a feeling of anticipation. As soon as she was strong enough, she thought, she would climb that trail to the old Byzantine town and perhaps even go over the ridge—the shepherds' country— to the next valley, where Demetrius owned orange groves, and where, he said, there was plentiful water and ruins still more ancient. Kathy, Australian-born, was reverent of ruins.

'It is just as though the baby isn't mine at all,' Milly complained, still wiping tears away with the back of her hand. 'Every damned old aunt thinks she is entitled to tell me how to have it. And the way they watch me, Kathy! And *prod*! As if I'm a sow or something. Sometimes I've a good mind to pack up and go back to England and have the baby at home. Whatever Demetrius said. And if it wasn't for you being here now, I would, I really would, Kathy.'

'But I am here, goose.'

And Kathy turned her fox-brown eyes from the mountain to the incongruity of Milly on a glazed chintz sofa pouring Earl Grey's tea from a silver pot. Beside her a kerosene stove, all white enamel and chromium, sent up an odourless hazy column of heat to be thrown down into the room from the already cracked plaster ceiling; the glass drops of the chandelier were misted and damp and trembling, like a cluster of Milly's tears hanging there in reserve for some real catastrophe. There was a fireplace under a marble mantel, with brass dogs and a stand hung with pokers and tongs and brushes and new bellows. Unfortunately it would not draw at all: Demetrius was still furious with the workmen. The room was cluttered with a great many little tables and stools and 'nests' of things, Jacobean in character if not in fact, and draped at each of the three long windows (for the room was a corner one) were curtains of glazed chintz in a pattern of purple peacocks that matched the upholstery of the sofas and chairs and built-in window-seats. It was a room reminiscent of an English middle-class country house. Very reminiscent, in fact—and Kathy's mouth quirked in comprehension—of her mother-in-law's sitting-room in the house in Gloucestershire, which had probably impressed Demetrius as being 'typical'. How like him to have imported everything, even to the young dam on whom he would sire a half-English generation. Who will probably despise him, Kathy thought, and looked with a sudden, wide, still interest at her sister-in-law, who was already involved in that future which Demetrius envisaged.

Milly's face, a little puffy with pregnancy and blurred with tears, had that familiar trapped look of the young wife who has just discovered herself, to her bewilderment, to be completely enclosed within the aims of her husband. Kathy wondered for a moment if it would be worthwhile prodding Milly into making a stand for her own right to existence. She was ten years older than her husband's little sister and had always had great influence over her. But she felt herself to be still semi-detached from life, her own hold too tenuous and her resolution too weak to instigate acts of subversion or defiance. Besides, the arrow forking between the tender blonde brows pointed only to complaint, not rebellion, and there was no pride in the set of the narrow shoulders. Milly was made for submission. And as Demetrius came cat-footed through the door and across the room to join them, Kathy's own shoulders straightened and her hand went up to her shorn hair; half angry, half amused, she caught herself deliberately turning up the wick of her own identity.

Demetrius was a big, sleek, handsome man of twenty-seven, already mature, even greying a little in a crisp and becoming black-and-silver way at the temples and the rather long sideburns that emphasised his very small round ears. He wore, as always, clothes from Jermyn Street—an Irish tweed suit and a Viyella shirt with a knitted tie, hand-made walking shoes that were soft-looking and polished to a deep burning glow, cashmere socks of a woody green that repeated the discreet fleck in the tweed of his suit. Everything just brawny enough. There was a momentary small pleasure in observing that the jacket was unbuttoned and the pants looked too tight—he had put on weight since his marriage—but his heavy male sweetness was insistent: the room was charged with it. He has only to appear, Kathy thought, to turn us into a harem.

'Girls' talk?' The glossy black arches quirked forbearingly on the broad low forehead. The thick ivory eyelids drooped. He would decline to comment on the obvious evidence of Milly's recent emotion. As yet, thought Kathy, who knew that much of the man already.

'My God!' he said, peering into Milly's cup and shuddering. 'A real cafeteria brew. Loverly cuppa.' His accent was slight and lilting, but his voice pitched higher in English than it did in Greek. 'Really, Milly, you must instruct Aliki to make the tea properly. After all this time. And is there no hot water?'

4

Milly pushed herself upright with clumsy and touching dignity and went to find out.

Demetrius annexed her place on the sofa, embraced the window-seat and Kathy in the unhurried sureness of his full-lipped smile that showed the small, white, gappy teeth, and folded his hands. Cushioned hands, almost womanish except for the dark silky hair that grew even on his fingers: the nails were a pale lavender colour, clipped straight and rather long.

'Well, Kyria Katerina?' He used the Greek version of her name, half mocking, half provocative, giving it the respectful prefix and sing-song island intonation of Aliki, who was so obviously fascinated by Kathy's convalescent pallor, stretch trousers, endless cigarettes, and cropped red hair: Demetrius had said with amusement that as yet Aliki disbelieved in Kathy's sex entirely and had been found at the keyhole of the bathroom, apparently trying to elucidate such a mystery.

'Do you think you will like it here, Kathy? Milly has found it difficult, as I am sure you have gathered already, to adjust her romantic expectations to the reality of this poor and primitive place.'

The oriental deprecation. She knew that in spite of his anglophilia he was sensitive on the subject of his native island, and she said warmly: 'I think it is the most interesting and exciting place I have ever seen, and I can't wait to explore a bit. It was good of you both to ask me to come to you. I am very grateful, Demetrius.' She meant it too, although she had come, in fact, only because she might as well come as not, and both the doctor and her husband Irwin had urged the trip with that depressing cheerfulness to which she had become resigned in the past months. She was, she knew, still utterly dispensable. So she was to stay with Milly and Demetrius for six months, when Irwin would come out also for a few weeks' holiday before taking her back to England.

Demetrius said courteously: 'The gratitude is ours, Kathy. Heaven knows, Milly needs a companion. She has been lonely here. And she needs a steadying influence just now. At least

5

until the child is born and steadies her willy-nilly. You would be doing me a great favour, Kathy, if you could manage to impart to her a little of your own . . .' and his full black eyes held hers for a moment before he smiled briefly and rather sadly and looked down again at his folded hands, '. . . serenity,' he said.

She was amused at his obtuseness in defining her like that. If she was still it was only because she was afraid to move. And certainly she had no intention of forming an alliance with Demetrius.

'Milly is very young.'

'My grandmother married at fifteen. My mother at seventeen.'

She supposed them to be represented among the family photographs ranked in tiers about the ikon box over the farther door . . . staring sepia men with curling sepia moustaches and faded flat-cheeked women who peered, unexpectant, from their nun-like headdresses. She tried to imagine them as brides. Grave, circumspect girls she thought they would have been, with gold coins at their throats and ears and soft strong eyes that saw clearly and accepted the weight of the responsibilities they would have seen ahead of them. Responsibilities familiar by precept and example since childhood.

Not so Milly. Pretty petted Milly, the family darling, born fifteen years after her brother and treated like a favourite toy, who had laughed and pouted and dreamed and danced her inconsequential way through debs' delights, little modelling jobs, minor TV roles, bit parts in films, and the thousand easy compliments of the inferior men who had courted her, until, out of her depth with a real one—and such a handsome one, so rich, so incredibly exotic—she had fallen in love, and had never doubted but that she would live happily ever after. ('An *island*, Kathy, *imagine*! Isn't it like a story? Oh, aren't Englishmen *dull*! I don't mean darling Win, of course,' she had added hurriedly, 'because, after all, you married him, dear Kathy, so he must be different.' But her glamour-filled eyes had been commiserating.) Pretty petted Milly, hurrying back egg-shaped, swollen-footed, and flustered from the kitchen with Aliki following, bearing the pot of hot water.

Demetrius permitted them to serve him: Milly anxious, guilty already, and Aliki a polished brown gargoyle from which poured a torrent of sickle-shaped words. She wore a white kerchief like a wimple about her face, a white apron over her high stomach, and under her skirt—voluminous, greenish black with age, ruched intricately at the waist—a red flannel petticoat which whisked about her dwarfed legs with every wrathful movement. She also had innumerable relations who inhabited the kitchen daily. Milly, with reason, lived in a permanent state of intimidation.

'She only pretends not to understand me. I wish you would speak to her, Demetrius.'

Aliki, in full spate, had retreated through the door. They could hear her banging pots and muttering to whichever cousins or aunts were waiting there for a glimpse of the new foreign lady.

'If I spoke to her, pet, you would lose what little authority you have. You must be firmer. Or try to sort out those terminations.' Suddenly indulgent, he laughed at her, ruffling her hair. 'Milly's Greek is something to marvel at,' he said to Kathy in real wonder.

Demetrius spoke four languages fluently, and was truly perplexed that his wife should find such difficulty in learning one. Finally he had put it down to her Englishness, and had even made it a secret source of gratification. Like a hallmark proving her to be the genuine article. The English were notoriously bad at languages.

2

He had decided to marry Milly at eleven o'clock on a winter's morning in the bucket seat of a brand-new green Bristol parked by the Tower at Broadway where on that day the North Cotswold Hunt was meeting. In his pocket had been a letter from his Uncle Paul which indicated that his father's illness was a good deal more serious than they had supposed and that it seemed likely that Demetrius, as the heir, would have to be recalled from the London office to take over the sponge business at source. He had at that time not told Milly of the letter.

It was his first week-end with her family in the country, and in a special sense it had been a revelation to him, as had Milly also, about whom his previous ideas and speculations (engendered in various London night-spots to which she and her crowd were addicted) had been much more directly carnal. Milly in her London role of model girl was one thing; Milly in her family context was apparently something else entirely. As also—and his thoughts had burrowed secretly through a series of impressions whose impact his calm and heavy face did not for a second betray— was a young Greek, however wealthy, handsome, and correctly equipped for a country week-end. (It had been Kathy, so very beautiful then, who had given him a wry look through the bewildering beef-red faces braying at one another over Lady Bassett's mahogany, a look conspiratorial almost, as if to say, 'You and I, poor foreigner, are alien here.')

The meet. His breath steaming weirdly across the windscreen. The suave Pinks oscillating under the elms' black arms. The polished hooves treading down the frost-spiked grass with a savage delicacy. His expensively gloved hands were still on the wheel of the expensively sleek car, and no tremor disclosed his physical fear of those terrible horses or the shiver that lightly touched his heart as Milly, wearing her young loveliness like a bright morning banner, moved confidently among them, familiar among the rearing and plunging and creaking of leather, tilting her head to a lifted stirrup-cup, stooping to caress the liver-coloured head of a fearsome slavering hound. He decided that she was almost certainly still a virgin.

Afterwards, with the sound of the horn still plangent among the Cotswold Hills, they had drunk mild-and-bitter at the Mount in Stanton, and Milly had talked hunting and horses with farming men in leggings and flat caps who had looked at him contemplatively from their light northern eyes and politely made room for him at the fire before they turned again to the Squire's daughter who belonged to them in spite of this foreign chap. It was the same excluding politeness he had experienced at her parents' table. Obscurely, it satisfied him. And standing there in his correct country tweeds, listening to the blurred and buzzing responses to her inquiries of wives and children, fields and crops and flocks and lambing, he had suddenly turned his head and looked long and deliberately into her English face that was as lovely and as empty as a flower and had seen the gentian eyes darken with half-terrified desire and heard her voice shake and falter, and he had known a deep sense of triumph.

(And again it had been Kathy who had supported the marriage against the disguised dismay of Milly's brother Irwin and the polite outrage of the chilling parents, who in the end had had to give Milly what she wanted, as they always had. Kathy with that expression of wry expectancy that disturbed him, the fox-brown eyes examining him with frank curiosity. 'The barriers are unjust and humiliating, Demetrius. But they are strong.' For a second she had glanced towards Irwin, and Demetrius had had a peculiar impression, despite the alert eyes, of a boredom that was nearly grief.)

3

'Irwin will miss you, Kathy,' he said gently out of his gratification.

'Oh, Win'll be all right. He's very busy with the spring list of books and all those literary luncheons and TV programmes. And Mrs Dapp pampers him shamelessly when I'm not there to stop her. Win has a way with those motherly women. Their hearts go out to his big blue eyes. Don't they, Milly? Actually he is perfectly capable of looking after himself, and I daresay this break will be as welcome a holiday to him as it is to me. And it's not as though I've been of much help for quite some time. At least he doesn't have the boys under his feet.'

'You're going to have trouble with Mummy about ever getting them back again,' said Milly, with wistfulness.

'Trouble with them, too.' Saying it, she was conscious again of that hopeless feeling of incapacity. Her husband and her children seemed as remote as travelling companions who had journeyed on while she had disembarked at a midway port. 'You can't imagine,' she said, with more braveness than they knew, 'how far away it all seems.' Carefully she rubbed the misted window-pane clean again and looked out at the mountain. Bronze and violet now, and rippled in closer. The twelve little chapels jumped in a vehemence of white and above them an eagle hung on stiff pinions like a scratch on the sky.

Demetrius frowned. Milly hurriedly conveyed four lumps of sugar to his cup and stirred it, her tongue pink and childish between her milky teeth.

'Then we must make quite sure you are well when Irwin comes for you. And fattened up a bit. Milly, pass the cakes to Kathy. And eat something yourself. You smoke too much, I think, Kathy.'

10

'Perhaps,' Kathy said, and refused the cakes and took another cigarette from the white-and-red Ethnos packet. She waited until Demetrius rose and lit it for her, a satisfaction of which she was instantly ashamed. *Why* do I do things like that? she thought. But the curious little current of antagonism that leapt between them was sharp and definite. She tingled with it, not quite unpleasantly. Milly obediently ate cakes. Little clouds of snow-white sugar puffed around her mouth and fingers and settled on the front of her blue maternity dress.

'You'll have to try the locally made ones. Ten for a drachma and guaranteed to smell the house out.' Demetrius smiled at her without rancour and lit for himself a cigarette from the silver box on the table—Churchman's: she had brought him her allowance of two hundred. He dropped his hand to Milly's stomach, which he caressed with the pride of ownership. The room was mazy now with the soporific warmth of the stove and repeated endlessly in the facing mirrors. Framed in gilt garlands, Milly and Demetrius on the chintz sofa behind the tea-tray recurred, apparently, into eternity—an unanswerable exposition of domestic felicity. On the farther wall, unreflected, the ranks of the family bore witness, and the stern and ancient faces of saints looked out from a smoulder of crimson and blue and gold where dragons writhed and unbelievers bowed before the swords of righteousness. In the kitchen Aliki sang a high harsh song.

He said: 'I meant to take you sightseeing today, Kathy. For what the sights are worth. But those oafs in the warehouse haven't finished the German orders yet, and I cannot trust them to get anything done without supervision. With Lazarus and Paul in Athens, there's no one to stand in, even for a few hours.'

'Please! Don't even think of it. I haven't come to be a nuisance. There's no earthly reason why I shouldn't go exploring with Milly. Or by myself, for that matter.'

'No, no, no. We cannot have you wandering about unescorted. Not done. Milly, why don't you take Kathy up to visit old Aunt Polymnia? It's high time you paid a courtesy call.'

'Oh . . . *Demetrius*!' Milly sat bolt upright on a wail of dismay.

'Yes. Yes. Come now, pet, it is a beautiful day. Almost like spring. And you need the exercise. Vassos said you were not to get sluggish. So no more excuses, now. Cheerfulness, my Milly. Cheerfulness and brisk walks.'

'Oh, honestly, do I *have* to? You can't imagine, Kathy, what a dreadful old sybil she is! Dreadful! She has *claws*! And she brews up ghastly things in an iron kettle and forces me to drink them, and she mutters incantations and makes mysterious signs over my stomach. Why must I go, Demetrius? She frightens me so much that I'm sure the baby will come out with two heads. I really am frightened . . .'

Demetrius smiled with gentle amusement. 'I have never met anyone with Milly's genius for putting a crumb on the table and climbing Mount Everest on it. In reality, Kathy, this Polymnia is a kind old island woman who acts as midwife and healer to the poorer people of the island. She was my nurse for a time when I was a child, so we give her the courtesy title of aunt. Of course you must go, Milly. As I have explained to you many times before, there are certain family duties allotted to every one of us. I realise that often these are boring and irksome, but they are inescapable, and you will save yourself hours of stewing, minx, if you accept that. Besides, you must consider our guest.' His eyes, ancient in their long almond shape, soft, moist, enigmatic, rested on Kathy. 'I know that it would interest Kathy to visit such an old island woman. Picturesque, eh? The genuine article. If you feel well enough, that is?' For it seemed to him suddenly that against the misted window-glass Kathy's pale face, with its sharp bones and deeply shadowed eye-sockets, took on the likeness of a skull. 'Are you all right, Kathy? Does your head hurt?'

She shook it experimentally and gave him a wary smile. 'All right. A goose walking over my grave. No, it doesn't hurt now. Not often, anyway.' But she put her hand up and her fingers moved cautiously through the cropped hair. The hard raised scar was healed now, but still tender enough to remind her that it was only lately that she had taken the first steps back from the borderland. It was a time, or place, she looked back on in shuddering wonder, and could not quite shake off. She had not escaped death, entirely.

'Do you know, Kathy, I've never properly understood how the accident happened,' Milly said curiously. 'Irwin didn't ever really give details in his letters.'

Kathy was rubbing at the window-pane again and did not turn her head. 'A moment of aberration. I put my foot on the accelerator instead of the brake.' (. . . The elms beating up in the headlights' translucent green and gold and crashing past like surf and the old forgotten exhilaration singing through her like madness and her foot of its own volition—yes, it was, it was! she couldn't have meant—stamped down on the accelerator and she rushed head-on into the rushing singing surf of light . . .) 'How about this visit, Milly? I've never met a witch, genuine or otherwise.'

'That's the ticket!' said Demetrius, and Milly pouted.

Her mouth was red and damp and lightly powdered with sugar. 'You will never want to again, either. Just wait. Yes, yes, Demetrius, I'll go. Don't *bully* me . . .' She was, after all, complacent with his caresses. Even a little smug. Kathy had lost her looks terribly since the accident. She found herself in the pleasantly novel situation of feeling a little bit sorry for her sister-in-law. Besides, Kathy was only married to Irwin.

Demetrius said decisively: 'Well, girls. This is not buying the baby a new bonnet. I'll walk as far as the warehouse with you if you both hurry. Wrap up well, though. The sunshine is deceptive yet.'

The flowery guest bedroom, white-shuttered and cold after the drawing-room, was still impersonal, although Aliki had unpacked the cases and placed on the bedside table the three-leaved leather case displaying the photographs of Kathy's husband and sons. The two boys were smiling at her with her own eyes, set a little too closely to the bridge of the nose and tilted under short sharp questioning eyebrows, but Irwin's well-bred face was carrying on its usual policy of concealment

13

and refrained from any sort of comment at all: even his moustache looked like a disguise. I'll write tonight, she thought. Or tomorrow. At the glass she carefully applied lipstick and brushed her hair with wary strokes. It was beginning to recover some of its old gloss and rippled under the bristles, but the deep sorrel colour was brindled lightly with silver now, like an animal's pelt, and the lipstick looked clownish on her thin sick face. She rubbed it off again, and tried to remember what she had looked like before the accident.

'Will you grow it again, Kathy?' Milly entered rather shyly, and well wrapped up as instructed. She was going to be huge in a month or so.

'I don't know. No, probably not. These white bits would look rather grisly dangling about. I wish they'd had the decency to grow in svelte streaks. I must say I like yours long, though. Very womanly and becoming.'

'It's a bore, but Demetrius doesn't want me to cut it again. He loathes short hair on a woman.'

'Most of them do. It's a strong mystique.' Kathy made a face at her own cropped head. 'Well, I'm ready. Is he cursing me for taking so long?'

'No, no. I mean, it's all right. Don't hurry.' In the looking-glass the blue eyes (so like Irwin's) avoided Kathy's. 'Do forgive me, Kathy, but I don't think you ought to wear trousers out of the house.' She flushed, in anger, or perhaps bashfulness: she had been little sister for too long. 'They live in the Dark Ages here. Really they do.'

'Oh?' said Kathy, looking at her intently, and then, cheerfully: 'Yes, of course. Thank you for warning me.' She gave Milly a reassuring hug—poor Milly!—and changed as quickly as she could into a pleated skirt and tights. The instruction, patently, was from Demetrius. *Touché* for the cigarette business, perhaps.

'Kathy . . . darling Kathy . . . I'm so *glad* you're here!'

They moved together down the stairs and along the wide hallway. At the end of it Aliki held open the grilled door on the still, heavy figure of Demetrius, waiting in sunshine among the tossing orange-trees to escort them—his foreign women, one for each arm—through the envious and admiring town.

4

The modern town, which was big for the Aegean, had grown around the harbour, where the port had been since the beginning, facing south, away from the autumn gales. The black ships for Troy had put out from there, and the galleys for Salamis, and later Saracen pirates had sheltered between those two appalling cliffs that hurtled from air to water. The town had been inland then, and prudently high, although the pirates had left it inviolate in exchange for sanctuary. It had taken an earthquake of unparalleled destructiveness to force the population down into the valley. Apathy, perhaps, had kept it there at first. Later, convenience. For by this time its trade was exclusively with ships and the sea.

Stumps of piers, like decayed teeth. And ships. Two hundred and more of them, built of good Samian pine in two distinct types—the broad supply schooners, floating wide and open like split melons, and the smaller, leaner diving-caïques, rather shabby now in winter, but graceful and workmanlike riding at their moorings.

A wide waterfront, a lopsided crescent in shape, paved with limestone blocks and crumbling badly at the sea edge. In the centre of it the Twenty-fifth of March statue, white marble, vaguely cubistic in feeling. Behind, a fringe of salt-trees, hung with tassels of drying octopus and crusted with hen droppings, and marking off the pavement in front of the taverns, the bakehouses, the coffee-shops, the clean barbering parlours. From the waterfront lanes ran back like veinous branches through the town, lined with other taverns, other bakehouses, other coffee-shops and barbering parlours. There were, besides, some dozen little cigarette factories, various workshops and ship chandlers, grocery stores, and a few shops displaying general merchandise—seamen's rubber boots, black peaked caps, cheap blue jerseys, strings of clumsy shoes soled with old motor tyres.

The residential section of the town, although here and there involved in a propinquity with commerce, for the most part lay behind the waterfront and between the lanes—simple cubes washed white or ochre or blue, which spread out over the flatland or were riveted in tiers—God knows how—to the cliff-faces that sheltered the harbour. There were many churches—almost as many churches as taverns—for the women were pious, a good deal alone, and often afraid. There was also a hospital, a police station, a post office, a covered market place, a primary school and a gymnasium, a town hall, and a number of huge barracks-like warehouses, one of which bore the sign, 'Casopédes and Heirs, Sponge Merchants'. Excepting only for the warehouses these public buildings had been erected during the period of the Italian occupation and were, in consequence, more elaborate than their functions warranted. They might even have altogether destroyed the severe harmonies of the town if they had not by this time faded to the colour of their rocky background: also, they were mostly falling to bits.

It was a town almost nude in its simplicity: although occasionally, and sometimes by the alchemy of light and texture and proportion even entirely, beautiful.

Aunt Polymnia's house was high on the cliffside above the harbour, in that area without a name that was referred to only as Epano, that is to say, Above. The town's skimpy electricity supply gave out a hundred feet below, and any attempt at paving. Here there were only goat trails scribbled through the clay, gouged-out watercourses choked with boulders, and crude elevations of whitewashed rocks to serve as steps. The back wall of every house in this area was the mountain itself, enduring, certainly, but damp also in the winter months. The women kept tins of charcoal burning at the ends of their rooms, and the bedshelf was invariably built at the other, but the infant mortality rate was far higher here than elsewhere in the town, and from early

17

middle age almost everybody developed swollen joints like rotten potatoes.

It was a vertiginous place, what with the mountain rushing up above and the square or oblong roof-tops rushing away below, and the harbour at the bottom so flat and small, with the boats spread like a flock of mallards come in to rest. The whole sponging fleet lay there that winter afternoon, but from such a height the boats seemed frail things, vulnerable, not to be relied on. The warehouse of Casopédes and Heirs lay by the water like an abandoned cardboard box spilling its contents right down to the sea's edge, where a long line of men and boys danced strangely in the winter shallows, treading the dark juices out of raw sponges.

Demetrius, foreshortened into squatness, waved up at them again, and went inside.

Kathy said, 'But why did Demetrius build the house in the valley when he could have had this?' She could see as far as Turkey.

They were both gasping from the climb, and surrounded by a swarm of children—grinning boys with shaved bullet skulls and thick candles of mucus hanging from scabby nostrils, little stick-limbed girls, silent and absorbed, who twirled always closer and closer, tossing long matted streamers of hair. Outside their doorways, where geraniums grew in kerosene tins, women squatted over smaller tins containing charcoal, stirring cooking-pots, and goats and hens foraged among sodden vegetable peelings and piles of rusted cans. The mountainside smelled of beans stewing in olive oil.

'Look at the neighbours,' said Milly, who was distributing greetings to the women in a placatory sort of way. 'Only the very poorest classes live up here. Divers' families mostly. People like that. Then there's practically no water. We have wells down there, and, besides, there was the garden already grown. Demetrius only had to pull down the ruin. Anyway, you'll see, the family stick together like glue.'

Kathy looked down on the town, spreading back from the busy waterfront to the point where the valley bulged obligingly,

18

as if to accommodate the group of solid Victorian mansions set within their high walls, and the new white villa which Demetrius had built for his English bride. She appreciated the point of the water and the gardens, but still thought it curious that when the sea had so splendidly prospered the generations of Casopédes they should choose to live with their backs to it.

'But you'd learn to fly if you lived up here, Milly. Almost certainly. Yes, certainly!' And she stretched her long neck up and spread her arms wide. The children all burst into laughter and began to flap their own arms wildly, and some of the bolder boys began launching themselves from the tops of boulders in comic parodies of flight.

'See! *They* know,' Kathy said, and the women in the doorways giggled, hiding their mouths in the folds of their headscarves.

'Kathy! They'll think you are mad!' But Milly, too, was exhilarated. Her cheeks were vivid, her hair blew out from its combs in glittering tendrils, and her coat blew also, exposing the curve of her pregnancy. She was brilliant in that barren setting, all gold and roses; the little girls twirled closer and closer, longing to touch her, and the boys shrieked and leaped and flapped in a frenzy all the way to Aunt Polymnia's door.

Aunt Polymnia's house was a white cube balanced among bare boulders. It was filled with other children, and apparently with drama also, for a woman sat sobbing with her head in her apron, and Aunt Polmnia (ancient, vulpine, and certainly witch-like in that indistinct interior) crouched over a screaming baby, rubbing its leg with something from a jam tin. The room reeked with a spiced and rancid smell.

'See what I mean?' said Milly out of the corner of her mouth, and stepped forward resignedly into explosions of welcome and explanation.

Aunt Polymnia, upright, seemed no bigger than the swarming children, but compelling in her shroudy muffling of skirts and shawls. And authoritative. Kathy felt that strongly. She stood in the doorway and subjected herself to the old woman's scrutiny. She had steel-rimmed spectacles secured to her black headscarf by a piece of dirty pink elastic, but these sat low on the saddle of her nose and she looked over them. Her eyes were dim, but crafty—the flesh fell down from under them in folds, stiff-looking, like stained canvas.

The sobbing woman took her head out of the apron to chivvy the children. A little girl brought rush-seated chairs and placed them ceremoniously in the centre of the room. An older girl picked up the baby (now convulsed with hiccups) and began to rock and shush in a practised way. Milly, surrounded, made faces at Kathy to come in.

And yet she did not move. Could not move, in fact, although she could not have said why. She continued to stand in the doorway facing the dim balloons of faces that bobbed at her under hanging bundles of herbs and sooty rafters until Aunt Polymnia pushed her way through the children and formally advanced and took Kathy's hand in both her own flecked and twisted ones. Her hands had a curiously unpleasant feel. Like leather rubbed with mutton fat or dubbin, Kathy thought, and for a second saw hard Australian sunlight and slip-rail fences and smelt the horses and the blue smoke. Then her hand was turned out to the light where the young escort still crowded, entranced.

Her palm stretched out to the fans of downcast eyes, revealed in the sunlight as supple and muscular, with fern-fronds of tracery, a small broken blister from a cigarette burn, and a tremor of long standing not yet under control. What prognosis there? The children were watchful, interested, as at a known ritual imperfectly understood, and they all hissed slightly when the old woman reached up to pull Kathy's bright head down to the myriad folds of her shrouded one and wipe her spittle on Kathy's brow and blow three times on her mouth and make the sign of the cross.

Then she sighed, apparently from some deep emotion—it could have been compassion, or only, perhaps, the unconscious wheezings of age— and led Kathy into the room.

'Do I pass?' Kathy smiled, but felt a little uneasy nevertheless. She would have liked to ask what, if anything, Aunt Polymnia had seen in her hand, and why she had blown on her mouth.

20

The old woman's breath had been startlingly horrible and familiar; cold stale stirrings from the grey no-time no-land that still called Kathy back in fear and sleep. I am still sick, she thought. And fanciful. That is all.

But Milly muttered with conviction: 'It gives me the *creeps*! For heaven's sake come and sit down, Kathy, and don't even *look* encouraging. We shall get it over as fast as we can.'

'What about this baby?'

It had begun to cry again, weakly, but from obvious pain. The leg protruding from the dirty wrappings was swollen badly and dark with bruises. The child's wan nursemaid looked at them dolorously, rocking and shushing as fast as she could, but Aunt Polymnia's interest had been transferred absolutely to her visitors, and at a sharp scolding word the girl pulled the baby's wrappings closer and carried it out of the house. Kathy expected the mother to protest at this, or to follow, but the woman continued to sit and nod apologetically and make embarrassed fluttering movements with her hands.

The ladies were not to be concerned. It was nothing. Nothing. Babies fell out of hammocks, into fires, children fell out of windows, off roof-tops, down wells, over precipices. Bam! Bam! Bam! It was nothing at all. Things happened. Things were always happening with children . . . (Or so Kathy understood.)

The woman was small and thin and worn, of an age impossible to determine. She wore a limp cotton dress with a shrunk and matted cardigan buttoned over a stomach as round and hard as a football. Over the stomach a plastic apron, quite new. Her head was coifed carelessly in a soiled scarf, originally white. Kathy, with a fresh and interested eye, noted these details and dismissed them as immaterial. Everything about the woman was subordinate to the fact of an entire set of stainless-steel teeth, which glittered marvellously every time she opened her mouth and gave Kathy an uneasy sense of the miraculous, as if the silver ikon above the bedshelf was making pronouncement.

Aunt Polymnia bustled and squawked, bringing saucers of jam on a plastic tray, and little thimbles of strega and glasses of cold well water, and finally a three-legged tin with a grey cone of charcoal which she placed precisely in the centre of the splintered plank floor. The remaining children had been herded to the railed bedshelf at the end of the room, where they crouched, whispering and giggling and peering, like dwarfs in a dark gallery, while Aunt Polymnia wheezed and cackled and questioned and Milly made her halting answers and Kathy turned her spoon in the jam and the worn woman smiled her ikonic smile. Soon the bundles of herbs hanging from the rafters began to stir in the heat from the charcoal tin, and little wafts of their outlandish scents blew about to dispel the lingering rancid smell. Plates glimmered bone-white on bright blue shelves.

'They are giving me the third degree on you,' Milly said. 'Hoo-blooming-ray! She won't have time to persecute me. You are a blessing, Kathy.'

And Kathy, locked out by the opacity of the language, and also more than a little spellbound by the strangeness of her surroundings, wondered very much indeed how she would appear in Milly's explanations. Katherine Bassett, aged thirty-one, wife of Irwin Bassett, publisher, of London, mother of two sons, convalescent after an automobile accident . . . where was she, Kathy, in that?

'Katerina,' Aunt Polymnia repeated, and the other woman after her. 'Eeeeh!' they said. 'Katerina,' and smiled at her in recognition of the familiar name.

'Damn!' said Milly. 'I can't think of the word for sister-in-law.' She giggled. 'Look at their faces, Kathy. I know I've made you into something incestuous!'

'What else do they want to know?'

'Oh, marriage and all that. Whether you have girls or children. Girl babies aren't classified as children here.'

Reassured on the sex of Kathy's, Aunt Polymnia made three approving spits in her direction, and three more at Milly's stomach.

'Filthy old thing!' said Milly. The ikonic woman now became voluble. 'She has eight,' Milly translated in disgust. 'As if we want to know. And two dead. Honestly, if you cut one of these

22

divers' wives open you'd find her full of *eggs*!'

The woman smiled dazzlingly and leaned forward and laid her hand on Milly's stomach and then on her own.

'And another on the way. Doesn't it make you *sick*?'

The woman sighed and shook her head and pointed at the ceiling.

'God sends them,' said Milly, giggly again, and a drop of spittle ran down Aunt Polymnia's chin and she cackled, wiping the end of her headscarf over the top of her glasses. Kathy felt that only Aunt Polymnia's respect for them as gentry restrained the old woman from making a lewd gesture, and even while she was thinking this the younger woman did make a gesture that was quite unmistakable, and repeated it, her eyes blackly avid on Kathy and her voice shrill in query.

'I *think*,' said Milly, hurriedly and confusedly, 'she is trying to ask you how you manage to have only two children after ten years of marriage.'

'Why don't you tell her? Somebody should.'

'Oh, *Kathy*!' said Milly, and turned bright pink.

The children snuffled and whispered behind the bedrail, secretive and absorbed, dwarfs from the background of a Velasquez group. Aunt Polymnia held her paunch and bubbled and spat like a boiling kettle. And across the charcoal tin the miraculous silver mouth shrilled louder and louder, desperate of communication, and the swollen hands with their dirty soft ragged nails despairingly pantomimed the unspeakable mystery of the beginning of life.

It seemed to Kathy afterwards that the diver had been flung into the room on the wave of pity that surged through her heart and broke, scattering woman and children like so many splinters and spars and leaving—stranded, confused, the violence knocked out of him—this man.

His upraised fist fell to his side, and a curse, bitten off in the moment of delivery, changed foolishly on his mouth to a drunken smile. Behind him the children crept down from the bedshelf and suddenly scattered out into the sunlight like a handful

23

of flung grain. The woman cowering against the wall uncovered her face and twisted it into an ingratiating grimace. Aunt Polymnia began furiously to scold, setting the chairs to rights. He lurched and stumbled taking one.

'You all O.K. here?' he said.

He was a slight man, a very drunk man, with a thin white exhausted face under a black peaked cap, and nervous narrow hands. He wore a seaman's blue jersey with a pattern of moss stitch and cables, and patched black pants tucked into high rubber boots. His belt had a silver snake for a buckle, and there was a gold seal ring on his finger. The stubble that showed on his jaw was pale and metallic-looking. His eyes—long, oblique, and at this moment confused—were pale also, but curiously so, as if the colour had been drained out of them suddenly once; in anger it could have been, or even fright.

He sat with a studied insolence, his head back-arched and the drunken smile still on his mouth, while Aunt Polymnia clucked on—but automatically now, already pouring the welcoming thimble of strega. The woman against the wall curved her mouth in pride and indulgence and made explanatory signs, circling her head with a furtive crown and rubbing her forefingers together.

'That Irini. That's my missus.' He jerked his head in indication, absorbed for the moment in the task of wriggling two fingers into the pocket of his skin-tight black pants to extract a flat tin. It had a blonde in a bikini printed on the lid. He offered it triumphantly. 'You like to smoke?'

Kathy liked to smoke very much indeed. She had been wanting to smoke for the last half-hour.

'Are these the locally made ones?' She smiled at him uncritically, testing his climate.

'Sure. They make plenty cigarettes here. Good stuff. Strong. You try one.'

'I'd like to,' said Kathy, but Milly looked frightened and despairing, and refused with an assumption of hauteur. She knew the nickname she had been given on the island. Lookoomi; that is to say, Turkish Delight. The diver grinned and screwed up one pale unfocused eye in derision. His teeth were broken, but white and strong.

'Just the job, eh?' From the other pocket he produced with the same difficulty a Ronson lighter. After a few attempts he managed to light the cigarettes. 'Good stuff, eh?' he said. 'Strong.' And beat his chest lightly with a closed fist.

'Yes. It's good. I like it.' She did. The taste was light, rank, and wild. 'Is the tobacco grown here?'

'Growing *here*?' His mouth twisted around the cigarette end, tipping it up so the smoke drifted like a veil over the top of his face. '*Here*!' He rubbed his hand across his chin, contacted the cigarette as if by accident, withdrew it from his mouth, and stared at it.

'No?' asked Kathy, smiling at him.

He inclined his head backwards, slowly, with deliberation, and clucked his tongue reprovingly.

Kathy laughed. 'All right,' she said. 'Forgive my ignorance. I gather the tobacco is *not* grown here.'

The women came back to their places around the charcoal tin, but silently, careful not to interrupt the male in his designs. His wife Irini sat forward on her chair, glittering mysteriously as she gazed with open mouth from her husband to Kathy and back again. Aunt Polymnia settled into the muffling of her greasy shawls and worked her jaws in the folds of her headscarf: she seemed resentful.

'I think . . .' Milly began uncertainly.

'You know what's growing here?' the diver said. 'Stones. Plenty stones. Stones growing everywhere. Plenty—plenty stones.'

'Kathy . . .'

'And you know what else?' He winked through the cigarette smoke and leaned forward to whisper confidentially. 'Bended legs. Sure. Growing here like trees. Every second feller growing one bended leg. Sometime two. Like this, see?' He rose from the chair and began lurching and hobbling around the room. The women shrieked and crossed themselves. Aunt Polymnia spat at him savagely, three times, and burst into vituperation.

25

'Kathy ...' Milly hissed again in desperation. They rose together, smiling politely in unison. The diver's mouth twisted arrogantly, watching them. Expensive women, sleeking their skirts over their thighs. Kathy, turning towards Aunt Polymnia, flipped her half-smoked cigarette into the charcoal tin.

'Here!' The diver was fumbling in his pocket. 'Here!' And thrust the tin at her. 'You take them. I got plenty. Plenty!'

'But I can't take all your cigarettes.' She half turned to look at him. She was puzzled and uncertain. He stood there shaking, waving the cigarette tin at her. But why? she thought in panic. What have we done to him? And as she stood there in astonishment, trying to grapple with the seething rage of the man (and would afterwards remember, with a curious detached pleasure, that they were exactly of a height), he suddenly emptied all the cigarettes on to the floor and ground them into the splintered planking with the heel of his boot.

She said, ignoring it, making her voice easy, 'Would you ask your wife if I may come and see her one day?'

He shrugged and hunched down into his jersey. His face under the shiny black peak of the cap looked almost luminous. A defiant face. Intractable. Unaccepting.

'Kath*eeee*!'

'Yes,' Kathy said, and hesitated for a moment. Then turned to the protestations of Aunt Polymnia, who kissed and crossed her. Irini touched her forehead to them both and stealthily stroked the expensive stuff of their sleeves.

They stepped out into the squashed crimson ball of the setting sun; into a torrent of running rose oils that poured off the shuddering spines of mountains retreating into night like herds of fleeing elephants. The harbour lay below them thick and still and dark, like a little pool of spilt blood.

They shivered going down and stumbled among the boulders. On a level with the green dome of St Nicholas the bells began to crash. On the opposite cliff-face St Stephanos responded, then I-Papandi, St Mummas, George and Demetrius, and the Holy Trinity. The evening was wild with bells.

Doors and windows throbbed gently with lamplight. There were families grouped, intimate, glimpsed for a second biblically breaking bread. A hand raising a blue platter. An aureoled head, bent. A child placing a lamp. Kathy was choked with it. Near tears.

'Now you know how the other half lives,' Milly said. 'Now, honestly darling, do you blame me for not wanting to go up there? I mean, *really*! I daresay I could put up with Aunt Polymnia, but I don't see why I should be inflicted with any drunken diver who cares to gatecrash the party! Some of them are no better than wild animals. Darling, how could you just stand there and be so *calm* about it!'

'Black ignorance. Waiting to see which way the cat would jump. Milly, isn't there a clinic on the island where the mothers could take sick babies?'

'There is a hospital. They just won't go. You talk about black ignorance! They're steeped in it. Uggh! I always feel I need a bath after one of these sessions. As though I have *picked up* something.'

Kathy pulled Milly's hand through her arm and patted it. *I have* picked up something, she thought. One's emotional resistance was lowered dangerously after sickness. Or perhaps Irwin's old accusation was true—she was low-life prone. But she wanted to know about these people. She did. She did.

'You look like a crystallised rose,' she said to Milly. 'Fortnum and Mason job. Was there ever such a light in all the world!'

Surprisingly, the diver came running down out of it, crashing above them, leaping down cataracts of boulders.

'Hey!' he called, waving at them. 'O.K. there?'

He stood straddled above them, hands in pockets, cap tipped back off his forehead. His face was as pink as a fresh salmon. His dark clothes were dyed wine-red.

'You ask for Fotis's house when you come up,' he called. 'Every feller round here knows Fotis.'

5

Nobody greeted him. He greeted nobody. Outside a coffee-house he stopped a passing cigarette boy and filled his tin from the tray. His hand shook and half the cigarettes spilled out on the pavement. He kicked them into the gutter with the toe of his rubber boot and went on down the waterfront, under the sparse salt-trees that were inimical now and rustling with roosting hens. His head was held stiffly, and the arch and fall of his breathing chest was harsh, to himself audible.

It was the time of day he hated most of all times. The time when his mouth was filled with bile and his intestines cramped. The grey time, silent after the summoning bells, when the last stain of day was sucked behind the mountains and the pale feathers of harbour mist drifted and curled on the stealthy sluck of the water, and even if he did not look at the ghosts of the diving-boats sidling up he could still hear them breathing with a woeful creaking of their planks, harsh as his own breath. The time when the cats scavenged and the men with crippled legs hauled themselves down to the port with their trays of cigarettes or honey-cakes or peanut-bars or six fresh eggs tied up in a check napkin and the bag of lottery numbers stuffed up a sleeve where the police wouldn't find it. (A drachma a dip! Only a drachma a dip and fine fresh eggs!) The time when the last spark of hope was extinguished in him and he was left exhausted as the day itself, empty of everything except the sourness of stale wine, needing another drink, a stronger drink, to bridge the time until the electricity plant started up. The violence of night would always abrogate fear.

He turned in from the busy waterfront, down the lane where the two foreign women had passed ten minutes before (he had watched them down the whole length of the pavement, the confident swing of their hips, the tilt of their shining heads, and heard their clear soprano voices belling through the dusk), and entered the coffee-house which he had lately come to patronise at this hour of the day because it was almost always empty and even when it wasn't it was as dark as a cave and other divers who might by chance come in for an evening ouzo or cognac might in fact not see him at all and so could not be said, or even thought, to be avoiding him pointedly.

Or even *thought* . . . that was the thing, not to think about it. Not to make something out of the fact that there were certain men who *would* always join him now. Unerringly. Stamatis, for instance, of the flicking tongue and running egg eyes, who was paralysed in both legs and so soft in the head that he could not even conceal his bag of lottery numbers so that the police would not find it. Old Captain Andonis, paralysed in only one leg, but senile ever since Fotis could remember, which was long after he (the captain) had lost his boat and all four of his sons and had taken to selling cigarettes for a living, hobbling around the town with a wooden tray slung around his bowed neck by a leather strap that had made a gall-mark, casting terrible shadows against the walls. Sullen Petros, who had turned so vicious in temper since they had had to cut his brother Tomás's air-hose that time off Benghazi that no Captain would sign him on for a cruise now, not even out of pity or sorrow or guilt, and he had come down to the ignominy of shearing sponges and trampling bales in the Casopédes warehouse. They saw Fotis all right, even in a coffee-shop as dark as a cave. And occasionally a couple of the young wide ones, the high walkers with the fancy knives in their belts and the fear already bitten into their boy faces. The ones of whom you knew, just by looking at them, that they would get it next season or the season after, if any captain signed them on, that was, because the captains always knew the smell as well as anybody and were not likely to take bad luck aboard if they could avoid it.

That was it—not to make something out of this unerring division of those who sat with him now and those who did not.

29

Not to admit that he was being pushed inexorably into a role he had not chosen but which he was being forced to play out. He needed drink for that. Strong drink to refute the reflection of himself in Captain Andonis's old and hopeless eyes, the echo of himself in the doomed boys' boastings, the knowledge of the corruption working in him as a sentence carried out in its inevitability. The others had decided the Evil Eye was on him. Not he.

No longer wild, despairing, and vengeful, but cunning rather, sly with himself, he entered the coffee-house which was not empty after all, but so filled with dusk that it was possible for him not to see that four men of his last season's diving team were playing cards at the window table. Or perhaps it was that the door, swinging back, blocked his sight of them, and with a drunkenness deliberately revived he hailed Petros and Stamatis, sitting at the very back of the shop under the category sign.

Stamatis had two packs of American cigarettes and the bag of lottery numbers out on the table among the ouzo and the grilled octopus tentacles. He was shaking the numbers hopefully before Fotis had even got his legs properly under the table.

'Shove it,' said Fotis, and looked away from the two curved sticks hooked one each side of the category sign behind Stamatis. Unless he twisted his chair and looked towards the voices and the soft slap of cards that he had not admitted were there, there was nowhere else to look except at Petros, so Fotis looked at Petros, recognising that he was lowering, baffled, carrying his sorrows like a great jagged weight in his intestines that no grunts of rage would eliminate. It infuriated him.

'Hey! You Petros! What's up? Caught your nackers in the sponge press?' For Petros still wore the peaked black cap and high boots of a diver, and did not care to be reminded that now he only bleached and snipped sponges instead of taking them from the bottom of the sea. Stamatis laughed, flicking his tongue in and out of his yellow face. 'What's the matter with you, cabbage-head?' said Fotis, and Stamatis stopped laughing.

Pantales brought the ouzo in a glass. 'Bring the bottle!' Fotis

30

yelled, grinning like a man at a wedding feast, so Pantales brought it, still without comment, and only lifted his hands in a brief, helpless gesture towards the other table as he turned away. (There in the livid light by the window the four quiet jerseyed men played cards. Silent. Concentrated. Only their eyes troubled.)

The one naked bulb hanging from the buckled brown-paper ceiling bloomed slowly, steadily, into light. The plaster wall paled imperceptibly. Their shadows emerged, dim but fixed. Fotis breathed out slowly, the constriction of his chest easing. It was night.

He reached for the bottle and filled up the glasses again, clattering glass against glass and slopping a pool of viscous syrup across the marble table-top. There was a wink of light caught in it, like a diamond. And behind him there was a chunk of knuckles and the slap, slap, slap of the cards, not to be heard, and before him there were the running red eyes of Stamatis, maudlin with comradeship, and the lowered beetling skull of Petros, brooding on his own despair. And he hated them both.

So he grinned, drawing his lips back from the sticky aniseed taste that coated his teeth and his tongue and the roof of his mouth and slid burning down his throat, and leaned over the table confidentially. 'I hear,' he said, 'that young Sponge Belly is going to employ girls in the warehouse next year. Says the work is too easy for men. Would that be right now, Petros?'

'Quit it!' snarled Petros briefly, but his scarred fingers, as thick and twisted as sea-weathered ropes, were squeezing tight around the little ribbed glass. Fotis could have yelped with laughter. The ouzo was warm in his belly now, loosening the cramp, lying inside him like a coating of courage. He poured another glassful down to fix the feeling.

'Eh, now, Petros? What do you say?' He wanted to goad, to prick, to stir the bafflement into frenzy. He thrust his grinning face to within an inch of the bristling moustache and broken teeth, almost as if he were tempting Petros to bite, and snapped his fingers in a dance rhythm.

'Eh?' he shouted. 'Eh? Eh? Eh?'

31

Petros brought the glass down on the marble with a splintering crack, and the pool of ouzo grew pink among the glass fragments. Fotis let out a yell of laughter. Stamatis laughed also. A silent wet hiccupping. Pantales brought a sponge and wordlessly mopped up the mess and placed a fresh glass on the table. The delicate slap of the cards was resumed with scarcely a pause. Two grey-uniformed policemen, wearing the blue-and-silver duty armbands, hesitated in the doorway and went on up the lane: they would come back in a little while.

Petros stuck his hand in his mouth and sucked on it and spat the blood out, carefully. A finger's width from the toe of Fotis's boot. He spoke to Stamatis.

'Fotis knows all about a man's work. Running through the town sniffing rich women. Nearly broke his neck getting close enough to bow.'

'That's right,' said Fotis, still laughing.

'Suck-arse!' said Petros.

Bubbles of exhilaration fizzed and exploded in Fotis's head. The warmth had spread to his fingers and gripped his nerves tight. Soon. Soon. His fist would smash into Petros's face . . .

'You wouldn't be jealous now, Petros, would you?'

Petros made a gesture with one finger.

Stamatis said without rancour: 'She's a nice little piece, that little Lookoomi. The rich always get the best.'

Petros wiped his hand across his moustache. It was still bleeding. He rubbed tobacco from a cigarette stub into the cut. He said, 'I suppose she's going to stand godmother to whatever Fotis has put in his wife's belly this time.'

'That could be,' said Fotis judicially, and tipped his cap down over his eyes and rocked his chair back on two legs and gripped the table. Ready.

Stamatis said: 'I wonder is it true that that skinny one comes from Australia. That's a good country, Australia. Plenty work. Anastasis had a letter from his third cousin . . .'

Petros's bleeding hand was also gripping the table's edge. 'You'd have to ask Fotis all about that,' he said. 'He's a personal friend.'

'That's right,' said Fotis agreeably, making it a taunt, 'I'll ask her when she comes up to visit Irini.' And even as he said it he knew, suddenly, that it was true. The one called Katerina, with that strange spiky unwomanly hair and the alert eyes that looked, not proudly, nor inquisitively, nor fearfully as the little Lookoomi looked, but straight, as a man looked at a man to judge his quality, one day she would come to his house and sit with his wife and accept what Irini would offer, and while he did not know why she would want to do this he knew that it would be so, and it was as if she had offered him a Good Eye which he had almost refused because he had been too drunk to recognise it. His hand loosened its grip on the cold curved marble, and his face, reflective suddenly and lit by something which was not quite yet hope, goaded Petros as none of his taunts had been able to do.

Then Petros said something that he had never intended to say. Something he could never have imagined himself saying. He said: 'Mother of God! Just wait till they pull you up from the bottom with your legs like Stamatis here, and see where your suck-arsing will get you!'

It was very quiet in the coffee-house then. One of the divers at the card-table crossed himself with deliberation. The others looked only at the table-top. Pantales set a long-handled copper pot on the black tin where the charcoal glowed and sat watching it with intense concentration. Stamatis's tongue flicked once, dryly, and he opened the little shrivelled hole of his mouth and closed it again. Perhaps he had wanted to apologise for his crippled legs.

Petros growled unintelligibly and drank two ouzos one after the other. Having said the unsayable he could be nothing now but defiant. Neither could Fotis, having goaded him to it, do other than continue to sit with his gleaming white face stretched in laughter, stretching his mouth wider and wider over his teeth until the nerves in his cheek twitched as convulsively as if the laughter had been real.

'Eh, Petros my boy, you needn't be worrying about me! Nobody's going to be pulling Fotis up from the bottom any more now!' He said it very loudly, so that the quiet card-players, whom he did not know were there, would be able to hear every word. 'That's a mug's game,' he said. He said, 'I'm not a cabbage-head.' And pushed his cap back on his brow and hooked his shaking thumbs through the belt with the silver snake for a buckle.

Petros laughed now. Shortly. Uneasily. 'I suppose a white woman has come in a dream and told you where to dig up some treasure. Or maybe that lady friend is going to write you the permit to go to Australia?'

'Sure,' Fotis said confidently. "Sure. She can do that. She can write the permit for me to go to Australia.'

6

Dearest Win, Kathy wrote, and crossed it out and tore the sheet from the block and wrote: *Win, my dear,* and lifted her face so that the sun fell on it and her eyes dazzled. On the porch she was sheltered from the wind, but she could see its teasing in the tumultuous leaves of the orange-trees with the sunlight skittering off them, and hear it in the clashing bamboos, and down valley, over the town, there were four—no, five—kites swooping and tugging up into the bright blown vault of the morning.

I am healing, she thought. I will tell him that. Win, my dear, I am healing.

Mrs Dapp would bring the letter to him at breakfast and perhaps there would be sunlight for him, too, even in wintry London, for the pretty Regency house was on the right side of Chapel Street to catch sunlight if it was about, and this was why Win always took his breakfast there in what he called the morning-room. He would have bathed and shaved already and would be wearing the brown quilted jacket over his suit trousers and striped shirt, and beside his plate there would be a little pile of pieces of cardboard torn from cigarette packets and covered with his round sepia writing. The coffee would be percolating. She could see it all so vividly. The tastefully reticent furniture. The pictures—the big gorgeous Lowry of hundreds of stick figures hurrying to factories through the Northern grit, a snippet of Christopher Wood's vanished Brittany, a tiny Constable that was like a gust of cold English air, the two Boningtons and the Cotman. The signed photographs above the mantel, proudly anachronistic—Arnold Bennett and H. Rider Haggard and Marcel Proust and Thomas Hardy. And on the table the two four-minute eggs, each in its own identical silver egg-cup, six tan triangles of toast in the silver rack, the Oxford marmalade, the black-lettered white china pot of Patum Peperium, the Gentleman's Relish, the tiny tall glass of Courvoisier which he drank each morning with his coffee. And then there would be the ring at the bell and he would listen attentively to the quick fluttering shuffle of Mrs Dapp's feet, with his smooth round brown head tilted. She would bring the mail already sorted and place it without comment in a neat pile on the side of his plate opposite the oblongs of cardboard. Then he would pour his coffee, arrange his sepia notes for the day in their proper order, dab his moustache with a napkin, brush a stray crumb from his knee, and finally, finally, after a careful and pleasurable examination of the beautiful stamps . . .

Kathy gave a funny little grunt that might have expressed anything and tore the sheet from the block and worked it into a tight ball, which she dropped into the empty flower-pot on top of the litter of cigarette stubs and burnt-out matches. Then she stretched her tightly trousered legs out in the sun and balanced the block on her knees, and wrote:

My darling Sprogs, I am sending you some beautiful sponges. They will look a bit flattened but if you put them in water for a while they will plump up nicely. They are called Elephants' Ears, as you will see by the shape. They are also called Silk Sponges. Touch them and you will feel why. They are rather special, since they grow only in one place off Benghazi on the African coast. There are many huge sharks there, so that the divers who go down to bring up these sponges have to be very brave. How are you, my darlings both? Does Mr Hotchkiss still let you ride the pony? And is the tree-house intact? Do write to me, you little beasts, and tell me about school and everything, and Granny and Pa, and what you do, and Danny will you please send me a drawing? One of the Ant sort? Be very good for Granny and tell her I am writing, and Aunt Milly too. I miss you so much . . .

And at the bottom of this letter she wrote: *P.S. The sponges*

36

are to WASH WITH. And then: *P.P.S. I have met one. A diver, I mean.*

7

She did not meet him again, however, for a long time. Although she did say, diffidently: 'I thought I might go up and visit that woman some time. If it wouldn't be presumptuous. I am haunted by the little baby.'

'That would be kind, Kathy.' Demetrius sounded slightly surprised. 'But I shouldn't worry too much about the baby. Aunt Polymnia is very capable. All these old women are. They know a great deal more about mending and curing than we give them credit for. But yes, it would be a kind action, and taken kindly. Go with Milly.'

Milly pulled a face.

Demetrius said in a spurt of exasperation, 'You might at least *pretend* some interest, my dear!'

There were, of course, tears. Which Kathy soothed tactfully, and did not mention visiting Epano again. In any case, there never seemed to be enough time.

The hospitality was overpowering, and strongly clannish, for there was Demetrius's Uncle Paul, and his cousin Lazarus, who had a younger brother also called Paul, who had married a young woman called Themolina, who was the daughter of another sponge merchant called Stephan Poulis, and in some way he was related to Aunt Sophia, who lived just across the street. (Kathy sometimes wondered where the blood links ended and the sponge links began.) There were innumerable other cousins of first, second, and third degree, and uncles and aunts in blood or by marriage, and godfathers and godmothers, and all of them, according to some carefully arranged protocol, insisted on entertaining Demetrius's foreign sister-in-law.

'But I am *not* your sister-in-law, I am Milly's sister-in-law,' Kathy would insist with a vehemence that surprised her, and

Demetrius would look at her with his calm black eyes and acknowledge that little current of antagonism that sometimes sparked between them, and he would smile as he pointed out that here relationships were different.

'Here you are my sister. Here I am your brother. And in the absence of your husband I am also your guardian and your protector. How do you like that?'

'You are a damned oriental,' she said. 'Demetrius Pasha!' In spite of the occasional sparks of antagonism she liked him more and more.

The truth of the matter was she found the whole family oriental. The men were all heavy, with the family likeness engraved in their gross chins, their slightly slanted eyes, their thick grape-coloured lips. Courteous men, soft of speech and manner, but withdrawn completely behind the barriers of maleness. Untouchable really. Ungetatable. And their soft, sluggish women, pallid as grubs, downed at lip and chin, diffusing always a faint sweetish smell of flesh and violet talcum powder and clothes kept in tissue paper. Indoor creatures, the women, belonging within walls, in dark shuttered rooms. Hearth, table, bed. Impossible to imagine them in sunlight. Even their gardens, in which they seldom walked, were still, shrouded, and protected by high walls, so that for these women the harsh valley did not exist, nor those bleak mountains, scoured and fissured, where nothing ever grew. Not a tree, not a terrace, not an ear of grain, not a thicket unless it was of thorns or those strange round bushes of acid green and yellow that oozed a poisonous milk.

'Our only pastures are in the sea, Kathy,' Demetrius said with that occasional sadness she found very touching in him, and she thought of the divers, crawling across the floors of the ocean to reap the oozy harvest which kept the high Casopédes walls intact and the heavy shutters closed on the rooms where the women ate honey-cakes and squeaked at one another like plump white mice.

I *will* go up there soon, she thought, but instead found herself being conducted to another luncheon or dinner in one of the

Victorian houses that stood in the valley with their backs to the sea.

She ate lamb grilled on skewers, lamb roasted on the spit, lamb stewed with winter lettuce, lamb with artichoke hearts, lamb baked with tomatoes and rice and cinnamon, lamb broiled with macaroni. Also boiled lamb's head. ('If you pretend the eyes are oysters they'll go down more easily,' whispered Demetrius, amused.) Then honey-cakes, almond-cakes, wheat-cakes, sugar-cakes, peanut-cakes, pastries filled with custard, walnut sweets, sweets of sesame seed, sweets of rose petals, sweets of pistachio nuts, bowls of yoghourt, bowls of walnuts dripping with honey, conserves of quince and fig and plum and peach and bitter orange.

Then, after the family rounds, the secondary island hierarchy—the bank manager, the police captain, the notary public, the mayor and the magistrate, the headmaster of the gymnasium, the Customs officials and the harbour-master, the despot and his senior priests—and another roundelay of eating and drinking in stiff, formal rooms of Western style where only the ikon cupboards and the inevitable ornamental sponge on the sideboard seemed to relate to the exotic cadences of the language she tried so very hard to understand.

When they were not visiting they were being visited, by the plump moustached women in their black dresses and shawls, who seemed to be content to sit stiffly in the drawing-room for hours at a time, watching and smiling and nodding and emitting strange little squawks of pleasure whenever Milly or Kathy attempted a valiant phrase or two in Greek.

'But, Kathy, aren't they simply *awful!*'

Kathy thought they were all very kind. Only terribly wearing. And so curiously unrelated to the surroundings which affected her so violently—the harsh mountains, the lean smell of the sea, the simple town of cubes and lanes where the other sort of people lived, the people whom, apparently, one did not ever meet. The involved people. 'If one could only communicate . . .' she said.

Milly looked aggrieved. 'Oh yes, it's all very well for you, darling. You'll go back to London and never have to see any of their stupid faces again. I mean, you don't have to live among them. For—all—your—*life!*' And she had looked up then, her face suddenly crumpled with fright.

'Oh, come now, don't be so silly.' Kathy tried to summon the reasonable voice she had always used with her sons on the occasions when one or the other of them was confronted by his own admission of reality, too dreadful to be borne, too late to deny or evade or twist into something less true but more comforting. 'You're not marooned. You don't *have* to live here all your life. There'll be trips back to see Granny and Pa, won't there? And Win and me, I hope. After all, Demetrius loves England as much as you do. More. If his father hadn't died just then he would probably have settled down in England. You know that. He'll take you back as soon as he has things straightened out here. He can always arrange another spell in the London office. Lots of spells, I imagine . . .'

'Yes, but when? *When?* I shall go mad, Kathy, I swear, if I have to rot here for years and years. Honestly . . .' The tears began to glisten.

'It's only because you feel so damned heavy and tired at the moment. So horribly *inhabited.* Things will seem totally different when the baby comes. That's a very sweet time for a woman, Milly. It is. You'll see.' And yes, yes, she thought. It had been sweet. She had wanted the babies and wanted them quickly, so glad and relieved in her own happiness in them, the happiness like a proof to offer to Irwin. See, Irwin, I *am* happy. Truly I am happy. And suddenly the diver's wife sprang vividly into her mind, her silver mouth and the grotesque pantomime of her hands. Had it been sweet for her the first time? 'Silly Milly,' she said tenderly. 'If you only knew how all your old girl friends are simply dying of envy. You and your glamorous husband and your Greek island. I mean, even if you were marooned, wouldn't it be worth it?'

'Kathy . . .' That glazed porcelain look the eyes had. Spode. Or willow pattern? So like. But Irwin's crackled in the whites with minute yellow lines. Milly's were like new china eggs painted

41

with forget-me-nots and set in fringed satin. 'Kathy, are you and Irwin . . .? Physically . . .? I mean . . . do you love Irwin *terribly*?' She blushed.

Kathy stifled a mad impulse of sincerity. What would it benefit Milly to hear of the scrupulous ways of companionship? Better for her to believe that sexual love would retain its shockingness and terror and delight for ever. A house-broken mystery would not be an appealing prospect to a very young woman passionately in love. Clearly. And how could one convey the terrible strength of habit and affection, that were not, as one had always imagined, dull and consolatory, but powerful enough to riddle one through and through? Like the roots of the bindweed, Kathy thought, feeling choked, bound, stiflingly entangled, and for a stinging second she was actually envious of ignorant empty Milly, who at least lived occasionally with the clouds and the lightning.

'*Terribly*,' she said, and kissed Milly and steered her on to the new *Vogue* with the stunning maternity patterns. The model girls were a new crop, and Milly found only one face she recognised. She was deeply nostalgic, and Kathy was sad for her.

Also irritated. Now, if she were Milly . . . She recognised the absurdity of the fantasy but persisted in it nevertheless. Or, rather, it persisted in her, like a nagging tooth. What she really envied Milly was the challenge presented by the island. The challenge. She saw in herself the need for challenge. And why should Milly, who was born, one might think, for the gayest and the emptiest of journeys, be faced with challenge while she, Kathy, with a mind and a heart that had always been wide open for the unprecedented, had been required to walk only in protected places? (Irwin's voice, filled with bafflement: 'But what *is* it, Kathy? Why are you never satisfied? What in God's name do you keep expecting?' And her own voice, vehement in defence: 'Nothing, darling. Nothing. I have everything.' But, obscurely, she had shamed or humiliated him from the first. She knew it, and had learned at last to disguise that look of expectancy he seemed to feel as a reproach, and to limit her giving to the measure

42

he found acceptable.) Protected places that had stifled her, and from the stifling she had fled that night in the black car through the elms beating up like surf . . .

Panic touched her. I was drunk that night, she thought. I was. It was that! Because I didn't mean . . . I could not have meant . . .

But with a terrifying clarity she knew what she had meant, and that soon she would need to examine that extraordinary act and to face its implications. Soon. First she must heal. And I will heal here, she determined. I will heal here because I must.

In this mood of determination she entered gladly into the arrangements made for her entertainment and pleasure, helped Milly with the household, was eager and interested in learning about sponges from Demetrius and about Greek cooking from Aliki, began on a phrase book, wrote cheerful letters to Irwin and her sons. She spent hours in the garden with old Stamatis, a crippled ex-diver, forking and manuring and pruning, or drawing water from the old well under the almond-tree. There were little nubs of bud on the branches now, and under the citrus-trees with their glowing globes of gold there were freesias and jonquils and tiny blue grape-hyacinths.

Irwin sent her parcels of new books which she did not read. Did not even want to read. Instead she let the silence work on her, the immeasurable silence which Milly's chatter did not disturb and which was only the more profound for the occasional sounds of bells or donkey harness creaking or the pit-pit-pit of hooves or the bamboos rustling. She looked at the mountain often, but knew that the mountain would wait.

Several times also, shopping with Milly in the public market, or wandering through warehouses and sponge-clipping rooms with Demetrius, she was caught by the flash of a silver smile or by some figure lounging in a blue jersey and black cap. But many of the island women had stainless-steel teeth, and most of the divers wore blue jerseys. Irini and Fotis would wait too.

Meanwhile, between the days of heaven blue, the last of the winter storms raged majestically, and at night the port was wild

43

with the music and singing and fighting and gambling of men whose time was shortening perceptibly. And the diver Fotis despairingly shadowed the tall foreign lady through lanes and alleys, waited and watched for her to emerge from church doorways, sponge factories, shops, market arches, and always she was accompanied and he did not dare approach her.

8

They met again finally on a cold yellow day on the waterfront when Kathy was returning with Demetrius from the warehouse.

Sky and sea and mountains were steeped in a solution of sulphur, and along the waterfront the wind came in gusts, rough as a cat's tongue. Down by the Twenty-fifth of March statue the labourers' handcarts were idle, and there were no tables out on the pavement. The taverns and the coffee-houses were crowded with men, and only men were out of doors—seamen in groups, looking at the harbour.

Demetrius slipped his gloved hand smoothly under Kathy's elbow and guided her on to the pavement behind the salt-trees. 'There may be trouble with the boats,' he said, 'if it gets worse. I must tell Lazarus to round up our crews to watch tonight.'

The boats were kicking and jolting uncomfortably on the heaving yellow water, and the mooring ropes in their cleats winced with sharp little squeaks like smothered cries of pain, and while they watched a wave sloshed right over the paving blocks and ran halfway across the waterfront. Out by the farthest breakwater, against which spray burst in sharp explosive clouds like bombs falling, the big empty supply schooners were rolling wildly.

Kathy felt as though she was vibrating like a tuning-fork. Her skin grew taut, her muscles tense; there was a clamp of excitement at the back of her neck like a strong hand making claim. Her own mysterious life rushed through her, strong suddenly in response to the rushing of air and water.

Beside her Demetrius sunk his head down into the fur collar of his thick reefer jacket and smiled, watching her. Waiting.

And just as she turned to him, her face sharp with imminence, the door of the coffee-house by which they had paused banged open and shut. Hands in pockets, shoulders hunched under the

45

blue jersey, the diver came towards them, his face twisted into a shaky, arrogant, white-lipped smile.

'You all O.K. there?' he said.

Demetrius nodded. It was a startled greeting which surprise made cordial.

'How are you?' Kathy said. 'How is your wife? And is the baby better?'

'Sure. Sure. That damn' leg swelled up all right, though. Like that,' he said proudly, and showed her with his blue, cold, shaking hands. And then, ignoring Demetrius, he said intently, sidelong, while apparently appraising the seething harbour: 'You coming up some time? You coming up and seeing Irini?'

'Yes,' she said. 'Yes.' That reckless white profile pointed to the wind. That thick beating excitement in her throat. 'When?'

'Any time,' he said, and then a squall snatched his black cap and whirled it along the waterfront, and Demetrius exerted a soft urgent pressure on her elbow, and in the moment that she saw that the diver's uncovered hair was streaky brown and fine as a child's she was being walked briskly up the lane towards home, with Demetrius's hand gripped gently about her arm so that it was impossible to turn and confirm what she saw in her mind—the huge, wrathful yellow day unleashing, and before it the frail black figure running along the waterfront beside the leaping boats, with peaked cap skittering before. Running, she thought, with a sort of joy.

'I didn't know you had a friend in the port.' Demetrius made 'the port' sound like a different country. Upper Kurdistan perhaps, or the Maldive Islands.

'He's the husband of the woman I was telling you about. The one with the sick baby who was up at Aunt Polymnia's that day.'

'Oh?' he said. 'Yes, of course. I remember.'

She hoped that he would leave it at that. For even though the matter stood as she had stated it, she felt guilty. She *had* picked up something at Epano. She knew it. There was an infection working in her. A sense of the nefarious, the dangerous, a hint of the expansive reckless world that lay outside the stone houses where the women sat eating honey-cakes and the men spoke softly to them out of grape-coloured lips in case they should guess what lay outside. Treasonable thoughts these, and intuitively she knew that Demetrius would be vigilant.

She was glad when Paul and Lazarus came to visit that evening, without their wives because of the weather. After the courtesies in English the men talked among themselves in Greek. Watching parties had been posted on the boats with spare anchors and ropes and grapnels on chains, and now the men sprawled heavy and comfortable on the chintz chairs around the steady blue flame of the stove with whiskies and cigars: Paul, a younger, less handsome, version of Demetrius, Lazarus older, shorter, already gross. Milly played records rather boredly, with the player turned low so as not to interrupt the men—Ella Fitzgerald and early Sinatra—and Kathy curled on her usual place in the window-seat, half muffled in purple peacocks, and listened to the wind blasting around the villa, growling for entrance, and thought of the wooden boats, wet and vulnerable, tossing in the seething dark, and the tavern windows cut sharply yellow like pumpkin lanterns, holding warmth, light, rough voices of men, old wisdoms of wine and lute-string. And the woman with the despairing hands and the silver mouth would be waiting, her hearth a charcoal tin, and she would be crouched, listening to the wind as Kathy listened, while the sick baby whimpered and the thin dirty children huddled like woodgrubs on the bedshelf for warmth. His woman. His children.

When Paul and Lazarus had gone, and Aliki was emptying the ashtrays and clearing away the glasses and Milly had begun to yawn and yawn, Demetrius said, 'Oh, incidentally, Kathy . . .'

She uncurled and stood and stretched, smiling at him.

'That family you are interested in,' he said.

'What of them?'

'Don't waste your time, my dear. They're a worthless lot.'

'Oh? How do you know that?'

47

'I thought I recognised the chap today. I was right. Lazarus knows him. He was on one of our boats for a few seasons. Just forget about him, Kathy. He's one of the worst trouble-makers in the port. A thoroughly nasty piece of work.' He shrugged. 'Drunk and violent. He's in trouble with the police every winter.'

'Are his wife and children drunk and violent too?'

He gave her a small, lenient smile. 'Oh, come off it now, Kathy! The point is that if you interest yourself in the woman and the children you'll never be rid of the man either. Believe me. I know these types.'

She said, 'I'm sure you do, Demetrius,' and kissed Milly good night and went upstairs to bed.

In the night worms of pain began wriggling in her head, the red, burning, hairy sort that would, she knew, eventually burrow down behind her temples and eyes and grip there with fiery hooks. It is a judgement on me, she thought, and tried to laugh, but that hurt too much, so she lay sweating in the darkness, trying to will it away according to an old formula that had sometimes worked in the really bad times. But it was obvious that she was in for a real bout, and there was nothing to do but resort to the pills whose efficacy had become so diminished with use that she never took them but despairingly. She lit the candle beside her bed—the electricity had cut out an hour before—and found the pills, but there was no water in the bedroom and she had to go to the bathroom for it, barefooted and freezing down the wind-shuddering corridor, shielding the leaping candle in her hands.

And it was in the corridor that Demetrius found her, the candle out, blindly butting her head against the plaster wall. She turned to his torch beam a face dazed and ravaged by pain.

'Sorry,' she gasped. 'I wanted water.'

'Kathy!' He closed the bedroom door soundlessly behind him and as quietly slipped an arm under her shoulders. 'Back to bed. I'll get the water.'

She let him lead her back to her room and help her into her bed, and lay there while he lit a brass lamp and brought a carafe of water and a glass.

'My God, I'll give Aliki hell for this,' he said pleasantly. 'And Milly too. There should be water in your room.'

'Shhh . . . doesn't matter . . .'

'It matters very much. But never mind now. Here.' He slipped his arm under her shoulders again to support her while she swallowed the tablets, then lowered her head to the pillow and tucked her arms under the covers. These ministrations he performed deftly, with a caressing gentleness. But at the same time a sort of stealthy intimacy, so that even in her pain Kathy was conscious of the insinuation of the yellow lamp glowing alone in the dark, wind-tormented villa where everybody else slept. Demetrius was wearing soft flannel pyjamas patterned with a blue Paisley leaf—Harrods, she thought, with a hard little bark of laughter exploding painfully inside her. The stuff was warm, comforting against her blazing face, sweet and musky-smelling as he cradled her head while she swallowed the pills. She managed to smile gratitude.

'So stupid.'

'You didn't tell me you still have these bad times, Kathy.'

'Only sometimes . . . don't bother any more . . . it will go away soon . . .'

'Hush,' he said. 'I'll wait a little while. Try to go to sleep.'

'No,' she said sharply.

'Hush, Kathy. Go to sleep.'

She frowned, no longer quite seeing him, and closed her eyes.

Aliki always left an extra rug folded at the foot of the bed. He took this and wrapped it around his legs and sat on the edge of the bed, very calm, very still, while the worms hooked in and hung and Kathy's skull, creaking, began to crack open like a rotten nut.

There was, Demetrius recognised, a sort of lechery in the observation of pain, particularly human pain, and heightened more when the victim was a woman. A desired woman. He accepted the admission without surprise; it had been on the frontiers of his consciousness for days now. Pain degraded utterly. Utterly exposed. He liked that she should be degraded before him, stripped down more absolutely than if she had lain to him in love. Silent, heavy, pleasurably aware of his own flesh still warm from Milly under the loose pyjamas, and even more pleasurably aware of Irwin Bassett's impotent presence in the leather frame on the night table, he sat on her bed in the intimate glow of lamplight and studied with a calm concupiscence the distinctive configurations of her skull, the loamy texture of her skin with the sweat springing, and trembling on it, the frailty of the exposed collar-bones, the hollow at the base of her throat, the shape of her eye-sockets, and the pain lines etching deeper between her tilted brows and on either side of her clenched mouth. In a way he rather hoped she would cry out.

9

The diver awoke for perhaps the sixth or seventh time that night and shivered heavily. He could feel the boards on the bedshelf through the thin mattress, and Irini was clutching him again, but he did not fling her off or bother to change his position. The howling wind had dropped and there was a little light coming through the cracks of the closed shutters, but it promised nothing, not even another day. The hillocks of his sleeping children were just discernible; their breaths were warm and musty all about him, and the incomprehensible choked sounds of their dreamings. He felt terribly lonely. More lonely than he had ever felt in his life. He was suffocating in the breath of his children, and so lonely.

An incredible dullness pervaded him. He had been very drunk the night before and almost happy, thinking about the red-haired foreign woman and that he had dared to speak to her at last. But nothing would come of it. He knew that now. What would she want with Irini or him either? She belonged with the rich in their big stone houses and all his experience told him that she would stay there. He yawned hugely. It did not seem worthwhile to sleep again or to wake up either, and his mouth tasted foul. There was still the sound of the *tsabuna* wailing faintly across the cliffside from Stathis's house where they had been marrying his second girl. Several times that night in his drunkenness and almost happiness he had thought of going to join the party, if for no other reason than that he knew he would be unwelcome. But even defiance did not seem worthwhile. And soon they would be locking the young couple in the little house below St Stephanos, as he had been locked into this house once with Irini for three days of initiation and proof, unspeakable days of flesh, to the end that he would at last lie suffocating in the living breath he had created.

51

The pressure of Irini's used body against his seemed intolerable, and the new life moving in it worse than intolerable. The trap. All these separate lives that were dependent upon his life. But he didn't want to live. To live without anything to look forward to seemed impossible. How could a man go on without hope at all? To see nothing ahead but the cigarette tray, the galled shoulder, the hooked shadow on the wall, the bag of lottery numbers, the shafts of the labourers' cart. To go on as a beggar or as a brute-beast. That, or to somehow persuade some not-too-choosy captain to sign him on again, in spite of the curse on him. But who would? And if one did? He stared straight up at the dim stuffed shape of the baby's hammock hung over his head, and the other image formed and he sank helplessly under its horror. He groaned softly, sweating in the terror that would never leave him now, and Irini turned against him and opened blackly glittering eyes.

'Are you sick?'

'No. Go to sleep. Why do you keep asking that?'

Her open mouth gleamed above him in the greyness. 'It has been weeks now. You haven't—'

'Mother of God! Haven't we made enough children?'

'But there is one inside now. You can't do any harm.'

'Shut up! Go to sleep.'

She whispered, bewildered, 'Shall I go in the morning to Polymnia and ask for a medicine for you?'

'No. Go to sleep.'

But she was shrill now, heedless of the children beginning to stir and whimper in the half-light. 'All winter you've been strange. Ever since the boats came home. You haven't been a man all winter long. I am ashamed with the other women.'

'Be quiet!' he hissed, and pushed her down roughly. 'Quiet or you'll be sorry.' And after a while she was quiet enough, although perhaps not sleeping. As long as she was quiet. He covered his eyes with the back of his forearm and groaned again.

To tell. To tell! If there was someone he *could* tell. If there was *something* he could tell. How could one tell it? Tell about a shape, a shadow . . .

10

It had begun in brightness. That was part of the terror now. Bleached emptiness above and the boat swimming in pale heat and the sun at its zenith above the Benghazi beds and down to the south a smudged blurry shimmer of hot mirage above the coastal *wadis*. And the shadow then had been companionship and comfort.

Stathis had been *colazaris*. The same Stathis who was marrying his second daughter in the house across the hillside where Fotis might have gone to be defiant. Stathis, a leathery man, sea-cured, with his brown fingers working delicately on the rope line and his knuckles swollen by heat so that they looked like knots on the rope. 'Flat sand,' Stathis had said. 'Not too much grass. Twenty-five fathoms. A piece of cake.' He said the first part in Greek, but 'piece of cake' in English, with the last word pronounced 'kek', because in the desert war Stathis had been attached to the British Eighth Army for a time and liked to preserve the English words and the slang he had picked up in those days. Often Fotis and Stathis spoke their bad English to each other, because in this way they shared a distinction from the others in the boat. Their only distinction, really.

So he had bolted on the shoulder-piece and slung the weights and had the big burning copper helmet locked on and he had cumbersomely gone down over the tilted diving ladder and dropped away slowly to the blessed blue coolness of twenty-five fathoms on the sandy Benghazi beds. A piece of cake. There was no darkness because the dayshine came up off the white sand bottom and there was no darkness because the sun was right overhead. Below the airy sea-blue that looked like well-water in a galvanised bucket there was a gently moving band— an indivisible blend of sea and sand—that was exactly the colour of new retzina. The shadow of the boat's hull circled around him on the pale rippled floor, and this was when the shadow was companionship and comfort.

The boat moved on the pivot of the airline that ran down to its coupling at the back of his helmet, not on a true circle, but more as a wobbly ellipse, so that in the thirty minutes he would be below the boat would make a traverse laterally across half a mile or so of the sponge-beds. Unless, of course, he encountered an area where good sponges proliferated, and then his double tug on the signal line that ran up to Stathis's knotted fingers would bring the slow traversing movement to a halt while he gathered in the crop and stuffed it into the mesh bag tied around his waist. A piece of cake.

But there were no worthwhile sponges on the sandy parts of the bed, and Fotis, awkward and slow and shapeless in the big boots and the yellow rubber suit and the great Cyclopean helmet, moved ahead through the jet and shimmer of his air bubbles, with the shadow of the boat above circling him rhythmically. In the passing and repassing of his shadow, dark and rippling on the corrugated floor of the sea, there was imparted something of the same sense of security that a man might feel in a besieged castle seeing a sentry pacing his slow, vigilant round of the battlements.

His uneasiness began when the brightness vanished, but this happened almost imperceptibly, for there must have been jerky interruptions of the circling of the boat's shadow before it disappeared altogether. But Fotis had not been conscious of this. He was only aware, suddenly, that the shadow was not there, and in an illogical need for reassurance he had to slowly roll over on his back and look up through the face-plate to see the blistery, globular coruscations of light and water on the skin of the sea which marked the passage of the boat's keel and the spin of its propeller in the wire cage.

Up there was all dazzle. Movement. Gem pricks and lively flares of light. But 'up there' was a hundred and fifty feet away, and where Fotis rolled the sea had turned dark and oldish-looking.

There was no sand here to pick up the comforting passage of the boat's shadow. He had come to an area of dense weed, coarse and black, that stirred sluggishly this way and that to the nudging of some vagrant coastal current. Inside the rubber suit he could not feel the grip and reluctant release of the weed fronds around his legs and boots, but even so he had the sensation of thick coarse files rasping at him, and things tugging insistently, with the touch of soft squashy fingers. It was still a piece of cake, though. He had been in weedy beds a hundred times, and he reminded himself of that when the weeds thickened and reached higher, coiling at his waist now. Pushing his way through with his hands he could feel the thick succulent black pods rubbing like cold treacle against his fingers and palms. The fronds were not rasping any more at all, but bulbous and silky and clammier than mere wetness, and underneath his boots there was no longer sand, but ooze and mud that was soft and slippery and which he knew to be black.

This did not explain his unease. Soft beds of ooze were common all the way from Alexandria to Tripoli. Indeed, even with the first stirrings of panic, he pushed on into the weed without any thought of stopping or retreating.

But only for a minute or two. And then he could not go on. An inexplicable fear clamped his body, and the fear was worse for being inexplicable. He could not define the danger, nor anything that was not common to his unfortunate calling. He had been diving for nearly twenty years. It was a piece of cake. And he could not move.

Beyond the thick glass of his face-plate the sea moved to its own lazy unrest. The weeds, inky black, rolled and lolled in heavy indolence. Tiny fish flicked, were static, cruised and curved in regimented formations. He could hear the hiss of air in his helmet, the sluck-sluck of the valve, the gulp of released bubbles. Far above him the bronze dark green exploded and flashed in silver sea-dazzle. A piece of cake. The metallic globe that encased his starting eyes thundered and echoed to the pounding of his own heart.

Waist-deep in the soft-sucking wavering blackness, he felt

that he was being engulfed in darkness, in blackness rather than darkness, as if all the shadows had coagulated into one shadow, one gigantic shadow, and this shadow was about to fall over him like an enormous smothering blanket. A black blanket. The appallingness of this seized him like claws at his throat, but he found that he could move, and in panic he rolled over on to his back in the weeds so that he might look up and find reassurance for the second time in the sea-gleam on the surface.

And there was no sea-gleam. There was only blackness. And the blackness was a giant manta ray that was the biggest and the most hideous thing Fotis had ever seen in his life. From tip to tip of its great pectoral fins its flattened and grotesque span was greater than the length of the boat above. It was only a fathom above him, directly above him now, like a huge-spread rhomboidal kite: its enormous black wings beat with a slow up-and-down gracefulness, and in the blanket of its moving mass there was the fearful face of the Devil, with a little fretful mouth grimacing, and below it the slashes of the gills pulsing in and out.

He pushed himself down into the ooze and the waving weeds, squirming like an animal into the mud, pressing his helmet back into the slime and the grappling weeds and squashy pulpy fingers, and the great ray went slowly across him like all the darkness of the world, with the long slender spear-tail arced down out of pink and fluttering membranes, and in the shadow of its passing Fotis for an eternal instant knew the uncoloured and lightless texture of death.

It was a long time before his cramped fingers found the rope line, and even then he had to exert a powerful effort of will to make the three pulls of 'emergency', and it was not until he was ascending slowly through the paling green, rising towards the quicksilver play of surface light, that he realised that he would not be able to tell it to Stathis the *colazaris* or to the captain or to any other man. The beds were a piece of cake. The great rays were not dangerous. And there were no sponges in the mesh bag, and there was no way whatever, and never would be, for

Fotis to explain to anyone the depth of horror that was lodged inside him. For it was not just that he was afraid. It was the stark realisation that he had always been afraid.

Not that they had needed explanations, of course. They had known. Divers always know fear in a boat. He had always known himself when it had happened to one of a team he was working with. And he had always done as they had done to him. Servants of a pitiless trade cannot afford pity. He had been marked and set apart from that moment. So that for the further month that the cruise lasted no single man joked when he failed time and time again to bring up a full bag of sponges, and no single man displayed anger or resentment at his obvious malingering. They had treated him with an aloof and formal courtesy, as one who had passed out of their community.

11

Lying on the bedshelf with his arm across his eyes, the diver could have wept. It was as though his whole being—the organism that bore the name of Fotis, walked, breathed, fought, got drunk, wore high boots and a jersey with moss stitch and cables—was actually disintegrating. Yet he had only done what other men had done. It had seemed enough to escape the dangers of existence if he could, and to take its consolations when they were offered. And for that he was condemned. Had been condemned from the beginning. Condemned without knowing who were his judges or of what he had been accused.

On the bedshelf the family began to waken. They moved and stirred and whimpered and snuffled all around him, but he lay there with his arm over his eyes and pretended to sleep. The baby began to cry and his eldest daughter Maria tried to soothe in her doleful child's voice. There was the heavy jerk of the shutter bars and a painful creaking as they were drawn back. Light poured over him. One by one the children rose from their rugs and descended the wooden ladder to the lower part of the room, where Irini cuffed and scolded, pulling at their sleep-crumpled clothes, pushing the smaller one out to the privy. He followed the morning sounds attentively—the splash of the tin dipper in the water bucket, the squeak of the knife against the bread-crust, the heavy slobber of the oil-can (for each child would receive a hunk of bread with oil poured on it to start the day), the soft thud of rugs being folded—seeing all the trivial rituals against his arm as if for the first time, but he did not move, not even when Maria came up the ladder again and stepped over him to stack the rugs away. At last Irini came and took the baby from the hammock and put it at her breast.

'You're sick,' she said. 'I will ask Aunt Polymnia to come.'

'No.'

'Then why don't you get up?'

'Why don't you leave me in peace?' he said wearily. But he got up presently and went outside to the privy and dipped water from the bucket to wash himself. The wedding party was winding down the mountain from Stathis's house. They curled down through the boulders and the cubes and he watched them descending—the violin, the *bouzouki*, the clarinet, the *tsabuna*—triumphant in the breaking morning. And the young couple pale and garlanded among the dancing guests. His own children were scrambling down after the wedding party, and Irini, with loosened hair and the baby at her breast, looked down with narrowed eyes and her mysterious smile.

That she can smile! he thought. That she can look at them and know what is to happen to them and still smile! It seemed appalling. It also seemed that he was seeing this worn woman in her ragged skirt and shrunken cardigan for the first time. Perhaps it was the loosened hair, still almost as black and lively as it had been under the wedding crown, when, half in modesty, half in fright, she had refused to look at him until, reeling with exhaustion, they had stood behind the door until the key grated in the lock and the last shouted jests and lewd injunctions and bursts of laughter had faded away down the mountain after the wedding music. She had looked at him then in the quiet still darkness of the heavily shuttered room, through her fingers spread over her face, and he had been less conscious of her ritual tears and beseechings than of the fact that the room was provisioned as if for a siege, and of the hand-made sheet spread glimmering on the mattress, waiting for the proof, and even while the wine worked in him and the smell of the girl and the arranged darkness and his lust leapt in savage eagerness, he had known dimly that it was all monstrous and a trap.

'Holy Jesus!' he said to himself, 'what have we done?'

'You *are* sick,' said Irini in a frightened, scolding voice, seeing his face watching her. 'And washing day and I have so much to do.'

'Then do it! Can't a man think?' He turned away and took his black cap and put it on and went out into the day. And the day stretched out before him. Those empty, intolerably stretching hours that he would have to fill. And after that all the days to come. The prospect of all the empty hours distressed him unbearably.

In the harbour below an engine spluttered into life, and another, and another. The sound of their exhausts settled into a broken rhythm. The captains would be testing engines this morning after yesterday's storm, and clearing bilges, and going over tackle and gear. There would have been men on watch on every diving-boat through the night: he had watched himself a score of times, and if he had not been on the watch he would have helped to drag the extra anchor chains and cables and the four-pronged grapnels through the shrieking dark with the smell and the sting of the sea angry in his face. The men down there would be feeling good now. He could see groups of them along the waterfront around the doors of the coffee-houses just opening. They had a proud stand to them and the amber beads were flicking in their fingers. Farther along, the public market was opening up also, and the women with their baskets swooping down on it for the pick of the fruit or the best meat cuts, and others were hurrying to the bakehouses with trays of bread or *moussaka* on their heads. Ant-like, the labourers were dragging their heavy carts along the mole to where a big timber schooner from Amorgos was unloading . . .

Everywhere was busyness. Irini had re-slung the baby's hammock between the bake oven and the lintel, and was arranging her flat tin washing-tub on two boulders. All along the cliffside women were doing the same, and the children were scrambling up among the higher rocks to fetch bundles of thorn to start the washing fires, or going down through the tiers of houses to the well with kerosene tins for water. The crisp activity of the morning overcame the diver with a feeling of listlessness that left him incapable of thought or action.

For a time he sat on the doorstep of the house, yawning,

watching the farther islands jumping up in peaks and pinnacles as the sun struck them, and the sea emerging from its dawn blandness into intense deep malachite, rough cut to the wind. But a fresh wind now, romping after yesterday's storm. The women's voices were beginning to rise on it in a work chant, and above the farther cliffside a kite suddenly tugged up eagerly.

So the time of the kites had come already. He remembered how every year, no matter how bad his hangovers, he had made a kite for his sons at this time. He had always liked doing things like that. Things with his hands. Making kites, carving halyard blocks in the shape of fish and dolphins or mermaids for the boards of the sidelights of whatever diving-boat he happened to be working with, decorating the New Year ship with the candles glowing through the coloured paper, glueing sponges and shells and coral and dried ribbon-weed to strangely shaped encrusted stones he had found on the sea's floor. For one boat he had carved a whole tiller two metres long in a twine of serpents and vines ending in the turbaned head of a Turk. It had always given him delight to use his hands in this way.

At least, he thought listlessly, to make a kite would fill in an hour or two of this wearily stretching day, and after he had smoked for a while he got up and went inside the house.

His seaman's chest stood against the wall under the wedding crowns. The crowns were yellow and dry, like two coils of dead seaweed with their sprays of brittle pods, and framed in an arrangement of shells: he had made and decorated the frame during the first year of his marriage and Irini had laughed with pride and pleasure. He had carved the chest himself, too, with coils and loops of rope and a mermaid sitting on a dolphin's back holding the ends of the rope in her hands.

The chest contained their separate treasures. A British battle-dress jacket dyed black, a silk cummerbund and the tasselled crimson scarf from Alexandria that he had always worn knotted across his white shirt at the Clean Monday dance on the threshing floor outside the town. A pair of pointed Egyptian shoes, tan and white, preserved on wooden lasts. Irini's native costume that she had had from her mother and would pass on to Maria in due course: she had used to wear it at Carnival but had not done so for many years. Her good dress wrapped in tissue paper, and the nylon stockings he had bought her still in their cellophane. He had brought her Alexandrian scarves, too, bright ones with pictures printed on them: they were folded there still unworn, with several sealed bottles of perfume. There were sheets folded there also, white ones with hand-made lace, with the embroidered tablecloths that were all meant for Maria's dowry when the time came: Irini had enjoyed doing such things before there were so many children. And in their sheaths his two treasured knives—the one from Crete, wicked-looking, and the other from Astypalaia, set all along the horn handle with little bright studs of glass and enamel.

He did not finger through these things as he usually did when he opened the chest, but only took the neat roll of coloured papers, the bundle of cut bamboo sticks, the ball of blue twine, and the half-rolled tube of strong glue. He yawned, taking out the things, and was of half a mind to put them all back again. What did it matter? But finally he shuffled out into the sunshine again, and the bright romping wind, and settled himself on a rock. At her washtub Irini broke her high shrilling chant and looked across at him with a worried, frightened expression. Then her face cleared and she took up her song again, working her arms vigorously in the suds. The boys, feeding thornbush to the fire under the kerosene tin, began to shove one another in their hurry to get it done and watch the making of the kite.

12

By mid-morning the sky was a carnival of kites, with the island suspended from it by hundreds of lively tugging cords: the wonder was that it stayed level.

On the waterfront everything was alive. Everything in motion. The salt-trees rolled and snapped. Loose shutters banged. Young girls carrying pitchers of water tried to beat down their ballooning skirts with free hands and young men loitered by the Twenty-fifth of March statue to watch them failing. Busy matrons, in long skirts and coifs like medieval women, swooped on the wind to bakehouse or market or well. There were boys with wooden trays of cigarettes and trays of honey-cakes and poison-coloured sweets calling their wares in high, rough, breaking voices. There were priests hurrying to their churches, beards down, cylindrical hats butting into the wind, black robes streaming and flapping. And the labourers trotted between the shafts of their laden carts, laughing.

Kathy felt like laughing too, for the joy of the morning and her freedom from pain. As always after a bad attack, she was frail and light and free, clear in the head as a fine empty bell, and her perceptions were like antennae responding to every colour and sound and smell. In the market she filled her basket with oranges and mandarins, and intoxicated with the smell of them she went on down the waterfront to the one dark and narrow pharmacy, where she bought vitamin tablets and a bottle of cod-liver oil, and might have bought the whole pharmacy too for her delight in the mahogany and the blue glass jars labelled in gold. She bought bars of chocolate and boxes of Turkish Delight. Then, without a glance at the warehouse of Casopédes and Heirs, she set out for Epano.

A heraldry of children swept her up and up into a smell

of thornbush smoke and green soap and a chorus of women's voices. The roof-tops had picked up a random crop of grasses and rushed down viridian to the viridian harbour where the boats jogged like facetious aunts bent on nursery amusement. There were old people sitting in doorways, warming their swollen joints, and one old man held his face in his hands as he returned her greeting, as if the gladness on it was surprising to him and he was afraid it might drop off. Aunt Polymnia's house was closed and shuttered and Kathy felt a stinging sense of inevitability and let the children whirl her on, pulling at her skirt and pointing and laughing like little conspirators. As if they knew perfectly well, had known from the beginning, where she intended to go. So she climbed on and up through shouts and laughter, tall, and with her hair shining like a rare red thistle being brought home for the May. The house was the highest of all.

Irini was bent over her washtub balanced on two boulders beside the bread oven. She shrieked when Kathy came panting and laughing among the children, but whether the cry was of dismay or of pleasure it would have been hard for anybody (least of all Irini, probably) to tell. And at her shriek—Kathy would remember this for ever—the diver rose from a crouching position among the scattered rocks and straightened and stood, holding before him a kite that was diamond in shape, half red, half green, with a bright blue dolphin pasted in the centre. He held this before him like a blazoned shield there on the barren mountainside, and his face above it was not showing satisfaction or pleasure or triumph, as it might have done, but looked out at her with an appalling expressionless tranquillity.

'I brought some oranges and some medicines for the baby,' she said, holding the basket out to the wet woman, but speaking to the man. 'Look, on both bottles the instructions are written in Greek, so it's quite easy and your wife can't make a mistake.' She was talking too fast, breathless, filled with a sudden shame at her own presumption, but unable to stop or slow up. 'And there are some sweets and things for the other children. I hope you don't mind,' she said, smelling the thorn smoke and the green

64

soap and the steamy sudsy smell of the soaking clothes, and seeing Irini's silver mouth and the cotton dress clinging wetly to the swollen breasts and belly and seeing and looking away from the crocheted scallops that edged the square neck of the diver's undershirt where his throat rose from the raw wool as thin and white as a soft peeled stalk, and knowing herself not yet totally committed to she did not know what, yet already committed too far to retreat. 'It's such a heavenly morning,' she said, 'and I was down there shopping and I saw the kites and I thought . . . well, you did say yesterday that I might come . . .?'

'Sure,' he said, unmoving. Then he laid the kite deliberately against a tall rock, considered it, and turned and barked briefly at the escort of children, who scattered for some distance before they began to sidle back again. Meanwhile Irini held the basket apologetically, standing with the steam coming off her wet skin and her hands red and swollen and soggy on the basket handle and the metallic smile coming and going among the furrows of her flat cheeks as if it was fulfilling some purpose of its own. And, after all, she was young.

A thin child ran inside the house and brought out one of the rush-seat chairs.

'Oh, please! I didn't want to interrupt you or anything. And I see your wife is busy. I only . . .'

'O.K. O.K. You sit down now.'

She sat. He spoke to his wife, curtly, and she went into the house with the basket and returned with another chair. She glanced at him in inquiry before she sat on it, but she did sit, formally facing Kathy on the other side of the open door with the cross smoked into the whitewashed lintel, and the diver stood looking at them with the closed face of an artist assessing a difficult composition. The difference in him today, Kathy thought, is that he is sober. And his wife is young. She smiled at Irini and the silver smile came and went, although perhaps not in return. Certainly it had nothing to do with her avid eyes. All the children had crept back to form a semicircle around the front of the house.

'Which are yours?'

He called them forward, naming them one by one. Apostóli. Yanni. Michalis. Three bumpy shaven skulls looking startlingly large and fragile over tiny old men's faces, or the faces of savages, and the skulls scored with old scars, and limbs like thin knotty sticks poking out from voluminous patched garments obviously cut short from their father's old ones and wrapped around and held with pins. Theodóra. Poppy. Two jetty little girls carrying bundles of thornbush. Black-haired, pale-skinned, looking tired already with an adult tiredness, even though they giggled. Doxouli, the toddler, wispily downed, dripping-drawered, covered in sores and bites, whining as she tugged at her mother's skirt.

'And Maria that one.' He indicated the washing-tub where the wan child bent staidly to the foam of soap. She had lank brown hair and large pink transparent ears with pieces of string tied through the pierce-holes.

'Plenty kids, eh?' he said, lounging against the rock with his naked feet and his naked throat, and the gold ring shuddering on his hand as he offered the cigarette tin with the blonde printed on the lid. And Kathy could not help but look at his wife's hands to see if they were repeating the gesture they had made in Aunt Polymnia's house. Instead they were crawling up the buttons of her bodice: her breast, long and melon-shaped, fell out and swung down into the open mouth of the toddler.

Kathy rose abruptly and walked over to where a hammock—made from a scrap of woven rug and a length of ship's rope—was slung between the roof projection and the bread oven. The crumpled grey face was sucking with resignation on a sticky wad of rag, and there was only resignation in the dull dark eyes, sunken like the eyes of the aged. It was swaddled tightly in scraps of blanket, so that she could not see its leg, but she stayed there for a while making foolish noises at the little grey hopeless face until Irini had buttoned up her bodice again.

'Is the baby better now?'

'Sure. You like a smoke?' If he was conscious of her embarrassment he did not show it.

'Do you think perhaps your wife should take the baby to a doctor? Just to be sure?'

He grinned derisively and shrugged and rubbed his thumb against his forefingers. It was the moment when she could, as she had intended, offer the doctor's fee. But she could not. Not to him, anyway. If she could have communicated with Irini, steaming away in the sun . . . (She wore, Kathy saw then, not string but real rings in her ears, gold, with little turquoise studs: perhaps he had given them to her once, after a good cruise to Africa?) But how to communicate to Irini except through him?

'Here,' he said. 'You have a smoke now.' He said it in a consoling sort of way, as though he had divined her difficulty and sympathised. And his eyes, wrinkling at her obliquely through a curl of smoke, were not washed-out, after all, but dense with greyness gathered there for the light to find, and the iris ringed with black. She felt that he was filled with intention, with design of his own, whose declaration he would decide in his own good time, so that she and Irini would just have to go on sitting there formally awaiting his pleasure and signal for release.

It was not my intention that brought me here, Kathy thought. It was his.

The child Maria wiped her hands on her bag apron and went inside to bring a blue-bordered plate with a glass of water precisely centred and a dish of dried figs, but when Kathy had eaten and drunk, as she knew she must, the tableau remained unaltered, and the silence went on with the women's voices and the kites soaring in it and the close wet slap of cloth where the girl bent again to the tub, until to break it (realising that Irini would continue to sit there, neither patient nor impatient, but just sitting, until the man made up his mind) she said:

'It is a very beautiful kite you have made.'

He shrugged again, dismissing it, the beautiful kite propped against the stone with its tail and fringes rustling in anticipation and the three gnomes quietly eager, waiting together with their fingers to their noses. She thought of her own sons, and was ashamed.

'It passes the time,' he said.

'I've been watching them all the morning and wishing I was a child. I wanted to fly one too.'

He moved the cigarette from one side of his mouth to the other and looked down at her with that closed secret look. Then he jerked his head slightly. 'Want to fly it?'

'Now?' she asked, startled. 'Why . . .' and looked uncertainly from him to Irini still sitting there with the smile coming and going mysteriously, and thought that she had not told Milly where she was going.

The diver watched her, and did not miss the involuntary glance she cast downwards to the harbour where the Casopédes warehouse was visible and the men trampling bales.

'Come on.' He picked up the kite and turned his back and started up through the boulders. The three boys followed him, still quiet, but bumping one another in excitement. Irini jumped from her chair and pointed after him; she even gave Kathy's shoulder a push. The man had made his decision. He went on climbing, with his sons trotting after, and did not look back.

'Well, then . . .' she said, and since the two gigglers were crowding her close she offered them each a hand. They tugged ahead of her so that she moved up through the rocks with her arms extended in front of her, like a sleep-walker, or someone blind. The boys and girls who had danced around her up the mountainside still sat around the house, absorbed in some game with pebbles. Irini had returned to the washtub, shoulders and arms violently in motion, while the melancholy Maria went primly from boulder to boulder spreading a patchwork of wet rags weighted with stones against the wind. The toddler staggered after her, clutching a tin can. Not one of them looked up.

Above, the diver went ahead barefooted in the clay—the yellow heels and the tendons tautening, the black legs, the tight flat buttocks moving up and down, and the three large fragile skulls bobbing behind. The path was a goat trail that led up and around the mountain-face to a whitewashed chapel the size of a doll's house from where the whole valley was visible and across it the ruined Byzantine city on its crag, so that Kathy came round the corner with a sharp bright shock, like walking into a pane of glass. There was a slope stupefying with the smell of wild thyme—the wind running across it and the eldest of his sons already trotting against the wind, streaming the kite. The diver leaned against the chapel wall, cigarette tin ready in shaking hand.

'Thanks.' Kathy looked out, breathless, the wind in her face. 'I want to go up there one day. There, to the old city.'

'Sure.' He held the lighter in cupped hands against the wind. Narrow, shaking hands, calloused, and the middle and index fingers tobacco-stained. 'Plenty old, that place,' he said.

'Yes, I know. Have you been? What is it like?'

'Old. Plenty old. They was *rich* then, them fellers.' He said this word *rich* with such intensity that she thought he might enlarge on it, but instead he looked at her and said slyly: 'Why you cut off your hair like that? That's not nice for a woman.'

'I hurt my head in a motor-car accident. The doctors had to shave my hair off. It's growing now.'

'Can't you drive a car good?' He was intent, derisive, the smoke whipping away from his mouth and nostrils. But the curious thing was that she felt herself on the brink of . . . of what? Confession? Confessing to him what she had not yet confessed to herself! A strange feeling . . . that he of all the people she knew might understand. But among the thyme the boy had turned, backing to the kite's eager lift, playing the cord.

'Look,' she said quickly. 'It's going up.'

'Sure. You want to fly it now?'

'Let the children. I am happy to watch.'

'What you want,' he said. The kite was plunging restively, but still going up, and the three ragged urchins backing away across the slope. 'Just the job, eh?' he said, watching it, and then the two jetty little girls were blown to Kathy with their dirty paws clutched around whole fistful of snapped anemones which they thrust into her hands. The petals were purple and red, with the texture of crinkled silk. The flowers spilled into her lap.

'You like?'

'Oh yes. So beautiful. Thank you,' she said to the little girls in Greek, and they giggled behind their hands and ran away over the slope again. And Kathy thought again that nothing in the world can be imagined beforehand: everything, everything is made up of unique particulars. One could not have foreseen the anemones or the smell of thyme and tobacco or the way the sun would fall on this one man's face. Behind him, in the dark interior of the chapel, a wick burned in front of some dim ikon.

'Where did you learn to speak English?'

He grinned at her with a sort of cautious deprecation.

'The war. Little bit English. Little bit Italian. Little bit German. Don't speak good, though.'

'You're all right.'

He shrugged, denying it, and then suddenly he said, all in a rush: 'I want to speak it good. Real good. Like you.'

'Why, then you will if you really want to.'

He grinned again. Derisive.

'Surely,' she said. 'If you want to enough.'

'Gotta talk. Nobody here to talk to.'

'Talk to me.'

He squinted at her sidelong and jerked his head in the direction of the white walled-in villa, shimmering below them in the valley in the mottled green of its garden. 'He going to like that?'

She said sharply: 'Demetrius? What on earth does Demetrius have to do with it?'

Again his shoulders hunched in that dismissive shrug, and for a while they were silent with the wind all about them and the kite high now and slanted in the gallery of toy shapes lifting and drifting in the air. Kathy was thinking rather uneasily of Demetrius when the diver said in a flat, casual voice:

'Is Australia a good country?'

'How did you know I come from Australia?' She was surprised and pleased, rather.

'One feller talking. Can't remember. Every feller here knows you come from Australia.' His lip curled. 'This place,' he said.

'Every place is the same about gossip. Even Australia. But, yes, it's a good country. A fine country.' She groped for something that might convey it. The long brown roll of earth and the tin roofs and the shadows under the wide verandahs and the redgums wading in the billabongs, and that train hurrying across the miles of wheat stubble and pasture and baked earth to take her away from all that, herself hurrying to get away, to get to It, the Big Thing, not knowing yet what it was going to be but knowing certainly she would recognise it when she found it, knowing too, it was not back there, although in terms of size back there was big enough, only too empty, too utterly and uncompromisingly empty to conceal anything from seventeen when it was clear-eyed and searching. What *was* it I was always searching for? she wondered. And why, oh *why*, did I never find it? 'It's bare,' she said. 'A bit like this, some of it. But bare. Bare. And the rocks like this, some of them. But big. Bigger than you can imagine. Enormous. Well, you could tuck all of Greece into one little corner.'

'Plenty work there, eh? Plenty jobs?'

'Yes,' she said uncertainly. 'I think so. Yes, of course there are.'

'You got one house there?'

'Oh no. No. I live in London. My husband is English, you see. It is eleven years and more since I left Australia.' Because Sydney had not been big enough, after all, but there had been so much time still ahead of her at twenty to find It, the Big Thing, whatever it was she was going to recognise the moment she came across it. It had to be somewhere else, somewhere farther on, and at twenty she had set out again, across thirteen thousand miles of seas and oceans, with an arts degree now and formal permission from the parents back there in the homestead beside the Murrumbidgee who had long since relinquished the right to permit or deny, not believing precisely that she would have walked it if necessary but knowing that she would have made the journey without degree or permission somehow or other, because London would be big enough to contain the wonder or the sign that it was her inalienable right to claim as her own.

'Lots of fellers here want to go to Australia,' the diver said, conversationally.

'Yes?'

'Sure. Plenty fellers.' He threw the cigarette stub to the wind and bent down and took an anemone from her lap and stuck it in the corner of his mouth. He looked up at the kite, high and steady now with only a languid flowing of the tail. 'Nothing here but the diving,' he said. 'Fellers don't like the diving.'

'You?' she said, watching him. 'Do you like the diving?'

Again the jerk of the thin shoulders. The anemone petals were trembling against his cheek. 'Nothing else to do here,' he said, his head tipped back, intent on the kite. A nerve in his cheek jumping, jumping.

She said, carefully: 'Do you want to go to Australia too? Like the others?'

He looked at her then, obliquely, but still with the nerve twitching, and his throat corded in tenseness. 'Don't know someone to write the paper. Got to have the paper to go to Australia.' Tiny pale points of heat in his eyes, silver hot like charcoal embers. The desire hot and fierce, consuming.

So that is what he wants of me, Kathy thought, and was shaken with disappointment like tears. She said cheerfully, to conceal it: 'Well, I don't really know anything about it. But I will ask Demetrius. He's sure to know.' The two points of heat cooling, or banked down, and the grin offhand, repudiating interest. 'I can find out,' she said quickly. I promise I will find out. I can do that much.'

'Sure,' he said, with an air of confidence that was oddly delicate, as if he was attempting to reassure her, and then he turned his head to the children and the kite and laughed on a sudden high excited note. 'Just the job, eh?' The kite was triumphantly aloft, higher than any other. Taut, fringed, emblazoned, it streamed up and up into the thin blown limitless morning, and the diver watched it with his head back-arched and his face held up still to the sky.

Kathy turned her own face up quickly so that the wind would whip the tears away from the corners of her eyes. There was no reason why his bare feet in the clay should hurt her so. But they did. They did. Intolerably.

13

Demetrius, in suède sneakers, picked his way delicately through the expanse of drying sponges spread yellow across an acre like a field of mustard.

'Kathy!' he called across, and on the steps Kathy hesitated, then waved, descended the last flight, and crossed the cobbles to the yard gate, swinging her shopping basket. 'What a nice surprise,' he said. 'Come in and have a glass of sherry with me while I finish up and we can walk back to lunch together.' He opened the gate and offered his arm with the courtesy of an Edwardian gentleman conducting a lady through the conservatory. He was wearing his working glasses, tinted slightly and with heavy black library frames: they added a touch of earnestness to his appearance that seemed theatrical: he was indeed a very handsome man.

In the shallows the long balletic line of men and boys, who had kept their heads politely lowered at Kathy's approach, now raised them again. Their arms were clasped behind their backs, their bare, blue, cold-mottled legs stamped up and down, up and down, treading a slow and stately rhythm on the chill ruffled sea.

'The Chorus,' Kathy said, and smiled and wished them a good morning. She received in return a battery of curious, considering eyes and a quick shy ripple of teeth: only one man, big, heavily moustached, brutal-looking, stared back at her with surly, unmistakable dislike.

'Not a very disciplined chorus. But articulate in their fashion. And terribly observant.' High against the bare rock, the house was visible. Even the bright scraps of clothes spread about and the bent pigmy figure of Irini at her washtub. Behind the crag the kite still strained up into the morning. 'How was Aunt Polymnia?' he asked.

'Not there. Out on a mercy errand, I suppose.' But she knew that he knew where she had been, as the men treading the sponges knew, and the men at the bleaching vats and the sponge presses and the men with the bagging needles and the men with the clipping shears. Walking down the length of the cool dark shed she was aware of the speculative eyes regarding her from the flanks of soft salty mountains of sponges, from ramps and rafters and piled wooden crates. 'Good morning,' she said, and called them by name. 'Good morning, Manólis. Georgios. Gregóri. Heraclés. Sotéro . . .'

'They like you very much, Kathy,' Demetrius said to her, pleased. 'Your knowing their names, they appreciate little things like that. They *do* like you.'

Demetrius's private office was at the very end of the vast building, on the street side, and beyond the big general office where Paul and Lazarus worked.

It was a room to which Kathy had become very attached, because of its air of immutability, she thought—an old-fashioned ponderousness perfectly pickled in the strong briny smell of sponges. Demetrius had not attempted to effect change here. The roll-top desk, the leather chairs, the heavy glass paperweight, the elaborate inkstand with its square-cut bottles of violet and blue and red, the mahogany bookcase stuffed with the cracking leather spines of old ledgers and ships' logbooks, the stuffed gull with its mad staring eyes fixed on the equally imbecile gaze of a mounted frigatebird, the walnut-framed photograph of an undistinguished London office building—one felt that these things had all survived, and would continue to survive, generations of change. The walls were a clutter of framed things. Three medals from an 1892 Trade Exposition in Brussels. A watercolour painting of the three-masted barque *Agios Nikólas* primly upright on a frenetic sea with gigantic flags streaming from each masttruck, all looking as if they were cut from buckled tinplate and the one at the mainmast bearing the name Casopédes. An extraordinary lithograph depicting a cross-section of the ocean, showing an armada of boats above and an army of divers crawling around on the sea-floor, each connected to the other in a mad criss-cross of airlines, weight-lines, and signal-lines (the picture was enclosed within a floridly decorative ribbon which bore the legend, *Nikólas Casopédes and Sons, 643 Lower Broadway, New York City, Wholesale Merchants of Fine Sponges*). Two photographs of tramp-steamers. The teeth and jawbone of a huge shark. A pair of builders' half-models of caïque hulls, darkly varnished over obscurely delicate laminations. A picture of a sponge-diving caïque anchored off a desert coast, with fiercely moustached men lined up along the weather cloth with their arms folded. An enormous glass-fronted cabinet containing an odd menagerie of curio-sponges shaped like animals or birds or reptiles. And sternly presiding over all this memorabilia of now-forgotten significance the yellowish marble head of Demetrius's great-grandfather, Nikólas Demetrius Casopédes himself, which appeared to have been vat-bleached and pickled also, and set upon a column of veined green marble to govern in perpetuity the affairs of Casopédes and Heirs.

The heir-incumbent opened the leaded doors of another cabinet and said: 'Tio Pepe or something a little less dry? There's Bristol Cream . . . Dry Fly . . .'

'What you're having,' said Kathy. He took out a square crystal decanter and two Georgian glasses with spiral-blown stems and set them down between the ornamental sponges on the sideboard.

Demetrius looked affectionately at the marble bust and said: 'When the old chap here came back from the West Indies he would never allow anything in his cabinet except rum. He had acquired a taste for it.' He poured the sherries and lifted his own glass in toast to the stern stone face of his ancestor with the frowning pouchy eyes and the fiercely curled moustaches and the sharp imperial and the sideburns hanging like leaden weights below his ears. 'Strange to think of him,' he said, almost with a trace of wistfulness, 'out there in those outlandish places with one little boat and seven homesick sailors from this island here, trying to do something nobody had ever done before. Out there in Turks Islands, and Tobago, and the Dry Tortugas . . . So strange . . .'

'He did it, though, didn't he?' Kathy said, oddly moved by Demetrius's expression.

'With a face like that how could he help it?' He smiled at her gently. 'Yes,' he said, 'he was the richest man in Greece when he came back here ten years later. He made Casopédes and Heirs, and he gave life back to this island. He was a man with scale,' he said, and looked away as if something had embarrassed him. 'How is the sherry?' he said. 'Too dry for you?'

She shook her head and smiled.

'And, more important than that, Kathy, how do you feel today? You worried me terribly last night.'

'It was good of you to take so much trouble. Did . . . did you stay with me long? I mean . . . I don't remember . . . I never do very clearly. It's humiliating.'

His slow full eyes were secretive behind the tinted glasses. 'I stayed until I was certain you were sleeping.' His fingers touched hers as he took her sherry glass to be refilled. 'You must not feel humiliated,' he said gently. So that she was suddenly uneasy, and to break the moment of intimacy he had trapped her in she made a wry little face and raised her glass to the blank stone eyes of the marble bust, smooth as sugar almonds.

'Your health, sir,' she said lightly. 'If you grew a moustache and imperial you'd look just like him, Demetrius. The very spit and image.'

'I wish I could afford to behave like him.'

'He would have been feudal, I suppose? Feudal and grand. I rather like that.'

'It was a different island then, before the occupation.' His wistfulness was apparent. 'He kept a liveried boat-crew and a private band of musicians. Even the sponge captains had their own musicians then. And on the old chap's name day—because Nikólas is the patron saint of seamen too—he had forty or fifty sheep slaughtered and roasted on the spit and all the island came and danced and feasted. They fired cannons from the terrace of the house—the house where Paul lives now—and to every orphaned girl on the island he would give a golden sovereign

77

towards her dowry. Good times, Kathy. They say that in the winter when the boats were laid up the Turks in Anatolia could hear the music of this island. We'll never see those days again.'

'Still,' she said reasonably, 'I've not noticed any evidence of dire want in your establishment.'

Demetrius rapped his forefinger three times against the desk-top. 'Please God! All the same, if we are in a sound position now it's only because I had the foresight to begin the strategic withdrawal when my father died. From this business, I mean. In fifteen years—well, twenty perhaps—the natural sponge will be found only in marine museums. A curiosity.' He shrugged.

She thought he sounded defiant, perhaps because of the stern presence on the green column and the disconcerting stare of those pale, pouched, lozenge eyes. She ran her fingers through the sponges in the wire sample tray. They were dry and hard to the touch. Dead things. Skeletons. 'Let me try now,' she said. 'That one is from off Tripoli. This one is Alexandrian. And this coarse one from Crete, no?'

'No,' he said, smiling. 'Pantellaria. But you are doing very well. An excellent pupil, Kathy. I wish Milly would display the same interest.'

'Did you expect her to?'

'No . . .' he said. 'No, I don't suppose I did.'

'It never occurred to me that you were marrying Milly because of her possible interest in the sponge trade.'

'True,' he said, and laughed softly. 'But at that time I didn't know how pleasant it would be to have a beautiful woman relieving the monotony of this old barn. It *is* very pleasant, Kathy. Did you know that?'

But she bent her head until he could see the red brush of hair and the bright wings of eyebrows sharp and pointed on her brow, and her hand went on moving among the sponges.

'It's so queer to think that these were living creatures once. All oozy and dark and mysterious at the bottom of the sea . . .' She sniffed at a triangular wedge of bleached sponge cut as sharply as a piece of cheese, and then her head came up and she looked at him ironically. 'It only smells of peroxide or something now you've finished with it. Well, what next, Demetrius? Synthetics?'

'But of course, my dear. Synthetics are the whole future. Cheap, durable, easy to produce . . .' All right, all right, he thought with a soft amusement. We will keep it at sponges for the moment. There are months ahead to change the subject.

'I think it's too revolting,' she said, and he thought that her eyes were the colour of marmalade. Little shreds of orange in them. Challenging eyes. So much the better. 'Those horrible poison-pink squares,' she said disgustedly, 'instead of these mysterious skeletons from Mersa Matruh and Derna and Tobruk and Benghazi. *And* Pantellaria. Can't you fight it? God, I would!'

'My dear Kathy, I would be fighting myself. The trade in natural sponges is doomed. Once upon a time there were half a dozen in every bathroom. They had a million uses in industry. Who uses them now? The high-class potteries, some sections of the automobile business, scraps to go into cartons with the tubes of shoe-polish. No, Kathy, it doesn't do any longer. I have been ploughing everything into synthetics since I took over. Every drachma I've been able to lay my hands on. Those two freighters there on the wall'—he pointed to the photographs—'sold,' he said, and spread his hands. 'Why pay for lay-ups in every little tramp tonnage crisis? Those two and eight others like them. Sold. Agencies now in London and New York and Berlin instead of our own offices. All that overhead saved, Kathy, to go into synthetics.' He laughed. 'Don't look so outraged, Kathy. Have a cigarette. And some more of that sherry. After all, shipping companies put their capital into airlines. It's common sense.'

'Of course I'm outraged. I think everybody in the world ought to be outraged. It's the end of the natural order. It . . . it's darkness descending for ever on the beautiful sensible mysteries. I wonder someone hasn't found a synthetic as yet for this sherry we're drinking! Demetrius, what is *he* thinking about all this?' she said, looking at the marble bust. 'After all that guts and effort and struggle . . . his little boat and those outlandish islands you talked about . . .'

'He had *his* day,' said Demetrius simply. 'His opportunity. Now it's my turn. This is a hundred years later, Kathy. It's a different world.'

'You're right, of course. And I am guilty too.' She glanced down at her white polo jersey distastefully and rubbed the shoulder of it. 'This isn't really wool,' she said. 'It's chemicals. Wears better. Doesn't matt in the wash or turn yellow in the sun.' And she saw, suddenly and vividly, the crocheted edge at the neck of the diver's raw wool undershirt. Irini would have spun the wool herself. Combed it and washed it in the sea and spun, and then knitted it according to a pattern so ancient as to be almost an instinct. 'What will happen to them, Demetrius?' she asked suddenly. 'The divers? When you are turning out your marshmallow squares what will they do?'

'There won't be any divers. Only a few old men sitting in the sun and boring their grandchildren with interminable stories of sponges and sharks and cities under the sea.'

He walked to the window and looked up the ramp to where the lanes spilled out into this far end of the waterfront, and the coffee-tables were packed along the whitewashed walls, out of the wind. Twenty men, perhaps thirty men, were sitting in groups over coffee and ouzo and brandy, black and white in the sunshine and the coloured tassels of the amber beads flicking like hummingbirds. He sipped his sherry and let the pale gold lie on his tongue a moment.

'The rest?' he said. 'Some will have gone to sea in merchant ships, some will have become fishermen, some will have drifted into labouring jobs in the town. Some will have emigrated. Some— a few—will have swallowed their pride and will be turning out that pink marshmallow. Blue too. And green. We produce a range of colours in the Piraeus factory, Kathy. We'll be ready to begin the final switch-over in a few years. There will be employment for some. Although I don't like employing divers.'

'Why not?' Her chin came up and her voice was sharp.

And his was angry, with the accent more pronounced suddenly. 'They're troublemakers,' he said. 'Every last one of them.'

He sipped his sherry with deliberation, a little startled at his own anger and trying to hide it from her. For he never admitted to himself that he was afraid of them really. Afraid of their lawlessness, their recklessness. Afraid of the force of their mass which in some way seemed to threaten the order of his life. Afraid because this order of his life was still dependent upon *them.* He had always felt like this about them, and since he had returned to London to take over the business—and to fight the opposition to his plans from his uncle and his cousins—the feeling had been more intense than ever. He had been uneasy many times in this last year, and had had to shake off a peculiar dread of the unexpected. For (not even Milly knew this) he was clinging tenaciously to the memory of the Pink oscillating under the bare elms and the horn sounding over the lovely hills, the green Bristol purring down English lanes, point-to-point meetings on churned fields, mild-and-bitter in country pubs and darts thucking into cork, safe and peaceful names like Chipping Camden and Bourton-on-the-Water and Stow-on-the-Wold. And for this dream he would be patient. Ten years, he thought, with a sweet yearning. Ten years. A gentleman's farm in the Cotswolds, and the children riding at gymkhanas, and Milly, in tweeds, opening the church bazaar. But in the meantime, he, the heir, was responsible to the other heirs of Casopédes, the complex of family that must be satisfied with investments and land and houses and dowries, marriages to be arranged, educations to be completed, futures to be discussed and settled . . . and all of this still dependent upon that handful of lawless men who were wild and unpredictable, and whom he feared.

Kathy looked troubled, watching him, trying to read the subtleties behind the handsome heavy mask of his face. She could hear the big presses thudding, and a sudden splintering of wood. Out in the shed the men began to laugh and shout, and then there was Lazarus's barking voice, loud in query. She said abruptly, as if this was a signal, 'Look, I wanted to ask you something.'

'Yes?' He was half listening to the disturbance outside, gauging its importance, and then a man began to sing 'White Ribbons', very sweet and laughing, and the regular work noises began again, and he turned to her, controlled, polite, gentle, assured. 'What is it, my dear?'

'Well, this morning I've been visiting the family of that diver— you remember, the one we met in the street. Yes, yes, I know you advised me against it, but it was something I felt I just had to do. Eight children, Demetrius. The woman pregnant again. A sick baby. I thought perhaps I could help . . .' I *did* believe that I could help, she thought unhappily. There had been something in the face of the diver held still to the sky that her whole being had recognised, an appeal like an echo to the rapt searching of her girlhood and youth, like a familiar cry caught and flung back on the wind, a passionate affirmation of that old lost desire to face challenge and danger, to be brave, to dare for the truth. Ah, but how to tell this to Demetrius! 'How can one help them? Such desperate poverty, Demetrius. And those heartbreaking children . . .'

Demetrius had taken off his glasses and laid them on the desk, and he was now regarding the end of his cigarette with darkly impenetrable eyes. 'Of course,' he said, guardedly.

'I mean . . . I thought . . . well, this question of migration. There must be somewhere I can write and get information. How he should go about it, I mean.'

'There is. The International Committee for European Migration. But why should you take it on yourself to make inquiries about a procedure with which your—er—your protégé is perfectly conversant already?'

'What do you mean?'

'There is not a man on this island who does not know every detail, every condition, of emigration off by heart. If this man were eligible—and I assure you emphatically he isn't—he would have made his own application long ago.'

'All the same,' she said with a show of confidence she was far from feeling, 'I think I will make the inquiries. I said I would.'

He gave a little puff of laughter, but it was as though his insides were growing as dark as his eyes, and the laughter came out like a small cloud presaging storm. 'I hate to say "I told you so", Kathy, but I knew that if you demonstrated any interest in that family you'd get yourself involved. Just leave it, my dear. Leave it. Your motives are commendable, but you are wasting your time and saddling yourself with more nuisance and trouble than you can imagine. Believe me, I've already told you, that particular character isn't worth a thought or a breath.'

'Yes, but even if that is true—oh, it may be: how should I know?—the dilemma appears stark enough. For his family, at any rate. And the man . . .' It was curious that neither of them seemed to be able to refer to him in any other way. The man. '. . . the man appears to be . . . desperate.' It needed a stronger word than that to convey the face lifted to the kite, the wild, the piercing hope of it. But she could not explain further to Demetrius. It would be like a betrayal.

'Good divers can make quite a lot of money, you know. Quite enough to support their families adequately.'

'But, Demetrius! Those children don't even have shoes! And I swear they are hungry. They look hungry. Undernourished, anyway. You can't mistake that look on a child's face.'

'I am not suggesting that you did. There is a great deal of poverty among the divers' families. But this is not because we are a bunch of Simon Legrees, Kathy. It's not because the men don't earn enough money. If you were down here any night through the winter you would understand better. Good God! why do we have a police force here big enough for a concentration camp or . . . or Alcatraz! Every night thousands of drachmas pass over the table . . . gallons of wine, cards, *tavli*, the toss of a coin . . . some of these types will gamble on anything. I've seen—I've actually seen, Kathy—the earnings of a whole seven months' diving go in one night! And their wives are invariably pregnant and their children invariably undernourished.' And on a flash of incipient triumph he looked at her. 'But I'll bet,' he said, 'that your protégé has a gold ring, though? And a cigarette lighter of the most expensive make?'

83

She said angrily: 'All right. Suppose that is true. And suppose that this man does get drunk every night and gamble away all his money. There must be a *reason* for it. Isn't it likely that they— the ones you talk about—drink and gamble because it may very well be their last chance on earth to do so?'

But anger had pushed her just too far, and now Demetrius pushed back his head and laughed. For he saw that her passionate idealism, which for a moment he had felt as a threat, was only, after all, womanishness. For a moment he had been ʋred into treating her as an equal. And she was only a woman. He laughed indulgently. 'Kathy, *Kathy*! You are the most shocking romantic about sponge-diving!'

She slid her hand into the wire tray again, and turned the sponges over one by one. She sensed the change in him and was suddenly uncertain. She said carefully: 'If it is roman tic to align oneself on the side of the victim—yes, then I suppose I am. But I don't *feel* romantic about it, Demetrius. I feel moved. Deeply, terribly moved. I feel shocked. Appalled. There is so little bravery left in all the world. And when I think of these unfortunate men dying at the bottom of the sea, being crippled, deafened, mauled by sharks ... well, I just don't think one should judge them by the conventional standards. I don't think one *can*! My God, Demetrius, you can't deny that the work is appalling? There are men killed every season. Men crippled. There must be hundred and hundreds of cripples in this town ... I see them everywhere.'

Demetrius covered her hand among the sponges with his own and smiled at her gently, with concern. 'And believing this, my dear, you condemn me for trying to bring an end to it? You really are being inconsistent, Kathy.' Women were always inconsistent. It was one of their charms.

Kathy bit her lip in vexation. But they were not communicating any longer. The conversation was on an entirely different level, and his masculinity was disconcerting to her. Somehow he had diminished her in a sexual way.

'You mustn't allow yourself to become overwrought about it, Kathy dear,' he said. 'Nobody has ever denied that the work is dangerous. But on the other hand you must not credit these very simple people with your own extreme sensitivity and imagination. To them it is work. Risky work, yes, but still only work. With the risks largely dependent upon their own skill, and the compensation of half a year's holiday every year.'

'Then why are they all so anxious to leave it? You said there isn't one of them who wouldn't emigrate if he could.'

'It is a very ancient Greek tradition, my dear. Since time began. We have always been great voyagers. Emigrants. Colonists. We are also, now, a very poor people. It is natural that these men should want to go and seek their fortunes, and it is natural that they should want to seek them at as great a distance as possible. The lure of the unknown. The belief in the fabulous. The golden apples of the Hesperides. Those green hills far away.'

It accorded well with her instinct about the diver. But it wasn't right. Not absolutely. His motivations were starker than that. More *necessitous*. His needs were immediate and primary and real. But she could not think clearly about this with the sweet dense maleness of Demetrius invading her through the cushioned pressure of his warm hand. My own motives need clarifying, she thought. Like a bowl of old dripping. She retrieved her hand and drank her sherry.

'Perhaps you're right,' she said with deliberate vagueness. 'You obviously know much more about it than I do ... All the same,' she added, and gave him a rather hypocritical little-girl smile that appealed to his male indulgence, 'I still think I will have to write that letter. After all, I said I would.'

She did write that afternoon, to the International Committee for European Migration, at the Athens address which Demetrius gave her with his eyelids heavy and his mouth tender and his fingertips held together in forbearance, and by the same mail (urged by a sudden, desperate need for contact) she wrote to Irwin, and another letter to her sons—those sturdy little boys with the sorrel eads and the fox-brown eyes who lived with their doting Granny in Gloucestershire and rode ponies and liked Madeira cake better than raisin bread for their afternoon tea. But she could not believe that the words she wrote would ever reach them. She had to make them up, imagine them piece by piece, and she broke out in a sweat at the sheer exertion of it. She could touch neither Irwin in London nor those little boys in Gloucestershire. There seemed no proof of their existence at all.

14

But what was real was this:

There came to the house one morning two men who asked Aliki if they might speak to the lady from Australia. They were both men of middle age, wearing the high boots and black peaked caps of sponge-divers. Very polite men. Their feet, following the indignant approach of Aliki's up the hall, sounding quite diffident on the polished boards. Caps held against chests in big salt-hardened hands. Shirts so newly pressed they showed scorch-marks from the charcoal iron.

They had a question to ask, which was put by the older of the two men in a slow, soft, clear, simple voice that did not really require Milly's flustered, incredulous translation. Australia, he said. Australia. Was it true what they had heard in the port? 'Could the lady write a permit?'

'*Well!*' Milly gasped when the door had closed on them. 'What on earth could have put *that* into their heads? And what impertinence for them to come up here like that!'

Kathy said hastily: 'No, no. Not impertinence. I don't think so. They've probably heard around the port somewhere that I've written a letter to the migration people. I imagine things get about in a small place like this. It was sensible of them, really, to come and ask me themselves.'

But she was disturbed when, after lunch—and so immediately after Demetrius had returned to the warehouse that it appeared to be calculated—a woman called with seven new-laid eggs tied up in a clean napkin, and prodding before her an embarrassed youth who wore a huge black moustache like a hand-me-down from one of his elders. The woman was ingratiating, but bold. Or at least determined.

Her son's name, she said, was Panayotis. He was a good

boy. A strong boy. He had never had a day's illness in his life. He could *work*. Work? Why, he could lift that table in his teeth to show the lady if she needed proof of his strength. This time, Aliki, having accepted the eggs on Kathy's behalf, stood inside the doorway with the napkin held against her stomach, nodding agreement and encouragement and occasionally offering an interjection.

'Really, Kathy, this is too much! The woman's Aliki's cousin or something. The boy's the only son among five daughters . . . they don't have dowries . . . something like that. Honestly, this *is* too much!'

The woman pleaded her way out, hand to forehead in the Turkish style, holding the boy's shoulder with the other, displaying him to the end. Aliki looked at Kathy without expression and made the slightest shrug before she conducted the visitors to the kitchen, where they remained for the rest of the afternoon in earnest conference. Stamatis came in from the garden to change over the gas bottles, and he too remained in the kitchen. Their voices warbled and whispered for hours.

When, at dinner, Milly told Demetrius of the episode he laughed, his eyes warm on Kathy's discomfiture.

' "Life is short, art is long, the occasion fleeting, experience deceitful, and judgement difficult",' he quoted. 'Especially is judgement difficult. Isn't that so, Kathy?'

The next day there were two more divers who came singly, and one who was accompanied by his wife, a skinny goitrous little thing with lovely skin and hands. By the third visit Kathy felt that her breath was being squeezed out of her, and it was an agony to have to depend on Milly—confused now, indignant, aggrieved—to explain the impossibility, the regret, the misunderstanding, while she herself could only smile sympathetically and shake her head or take refuge in gestures against those eyes—the grave ones of the men, the incredibly starting ones of the woman. They were all such polite people, so quiet, with the hope held in, tight, and when they left they went as politely as they had come, without reproach or insistence,

88

but only that last backward look, direct, dark, considering.

Over the coffee and brandy Demetrius said: 'Maybe you would prefer to work in my study, Kathy? Where you could deal with your applicants undisturbed.'

'You mean that *I* could deal with them,' said Milly with sudden snappish superiority.

'Splendid! Couldn't be better for your terminations, darling. Excellent practice.' His eyes were very merry. 'Oh, I forgot to tell you, Kathy,' he said, 'that I have four more for your consideration. Workmen of mine. They asked if I would tender their applications for them. Shall I submit them formally now or do you insist on personal interviews?' He was laughing all over. Masculinity ascendant.

'After all,' Milly said, smugly ascending on her husband's triumph like a basket under a balloon, 'we did warn you that if you mixed yourself up with those awful people . . . I mean to say, one simply *must* keep one's distance. If you'd been here as long as I have, ducky, you'd realise there's just no other way.'

'If Kathy had been here as long as you have, my pet, she would have been elected mayor by this time. She has learnt more about the island in a few weeks than you have done in two whole years.'

Milly's eyes glazed over and she bit her lip unsteadily, but she controlled her tears until Demetrius, still imperturbable, had retired to his study to check through a new batch of foreign orders.

'Oh, damn and blast his island!' she cried. 'I hate it! *Hate it!* And now that I look hideous he doesn't care about me any more. He cares about you more than he does about me. He *does*, Kathy. He thinks I'm ugly and stupid and good for nothing. No matter how I try to please him. God, I wish I was *dead!*'

And although Kathy smiled a little at this, having heard Milly wishing herself dead at intervals since she was ten years old, she was troubled. More than she cared to admit. She felt muddy, clouded, unsure. She started having headaches again. She was tempted to return to London, and confided as much to Milly, who at once went into a passion bordering on hysteria.

'If you abandon me now, if you leave me to these black

crows, I . . . I don't know what I'll do! I'll do something awful! I swear I will!'

Sighing, Kathy reassured her. She didn't want to leave the island really. Not yet. Even though she was beginning to feel that she had made rather a fool of herself. It had been a presumption to meddle. Her intuition had been unsound.

Try as she would, she could not recapture the certainty that had seemed to reveal itself to her on the day of the kites. Instead was only the certainty that the diver had been boasting in taverns and coffee-houses—a nagging grain of humiliation, this, which she dealt with oyster-like, growing it over with stealthy secretions of pride. She had fulfilled her promise to him in writing the letter to the migration committee. As soon as a reply came she would communicate it to him and wash her hands of the whole business.

But when she saw him again she still had heard nothing, and felt as guilty as if she personally were responsible for the workings of bureaucracy.

It was in the crowded lane where the shoemakers had their shops, and the ironmongers, and where there was a tavern called The New World, a dark long room with a bamboo ceiling, lined with numbered barrels, and with trestle-tables and benches on the sawdust-sprinkled floor. It had a vine outside the door and on a stormy day you could hear the sea growling under its gutters, louder than the shouts and laughter inside.

He was leaning in the doorway, looking dejected. Looking sick. He's drunk, she thought, and was glad, because of her pride, because of the humiliation that pride covered, because of her guilt on behalf of the migration committee. And she was glad because of her own elegance, for she had been at the bank cashing travellers' cheques and had dressed rather formally in a dark pleated skirt and a corded blazer of fine purple and black stripes. The vine outside The New World was valiantly trying to bud, and the sea growled tentatively beneath the gutters, and he swayed a little against the vine.

She stopped, conscious of the sudden silence within the tavern, of the suddenly immobile figures in shop doorways, and she smiled

90

at him pleasantly and said: 'There's no news yet. I am sorry. I will let you know.'

'Sure,' he said, and waved a vague hand. 'That's O.K. Sure.'

'How is the baby?'

'O.K. O.K.'

'And your wife?'

'Irini? She's fine,' he said. 'Fine.'

'Good. That's splendid, then,' Kathy said cheerfully, and still maintaining an expression of impersonal friendliness. 'Incidentally,' she said, 'lots of men have been coming up to the house to ask about going to Australia. Divers. Friends of yours, I expect.'

His mouth twisted. 'Plenty fellers here want to go to Australia.'

'But . . .' She hesitated, summoning patience. 'But you do see that I *can't*, don't you? It isn't fair to them to let them think otherwise. All I can do is write a letter and find out how you go about it. Couldn't you tell them that?'

'Sure,' he said nonchalantly. 'I'll tell 'em.' And then, 'They're jealous, them other fellers.'

'*Jealous?* What on earth . . .'

'Sure. Plenty jealous. I tell 'em you write the letter for me, not for them.'

'But—*look,*' she said, exasperated. 'It isn't at all certain that anything will come of it. You *must* understand that. I don't want you to be disappointed. Don't you see?'

'Sure,' he said, and his uncanny grey eyes crinkled at her in sudden gentleness, and he smiled with that queer little air of reassurance. 'That's O.K. Not to be worrying now.'

And then, as she stood there indecisively, not sure whether she wanted to march off in anger or burst into laughter, he said:

'When you like to be going up to that old place?'

'What old place?'

'Up there. Where you said you liked to be going.'

'Oh, the old city? I don't know. Some time.'

'Today?'

'No. Not today. I must go visiting today.' Aunt Sophia and

the sluggish daughters. Stiff chairs. Honey-cakes. Glandular children in embroidered bibs.

'Next day?' he asked, very soft and insistent.

'I don't know. I hadn't thought about it.'

'O.K. Next day.' He looked at her directly, intently, eyes fiercely hot, fiercely pale in the pale sick face swaying a little against the budding vine. The sea grumbled under the gutter and the smell of it came up, thin and harsh. The people in the street were still immobilised with interest. 'I wait for you down the road a bit. Not near your house. Two o'clock,' he said.

She went on with her head high, through the pots and pans and the strings of sandals soled with old motor tyres and the festoons of steel nuts. Through the interested eyes watching from doorways. Through the formal greetings and responses. She was filled with a nervous dismay.

But, after all, I needn't go, she thought. I didn't say I would.

15

Next morning after breakfast—Maxwell House coffee, Danish bacon, American canned milk, Dutch butter, English kippers, but the grapefruit and oranges from the garden and tasting of sunshine—she said casually: 'I think I might go exploring up in the old city this afternoon. I've been meaning to for ages.' Through the dining-room windows she could see it on its crag. The little chapels had a pink tinge in the morning light.

Aliki was clearing away the breakfast things with the help of a very small girl who had lately attached herself to the household, and Demetrius relaxed under the hands of the barber who came up from the port every morning to shave him. The dining-room was long, and furnished in black oak. There was a carved buffet loaded with old brown Wedgwood, very fine and dim and beautiful, and the chairs were high, with heavy carving around the woven cane backs and seats. There was a set of Leech's comic hunting prints on the walls, and some good horse brasses that Demetrius had picked up in Broadway. The windows were curtained in frosty white muslin, and pots of basil sat on each ledge in white wire holders.

Kathy remained at the table, idling with the littered pages of a two-day-old *Akropoli*, while Milly, in a yellow woollen robe, came and went from the downstairs washroom, bringing (or bearing, for this was a ritual) the ceremonial articles for Demetrius's toilet: the leather strop, dark with age and nicked along one edge, the damascened razor in a case of morocco leather lined with blue silk so old and frayed that one might almost blow it into a puff of blue morning, the silver mug misted with steam and the silver-handled brush with the bristles worn down to a stub like a docked tail, the towels white with that utmost whiteness of snow or sails or gulls' wings or the crests of waves, the tortoiseshell combs and the silver-backed brushes, the tubes and pots and jars of extreme and expensive packaging—shaving-cream, after-shave lotion, cologne, rosewater, talcum, bay rum—whose elegance competed with those other articles lustred by age (although Kathy thought that spikenard and myrrh and frankincense would have been more absolutely suitable, in porphry pots, with jewelled stoppers. She had once suggested it to Demetrius.).

The morning sunlight chanted over all this in little rilling cadences, and over the crumbs and a topaz of spilt marmalade on the white breakfast cloth, over a glittering lock of Milly's hair and the piercing white note of the diamond on her finger, over Aliki's hands, as hard and dark as the earth, moving patiently among the soiled plates, over the face of the barber Tomás—which was pale, plump, and obsequious as befitted his trade, but with dense thickets of eyebrows that jutted and curled over according to some timeless instinct, giving the top half of his face an expression of extraordinary belligerence. He bent to the razor caressing the strop, and behind him, through the open garden door, old Stamatis limped painfully down the path and stopped to look at a young almond-tree that had foamed into blossom overnight.

'The old city? But . . .' Under the rapidly circling brush Demetrius's cheeks and chin, massaged with shaving-cream, began to froth like whisked egg-whites. His lips grew as dark as slices of aubergine. His little gappy teeth turned faintly yellow.

'. . . alone?' he asked.

Tomás turned his face deftly, stretching the skin between thumb and forefinger. The razor, right-angled and hurling light, swept a glossy blue swathe down his jawbone.

'Dear girl,' he said, 'it's a terribly out-of-the way sort of place.'

She waited until his mouth, contorted under Tomás's skilfully stretching fingers, came back to where it belonged. The smooth blue cheek was turned and Tomás began on the foaming one. She said to it: 'Good heavens! Don't tell me it's *dangerous!*' Laughing a little. 'Are there bandits in them thar hills?'

'My dear. Of course it isn't dangerous. You are as safe anywhere on the island as you are in this house. It's only that . . .'

'It's only that they live in the Dark Ages here,' Milly dubbed for him. 'Women are not supposed to traipse about unescorted. Nobody would even understand why you *wanted* to.'

Tomás raised one finger and those two belligerent eyebrows that denied the obsequious smile. Milly quickly folded a clean towel and took the scummy one from Demetrius's shoulder. Aliki stepped forward and took the scummy towel from Milly, and the small girl took it from Aliki and left the room. Tomás completed an upstroke with a commendable and excusable flourish, stepped back to admire, and moved in to the delicate job of the upper lip. Small scratching noises and Demetrius's mouth pulled into a gargoyle shape. The dining-room smelt delicious.

Upright for a moment and tentatively touching his cheeks, Demetrius said: 'Why not wait until Sunday, Kathy? I would very much like to come with you. It is a fascinating old place, but actually you do need a guide to get the best from it.' He leaned back and presented his throat to Tomás.

'Let's *do* that!' Milly cried in pleasure. 'If it's a nice day we could make a picnic of it.'

Demetrius stayed Tomás's hand. 'And how do you think you are going to climb a mountain, my pet?' he inquired gently of the cracked plaster ceiling.

So that's it, Kathy thought, and knew that she had been expecting some move from him for quite a long time.

'We could get donkeys at the village, couldn't we?' Milly asked. 'Let's do it. Yes, let's.'

Demetrius's thick smooth throat emerged swathe by swathe from the lather. His thick smooth eyelids were closed in sensuous pleasure, and his hands fell limp and dreamy from his wrists resting on the carved chair arms.

Tomcat's paws, thought Kathy, waiting.

Tomás stepped back a pace and Demetrius sat up and began

95

twisting his face about, working the muscles. It was bare and shining and faintly blue, and still frothed a little at the nostrils and ears.

'My darling little idiot,' he said forbearingly. 'Have you the faintest memory of what that path is like?'

'But Vassos *said* I should have more exercise. *You* said I should have more exercise.'

'No, Milly,' he said gently but firmly, and reached across to pat her hand. 'We are not going to risk a miscarriage just for an outing.'

'Well,' she replied in an aggrieved tone, '*I* think that having a baby is the most overrated pastime ever invented. Evidently I can't do *any*thing.'

'Never mind, darling,' said Kathy easily. 'Although I do agree with Demetrius. That path certainly looks as if it might be a bit much. But suppose we picnic on Sunday, anyway? All of us. Somewhere else. What about the old shipyard? I haven't been there since the boats began fitting out, and I'd love to see it. Some of your boats are slipped already, aren't they, Demetrius?'

He emerged from the towels, pink now, glowing, touching his smooth cheeks with his fingertips. Tomás unstoppered the lotion and held it poised.

'Four of ours are up, yes,' he said. 'But why should you indulge Milly in her selfishness? She's a woman, not a little child. Why go to the shipyard when you want to go to the old city?'

'I'm indulging myself, not Milly. I'd love to picnic at the shipyard on Sunday. And I can wander up to the old city myself this afternoon as I had intended.'

'But I don't like to think of you going alone,' he said through puffs of talcum powder. 'I don't like it a bit.'

The sunbeams were clouded and whirling madly. Alone. Alone? The question was not to be avoided then. As if it ever was. All questions have to be answered sometime. But she felt a keen exasperation at being pushed to this point, an exasperation with Demetrius for pushing her, and an exasperation with the diver who was the cause of it all. Obviously she could not go at all now, without telling a lie or telling the truth, which in either case would aggravate a situation that seemed already to be out of proportion.

She shrugged her shoulders in the thick brown robe. 'Oh well, let's leave it,' she said. 'It doesn't matter, anyway.' But she looked out the window and saw the city on its yellow wave and thought angrily that it *did* matter. It mattered very much indeed.

Tomás snipped delicately at one last hair in Demetrius's nostril and stepped back with a little bow. Demetrius rose in the fullness of perfect physical content, the morning ritual completed, and Milly stood on tiptoe to brush his shoulders and pull at the knot of his tie. While the barber was packing up, Aliki brought the post on a silver tray.

'Something for you, Kathy,' said Demetrius, and held it out to her in the tips of his fingers, his eyelids half lowered, sleepy-looking. It was a long brown envelope on which was printed International Committee for European Migration.

'Well?' he asked, still with that sleepy look, watching her read the one flimsy typewritten sheet. 'Was I right?'

She glanced up at him, then looked back at the letter. Her face was troubled. 'Yes. You were right. Single men aged eighteen to thirty-five. Married men with no more than four children. Of course he isn't eligible. Just as you said. And now you may say "I told you so" if you wish.'

But he went on sorting through the stack of letters and his smile was bland and his voice peaceful. 'Never mind, Kathy. You have done what you can. And just to ease your mind I have spread the word around the town so that you shouldn't be troubled with any more of this nonsense. More mags for you, Milly. Here. *The Queen*, looks like, and *Town and Country*. Now, *Kathy!*' he said, 'stop worrying!'

She flushed in mortification. 'I know you think I've acted like a fool. And I suppose I have, really. But he seemed to be in such a desperate plight, Demetrius. I . . . felt it so strongly. I can't explain it quite.'

'Why don't you forget it?' he said. 'That particular one is

a bad type, anyway. Everybody knows it. Ask Aliki here. Ask Tomás. Another thing—I happen to know why he is so anxious to emigrate.'

'Why?'

'Because he would have to be very lucky indeed to be taken on by any captain ever again. He's through as a diver.'

'But why, Demetrius? Why?'

He looked at her sidelong and smiled briefly. 'Turned yellow. All the town knows it.'

Kathy swallowed a shout of hysterical laughter. Had he turned yellow gradually, like a plum ripening? Or had that pale face suddenly been suffused with ochre, jaundiced eyeballs glaring into the African sun through the window of his diving helmet, and his shipmates drawing back in terror on the hot planks?

But Demetrius was interrogating Tomás, who turned his obsequious smile and pugnacious forehead to her and with an inexpressibly contemptuous gesture rubbed the lapel of his starched jacket between his thumb and forefinger. And Aliki touched her arms and spoke to her earnestly and spat three times very quickly.

'Would you like to know what she is saying?' Demetrius asked.

'Why not? Yes. Of course.'

'She is telling you that he has the Evil Eye on him.'

Kathy did laugh then, a shade too loudly.

'Do you believe in all that too? Really, Demetrius!'

'*They* believe it, my dear. That is what you must remember.'

'Then it sounds as though the poor wretch needs a friend more than ever,' she said with a certain stubbornness. For she had already decided that she would meet him in the afternoon. She would have to now.

16

The day turned nasty after lunch, with a nervous wind and a lot of scudding cloud. But when Demetrius had returned to the warehouse, and Milly to her bedroom to rest, Kathy left the house, still feeling exasperated, mistrustful of herself, and conscious that Aliki was watching her from the kitchen window. This is cheating, she thought, and I don't want to cheat. I hate cheats. She wished she could go back to the luncheon table and plainly declare her intention. She wished she could go back to breakfast and do it all again. After all, she was a grown woman and there was no reason on earth why she should not go for a walk if she wanted to, in any company she chose.

She hesitated when she reached the automobile station, where the half-dozen decrepit old tourers and sedans that served as buses for the inland villages stood silent with their drivers asleep on the seats. But she went on, between the walls of the sober, heavy houses, all shuttered, where the grub women would be taking siesta too. She passed the donkey stables and the last of the paved streets, and continued along the dirt road between rough stone walls grown over with spiky grasses and poppies tossing in the gusty wind. The dust whirled up around her legs, and the road was empty except for a shepherd heading for the port with a donkey bearing two panniers that had a trussed goat in each. She greeted the shepherd and the shepherd greeted her, and the goats rolled their frantic eyes and pulled their soft lips back soundlessly. After walking for half a mile the road was still empty, even of shepherds and donkeys and goats, and she began to wonder if the diver would not turn up. Began to hope for that, rather, and at the same time to feel foolish and irritable and unable to decide whether to go on alone or to return to the house. She wished profoundly that she had never met him.

He was waiting just where the road curled round a bluff that cut off from view the stone houses and the white villa. He had a red poppy stuck in his mouth and he was leaning against the rock looking out across a dried-up rivercourse which was choked with thistle and spears of asphodel.

And she had to come upon him like that. So suddenly. So suddenly that she saw that the man leaning against the rock had nothing whatever to do with her conception of him. The conception was something she had built herself, piece by piece in her imagination, the pieces arranged and rearranged according to her own moods and fancies and other people's impressions—the barber's contemptuous gesture, for instance, and Aliki crossing herself. As a conception it was worthless. For a single moment, before he sensed her and turned, he was undisguised, and there had been nothing—no, nothing: not even the day of the kites—to prepare her for that single red poppy clenched defiantly in a face so bleak, so bare, so pillaged, so utterly divested of every hope or joy that her heart constricted. But it is true, she thought wildly. He has the Evil Eye on him. And he *knows* it.

Then his arrogant grin arranged itself. His shoulders straightened in the blue jersey. 'O.K. there?' he said jauntily round the red poppy, and stuck his thumbs through the belt with the snake buckle and screwed up his eyes at her. 'Let's go?'

And of course she should have told him then, with her fingers crumpling the envelope in the pocket of her skirt. But she couldn't. Not then. All she could do was to nod and follow him.

They walked . . . not together . . . she did not have the sense of their being together, although they were of a height and afterwards she remembered noticing that again with the same curious detached pleasure, and they were certainly walking along the same road, with the flurries of dust blowing and the cloud shadows chasing over the barren fields. That barren valley. She felt its depth and its dreadful sterility. The earth half bald, scarred, tufted here and there with big squashy-looking bushes of a chemical green, thistles and nettles and spiky things, giant asphodel sparkling ragged white stars. Thin, dirty, tinkling sheep and the wild yellow eyes of goats with their horns curving away like barbaric head-dresses. There were some farmhouses. But farm was a euphemism. There were no pastures. (*Only in the sea, Kathy. Only in the sea.*—With that sadness she had found touching in him.) Small houses washed blue or white and rippling in the scurry of cloud shadows as if they were painted on canvas backdrops. Around them were almond or fig trees with branches like finger-bones and silver olives tossing among the small sad patches of wind-bowed wheat. She thought that all these pathetic little farms must be built around ancient wells. They were a grateful sight, if sad, and there were dogs barking, and women and children peering from doorways, shyly, like savage people. Once they passed three strange high mounds, tufted all over with queer patches of a coarse, dun grass. She wanted to ask about them, but did not. Demetrius, of course, would have known.

The road led diagonally across the valley, and they walked it side by side but not together, although the same dust kicked up around their feet and rose and whipped away across the fields, over the thistles and the asphodel and the curled horns of goats. She could see his shoulders moving and the hook of his nose and the slant of his cheek bone under the tilted cap, and one ear which was pale and delicately convoluted like a wax impression of an ear and had no hair growing in it at all as Demetrius's ears had. And she watched him walking along like that, with his cap tipped back and his hands in his tight pockets, and she held the envelope in her own pocket and thought of the corruption working in him like a sentence being carried out. She tried to remember what she had heard as a child about bone-pointing among the Aborigines, for the diver's affliction seemed to be equally mysterious and awful. (Dinga in the Blacks' Cutting, down near the claypits where the Murrumbidgee made the big bend around the old billabong, wasting away in his humpy, refusing to eat. His skin already faded to a dull dirty grey with the knobs of bone stuck up in it, and very dry. Death is terribly dry. The moisture dried up. Then that pungent racial smell also? The prickly grey lantana leaves and the little flowers scattering and the straw-like yellow grass poking through the bark fallen from the river gums. All very dry. 'But why, Dad? Why?' she had asked, and her father had said: 'Because, Kate, he knew from the moment the bone was pointed at him that there was nothing more for him to do. No, there was nothing we could do, either. We cannot interfere in these things.')

After they had walked for half an hour they came over a ridge and descended between high stone walls to the village at the base of the crag. And this was just about the most curious village Kathy had ever seen, for it was blue, entirely blue, and the blues ranged from the merest brightening of stark white, like a blue-rinsed sheet, to a rich, thick ultramarine, so that the whole place seemed to be an optical illusion. Stairs melted into walls, corners curved, pavements swelled into domed ovens, houses thinned out into pure atmosphere, or the sky swept down, solidified, with two darker blue windows, a pot of green basil, and a human face drawn on. The black-clad women, who came running, were as emphatic as exclamation-points, the children's clothes brilliant. There was a threshing floor and a mulberry-tree, and under the mulberry-tree a well with a conical iron cap. He drew ice-cold water for her to drink while the women and children crowded around, squawking like seagulls, pushing and touching. She heard the word 'Australia' over and over again, pronounced queerly, but unmistakable, and she smiled at them and nodded while the diver drew water for himself and drank it out of his cupped hands.

Then they went on again, out of the fantastic blue, and beyond the village they began to climb, leaving the roof-tops with their whirling smoke—another blueness—and the women's voices rising after them, excited and conjectural, and for a little while a pack of lean children pursued them until he threw a stone and cursed them and they dropped away.

And it was like the day of the kite. He went ahead, not looking back, but now with the heavy scuff of his dusty rubber boots on the hard earth, and the blue jersey instead of the raw wool undershirt, and the wafts of cigarette smoke blowing back over his shoulder—acrid, sharp. Then they were on the mountain-face, crossing it diagonally, always up, zig-zagging up the petrified yellow wave. Only stones now, even the path rocky, difficult underfoot, agonising to ankles and heel tendons. Her head began to thump and it hurt her to breathe, but because he kept going she must keep going too, until there were iron bands around her chest and her breath had a tearing sound and she felt as though her spine was being sliced open with a rusty razor blade. She stopped counting the diagonal turns. Every time it was as if they were retracing their steps and never getting anywhere, although they never stopped climbing. And after a while she even stopped trying to remember how many zig-zags she had counted from the house when she had been looking at the mountain from the window-seat, and after that it occurred to her that she and the diver must be perfectly visible from there, and after that she didn't think about anything at all except how to keep her lungs from tearing and knew that this was impossible and that they would not, could not, stand it any longer, and the diver would have to run down to the village and find help to carry her back, and then she walked into shadow that was pansy-coloured and freezing cold and sat down abruptly because her legs wouldn't hold up any more.

'O.K.?' His voice asked from somewhere above her, and there he was looking down with that derisive, impossibly shaky grin, one hand propped nonchalantly against the stone gateway in the shadow of which she sat while the breath roared and whistled in her hurting chest and her black-stockinged legs shook and jellied as if there were no bones in them at all.

He handed down a cigarette, lit. It passed from shaking hand to shaking hand with such difficulty that she began to laugh.

'What a pair we are!' she said, and found that she was shivering violently even while sweat was pouring down her face and spine.

'Ah, you come on,' he said above her. 'Rest inside. Better.' And he was gone at once round the worn angle of the stone. She hauled herself upright on those madly trembling legs to follow him, and as she did so she felt the stiff crackle of the envelope in her pocket. Well, she would tell him now. But still she paused irresolutely. The valley spread away below, the tufted and half-bald earth with the shadows fleeing across it, the blue enchanted village, the few sparse farms, and down in the mouth of it the town flung like a patchwork quilt draped carelessly and buttoned down with church domes, and then the sea, the matchstick boats, and two tan sails taut and scudding towards Anatolia.

Then she turned and entered the gate of the city. It was a small plateau, shaped like a tilted plate within the rim of its crumbling walls, and what was evident was that it was dead. Truly dead. She had not expected that. The stone grown over with paper-dry lichen of no colour at all, so that the pansy shadow was more real than the substance. The gate only a blind eye. Trachomaed. Blind gate, blind walls, blind keep, blind stones lying sightless to the sky, and the sky so close here, the clouds almost within fingertip reach, oyster-grey and scudding, so that the tumbled stones inside the gate seemed to shudder, and the twelve tiny chapels dimmed and leapt back to white again one after the other, flicking on and off like signals.

The diver beckoned her with a jerk of his head, and she brushed slowly through the nettles to where he stood among the stones. She had the envelope half out of her pocket then.

'See?' he said. 'See?'

His gesture—wide, encompassing—was proprietorial and proud. Even his voice had a new, imperious ring. He had somehow invested himself with hauteur. Between the vivid washes of sunlight the cloud shadows rolled over him and streamed out behind like garments. Rich garments. She knew then that he played at princes here. Among the blind stones, the gutted hearths, the fallen roofs, the walls toppled to dust. Fotis the diver, playing at princes where the regnant nettle choked hearth, stone, roof, wall, thistle, asphodel, and even the invading thyme.

'Look here . . .!' he cried. 'That was one house there. See? See it? Big. Look how many rooms. Here . . . here . . . here. Plenty rooms. All the houses was like that. Big!'

She stretched out her hand, perhaps in appeal, but he beckoned her on again, excitedly, and she scrabbled after him over mounds where the nettle purses stood as high as their waists.

He said: 'I bet this street is where the shops was and all the processions was coming down. Look how wide. You look at that. I bet the king was coming down here . . .'

She could have cried. He stood in the weeds like a conqueror, gathering to him in wide embracing gestures the desolate stones, the cold shadow scud, the flying light, and building with them palaces and thrones, mansions and towers. How did he know of such things? The city had been abandoned for nine centuries. Was it a race memory? Or were the stones themselves communicative, if one knew how to listen?

The cloud shadows were moving slower, had grown darker, as if gradually solidifying. She was cold now, but scarcely noticed it. She let him lead her to an ancient cistern, tomb-square, tomb-black, with a stone shaft down which they looked to see their faces mirrored minutely against a circle of sky fifty feet below.

'Listen.' He picked up a pebble and dropped it down the shaft. It seemed a long time before the small dismal impact, and then the impact multiplied into an awful, rolling howl, as though the pebble had released the sorrows of centuries.

'Plenty of stuff down there,' he said. 'Gold. Jewels. Rings. That sort of stuff.'

'How do you know?'

He gave her a small, haughty smile. 'They was rich then, wasn't they? Pirates down there . . .' He gestured towards the sea.

'Oh. And you think they buried their treasures for safety?'

'Sure they did.' And then (the *yearning* in the febrile voice): 'They was *rich*! Gold. Rings . . . You come here one minute.' He bent and began tearing at the camomile daisies and wild growths and scratching at the earth beneath, the shadows lapping over him, dark now, dark and cold, and after a while he picked something out of the earth and spat on it and rubbed it carefully on the sleeve of his jersey and handed it to her. It was a fragment of glass as big as a fingernail, curved, bubble-thin, iridescent.

'That's nothing,' he said, rather deprecatingly. 'Nothing. Plenty stuff like that.'

But holding the fragile piece of glass she too was suddenly shaken by longing.

'But has anybody ever *found* anything? Gold, rings, necklaces . . .'

Still crouched, he looked up at her slyly. 'He never told you nothing?'

'Who? Demetrius?'

He nodded.

'Why?' she cried in astonishment. 'Did *Demetrius* find something here?'

He tilted his head back in negation and clucked his tongue the Greek way. 'Not *him*. The old one. She was dead before the war. Old, she was.' He straightened up slowly and delved in his pocket for the cigarette tin. She assumed he was referring to Demetrius's great-grandmother, that long-lived widow of Nikólas of the marble bust on the green column. She had ruled the whole clan of them for almost fifty years, and the whole island too, and had never moved out of her high dark-curtained rooms for thirty of those years until they carried her out with the coffin lid going before. 'She knew something, all right,' the diver said.

She shivered. 'Ah . . . tell me . . .'

He lit a cigarette, picked a scrap of torn paper from his bottom lip, and examined it carefully. 'One man I know,' he said, 'his grandmother worked there. In the house. She was crazy, all right, that old one.' He tapped his forehead significantly. 'One night one woman comes to this old crazy one—white dress, white veil . . . everything all white—and this white one tells the old crazy one to come up here to this place in the night and dig in the place the white one tells her about.' His voice, grown sing-song in the telling, paused, and he stood dragging on the cigarette, not looking at Kathy but at some point far distant. Speculative. Even for the moment tranquil.

'Yes?' she urged softly, with the fragment of glass in the curve of her hand. 'Go on. Tell me.'

'Three nights this woman comes, this white one. White dress. Just the same. Everything white. Three nights she's saying this same thing to that crazy grandmother of this man I know. And you know what that crazy one was doing?' He turned to face her, amazed, angry, shaking. 'She *tells* it all to that rich old one up at the house! She tells her *everything* that the white one said to her. Crazy, she was. *Crazy!*' And still he stared at her, his face incredulous and raging, while she grappled for understanding among his few crude words where the real meaning lay deep and significant, like a half-remembered language.

'But what *happened?*' she cried in bafflement, and his face cleared of its fury and he gave her that little grin again—quick, sly, personal, mocking.

'You ask him one day,' he said. 'See if he tells you.' He dropped the cigarette and ground it into the daisies with the toe of his boot and the smell of camomile came up at her. 'You like to be looking inside the churches now?' he asked.

Still dazed, still uncomprehending, still with the thin cool curve of glass in her fingers, she followed him.

The day had changed. It had grown very dark. Very hushed. Brooding. The sky was close. So heavily hanging over the stones of terminated purpose and the nettles drooping a little now. Hanging like a heavy purple arras. Or a pall. Ceremonial certainly. Prescient. The twelve scattered chapels glowed softly like distributed pearls. Luminous. Every one distinct and separate. There was a lizard on a stone.

Inside, the chapels smelt stalely of nothing. It was almost too dark to make out the dim faces of saints peering pallidly through the smeared whitewash. The Turks had put their eyes out centuries ago, and generations of old women from the village below had carelessly paled them, reduced them, year after year, with washes of lime. Old black women toiling up the mountain path with their brushes and whitewash pails like old goats toiling to half-remembered pastures. Piously, patiently, with guano-dropping patience, year after year whitening over the impotent, sightless, Byzantine eyes.

But the diver was alive. Fiercely containing his own defiant life as he moved beside her from chapel to dead chapel under the still draped pall of sky. She walked now like someone half asleep, while the stillness deepened into a silence as profound as death, and whether the blind saints of Byzantium peered from walls or nettle-beds or death-still sky she no longer knew. The first drops of rain—warm, heavy, hugely splashing—could have been tears. The diver held his face up to the rain and laughed suddenly, and when he turned to her his eyes were hot and interrogating.

The smell of wet thyme was overpowering. It flowed in and filled the last and highest chapel of all, where he led her at last through the rain, but without haste, as if the rain were of no account at all. She caught her breath at the stillness of the chapel, with the smell of thyme trapped within it. The heavy drumming of the rain on the roof did not seem more audible than the beating of her heart. His wet face glimmered white and hieratic, turned on the exact level of her own to look at her with a long, still looking.

She said, very distinctly: 'I have received the letter. There is no possible hope of your emigrating.'

For a moment she thought he had not understood, but then, without haste, he turned from her and went to the cracked altar slab and took a stick of burnt charcoal that lay there beside the terracotta incense-burner. He walked to the opposite wall and deliberately, with great savage strokes, he wrote the beautiful Greek characters of his name, huge, right across the peering dim faces.

'Fotis!' he said, as if in triumph.

And having nothing else to give him, Kathy said: 'I must tell you. That car accident. I was trying to kill myself.' And she thought insanely: It is all right, really. He didn't really need to write his name like that at all, because they're all blind anyway. Whatever happens now they won't be able to see at all.

As he came towards her she clenched her fist, and the thin curl of iridescent glass, forgotten, crunched against her wedding ring and bit swift as a snake into the flange of her finger. So that there was blood on his face as well as the rain or the tears.

17

It had never been his intention, probably. Or never his conscious intention. In fact he had scarcely thought of her as being a woman at all, in the sense that Irini was a woman or the little Lookoomi was a woman. Irini was a familiar woman he could have whenever he wanted, and the little Lookoomi was an unfamiliar woman he could never have but might imagine having—although there was no question but that they were both women, with unambiguous womanly functions—and Kathy was the woman he could simply not have imagined himself as having. She had appeared to him more as a force or a power which might be appealed to or coerced if necessary to his advantage, a piece of luck come surprisingly his way and as yet but dimly understood. So that he was amazed at and frightened of what he had done as soon as he had done it, and her abandoned weeping seemed to him the most terrifying thing of all. He had the feeling that his act had been utterly sacrilegious, not because it had occurred in a chapel, but because of his own appalling temerity in taking her like that: he attached infinitely more superstition to her than to the church which sheltered them. At the same time he felt a dark and palpable joy he had never known before: there had been no intimation of such a thing in all his usage of Irini. This one might have been the first woman in the world, or a completely new species. So perhaps some remote shepherd-boy ancestor might have felt on discovering that the nymph with whom he had just dallied was not, after all, mortal.

As for Kathy, she wept because she could not help it, because the physical release from long celibacy was violent in itself, because she did not know what this man would think of her now, and because she was hopelessly and utterly in love with him and knew it to be unreasonable and that no good could possibly come of it: and she wept because Demetrius had been right to warn her, and she wept in shame and disgust for her own womanish weeping.

In abject distress the diver stroked her dim wet face with hands now uncontrollably shaking, and he made foolish little murmuring noises that burst every now and then into phrases of absurd coherence—'Did I hurt you? . . . Are you hurting? . . . Say . . . say . . . you are liking me to go away now? . . . Ah! . . . you are . . . you are . . .' But only Greek words could express his stricken consternation, and he used them humbly, in a kind of childlike adoration, calling her a flower, a star, a golden one, a crown of jewels.

'If you want I kill myself,' he said, and meant it. He would have, at that moment, in worship or gratitude or possibly expiation.

This passion of tenderness and endearment was completely unlike anything she had expected from him, so that she felt his hands and heard his voice with astonishment. She was scalded by sweetness, too sudden, too new, and through the tears that still came she smiled up at him with a radiance as yet uncertain.

'Fotis!' She formed his name experimentally. 'Fotis,' she said, and touched his streaky fine hair and the slanting planes of his face, learning both the sound and the feel of him. 'I've put blood on you,' she cried, and he grasped at her bleeding finger and took it in his mouth and sucked it clean.

'Wait now. Wait now,' he muttered distressfully, rummaging for the cigarette tin, and he undid a cigarette and rubbed tobacco over the cut to stop the bleeding, then found a red handkerchief and clumsily began wiping at her face, and dabbed at her, trying to stop the tears too. But by this time she did not know whether she was crying or laughing, and she let him kneel beside her in an agony of service, wiping at her cheeks and straightening her clothes, and when he had arranged her skirt modestly again he pulled off his jersey and wrapped it tightly around her shoulders and lit two cigarettes and put one in her mouth, and she sat up then and looked at him.

'Fotis,' she said, and marvelled at the intensity of her happiness to be sitting on the cold damp stones of this spooky little chapel and at her outrageous pleasure in the lean male smell of the blue jersey. This is being in love, she thought, looking at him, and on a sudden choke of laughter she wondered whatever they would talk about now.

At once he said, accusingly: 'Why you trying to kill yourself? Eh? Why you wanted to do one thing like that? That's a crazy thing to do! You're one crazy woman!' He was really in a fury at the thought that she had so nearly escaped him, and in a special sense she understood and appreciated the justice of his point. How very curious that I should have told him that, she thought, blissfully conscious of the rank wild taste of the tobacco, the smell of the jersey and of thyme and must and mildew and age and a lingering of incense, the sound of the rain still drumming and drumming, the feel of her damp clothes and the soreness of her body, her absolute positive sensation of being alive: and thinking at the same time, *Was* I crazy then? She had always been aware of a certain perilous desperation in her own nature, which Irwin had feared and balked by a solicitous, protective attitude that had suffocated her. Had she then wanted to die positively in preference to living half-heartedly? We are alike, she thought, and looked at him with fox-brown eyes grown sly and smiling. You are a desperate one too. She was incredulous that she should be happy when it was so perfectly clear that the situation was impossible, could not possibly last, and that in any case this man was doomed already.

'I tried to kill myself,' she said carefully, 'because . . . because I had already lived thirty years of my life and still hadn't found you . . . ah . . . you . . .' she said, laughing.

'You are one crazy woman. Crazy!' he said again with that same retrospective anger at her lack of faith, and turning to touch him she felt the envelope crackle again in her pocket.

'Do you really mind about Australia?' She looked at him closely and cried on an intuition: 'But you *knew*. You did know, didn't you? Demetrius said you knew . . . It was

112

something else you wanted me to do, wasn't it? Something more. Tell me,' she said. 'You can tell me anything now.'

He looked very young bareheaded like that in the raw wool undershirt with its crocheted neck. Very young. Shy suddenly with too much happiness. Uncertain. He dribbled smoke through finely flanged nostrils and eyed her obliquely, not quite believing any of it. 'I know one feller . . .' he began and stopped.

'Yes? Tell me.'

He examined the tip of his cigarette. 'One feller went to Australia because he got a paper from there. *From* Australia, see? Some feller sent him the paper to say there was work and a place to stay. If a feller's got that sort of paper written from there, then he can go. Sure.'

'I see,' she said, and thought about it. 'So if a job is guaranteed, and accommodation . . . it's like your having a sponsor, really. Then you could go. Wait. Let me think. I could write to my father—I don't know if he could do this but he might know somebody who would . . . Is that what you want me to do?'

'If you want,' he said diffidently, and as he looked at her the grey eyes grew hot again and he sucked in his breath sharply. 'Ah, you are . . . you are . . . Ketty. *Ketty!*' And he laughed on a high wild note, a surge of laughter that quivered right through him and broke and splintered among the dim eyeless saints. Rather frightening laughter, really. Rather reckless, springing from a source so untrustworthy as a sudden blind faith in miracles. 'Crazy . . . crazy . . . crazy . . .'

They found a taxi in the village below when the rain eased off for a time, an old Hudson tourer with celluloid side-curtains and broken seat-springs covered with torn sacking that had brought two nuns from the afternoon steamer, and bumping back to the port they sat discreetly apart and looked at each other with the same faintly narrowed eyes and faintly smiling mouths. Kathy paid for the taxi at the automobile station and walked away across the square without looking back. All the bells were ringing for *espéres,* surging and crashing, and down by St Mummas she could see Demetrius, fur collar turned up, hands deep in the pockets of his reefer jacket, padding up the lane towards her. She waited by the gate of Uncle Paul's house. Now, she thought calmly, the lies will begin.

18

That was the last of the winter storms. Spring came suddenly, with a smell of the south. Moving softly, softly through the town in those soft new days, Demetrius was uneasily conscious of the tempo quickening. The pace of all the year's activities was in acceleration, like the sand in an hourglass hurrying as it comes to its final drop. In the harbour now there was the thud and sputter of caïque engines testing all day long and whirling grey smoke-rings jetted up above the broken rhythm of their vertical exhausts. A number of the diving-boats had already moved down to the nearby shipyard for slipping. All eight of the Casopédes boats were slipped, together with the big mothership *Calliope*, and their captains were beginning to sign on diving teams for the seven months' summer on the African beds.

Along the waterfront the labourers sweated at handcarts piled with paraffin drums and ballast weights and coils of hempen rope. The coffee houses were more crowded than ever, but the atmosphere was different—heightened: these were no longer men passing the time but greedy of what was left of it. Demetrius responded to their expansiveness, their recklessness, with a strange dread, as if his whole moral being was at their mercy. Often he would stop in the doorways of smoky little forge-glowing shops smelling of brass and rubber and lubricating oil, where the yellow diving-suits hung in the racks like flat cut-outs of giants to be used in some *Karagiósis* shadow play, and the dark moustached faces would turn to him, polite and expectant, and smile deferentially at his slightly over-hearty jests and comments, and wait for him to go. It affected him unreasonably, profoundly.

Yet this season of preparation was in no way different from all the seasons that had preceded it, back through his father's lifetime, and his grandfather's, and his great-grandfather's—those unquestioning patriarchs whose boat crews had worn livery, and who had given poor girls golden sovereigns for their dowries. In these weeks before Lent there had always been this heightened activity, a sense of movement, of forces mustering. The glint of copper couplings, the marline-antifouling-pitchy smell of the ship chandlers, the shackles and brass sidelights and the casks of copper nails, and in some doorway, then as now, a pile of lead chest weights and an air hose coiled like a serpent. Out too in the little religious shops that sold incense and candles and silver beads to ward off the Evil Eye and talismans to ward off sickness or peril there were flat little silver amulets on sale in the shapes of diving helmets or boats or just the form of a man's leg. In the two big waterfront churches—of St Nikólas the patron of seamen and of St Stephanos the patron of divers—forests of candles burnt nightly. And at night, too, the first of the masked figures heralding Carnival were beginning to appear, little bands of them running from house to house, shaking gourds and tin cans—demoniac figures, disguised out of humanity. It had always been so; it was the time of the year . . .

Ah, but they—the Casopédes who had preceded him—had accepted the preparations and fulfilments of the seasons as willed, predetermined, immutable. Demetrius envied them, the unquestioning patriarchs, the unquestioning exploiters. And unquestioned, too. Their moral beings had never been undermined by the fact of lawlessness. Lawlessness had been something to be controlled, governed, put down, put upon, manipulated. They had been lawless themselves. He was not as they had been. He was a modern man, Western-educated, enlightened, far-seeing. Well, I can see far enough to the end of this, anyway, he thought with a satisfaction so savage it surprised him.

But if the year's activities were hurrying towards the imminence of action there was still the residue of the past year to be dispersed. The Customs House was stacked to the roof-beams with pressed and flattened bales bearing the black stencillings of New York, Paris, Hamburg, Dusseldorf, Stoke-on-Trent, Sydney . . . And still the warehouse was filled with

116

soft salty mountains where the shears clipped with an insectine chirruping all day. There were sponges in the bleaching vats, sponges in the presses, sponges in the sea being trampled under the blue legs of boys, sponges drying in every available flat space like a strange fungoid growth sprouted from the paving-blocks. Hung in boats' riggings, too, and in the trees with the drying octopus and squid.

The buyers came in on every steamer from Piraeus now. It was a busy time. And important. Too busy and too important for him to be much at home, excepting for the entertaining of the visiting merchants, who were so gratifyingly impressed by the new house, the lavishness of the offered entertainment, by the beauty of his English wife and her maddening sister-in-law.

Maddening. Maddening. She obsessed him. Since the day of the storm when she had waited for him at Paul's gateway with her soaked clothes clinging and her face so wet and strange he had been almost afraid of her, afraid of what she represented— an implacable will that he could not govern, could not coerce.

'Kathy! What craziness is this? Do you mean to tell me you've actually been scrambling around up there in this sort of weather?'

And she had said, holding up a finger with shreds of tobacco clinging to it, 'I found a piece of glass,' and turned up to him a face transparent and serene under the wet red cap of hair.

He wanted—he did not know what he wanted. A whip, perhaps. That she was free. Women ought not to be free. It was unbearable that he should be forced to *reason* with her when his blood was choked by choler. A whip. Yes. That was what he wanted really.

For she had been writing letters again. Writing on behalf of that drunken lout of a diver. And quite openly.

'Surely you cannot intend to persist in this absurd philanthropy? It's all quite ludicrous, Kathy. You *must* be able to see that!'

She had looked at him directly then, eyes like hot chestnuts, that full upper lip of hers rather tremulous. It had been, he knew, an appeal. 'There *is* another way to emigrate. If an Australian in Australia acts as a kind of sponsor, guarantees work, puts up the passage money, and so on. Daddy could, I think. I have to try, Demetrius. I *have* to!' she had cried in sudden passion. 'Don't you understand? I have never done anything good in all my life!'

It seemed to him to be the most terrible childishness—a total incapacity to perceive the reasons for things, a complete blindness to the true nature of people. Idealism. Stubbornness too. It infuriated him, obsessed him, and he could do nothing about it. She had become inimical to him by aligning herself with the lawless forces he feared, and she had become humiliating to him, for she was a woman and he had no control over her.

And now, as he walked brooding and soft-footed through the busy town, he seemed for ever to be encountering the hated diver. It was as though there was the most violent attraction operating between them.

They would look at each other slowly, with a curious intentness—Demetrius big, heavy, padding soft and handsome in his polished brogues and expensive Irish tweeds, the diver thin and skimpy-looking in blue jersey and high boots, lounging in a tavern doorway, or sitting under the salt-trees at some coffee-table. As though he was waiting there deliberately. Or perhaps it was that subconsciously Demetrius was seeking him out.

Did Kathy meet that man? He could not bring himself to ask her, could not demean himself by asking others. She was out of the house often, he knew, and she did not come to the warehouse now as she had liked to do. She had been seen in strange places, walking to the shipyard, climbing on the road to High Lady.

'I was exploring today,' she would offer serenely at dinner. 'This gorgeous weather . . . what a beautiful place your island is, Demetrius.' Or, 'There was a woman weaving rugs,' she would say. 'I walked around by St Stephanos.' Or: 'I followed a funeral this afternoon. How barbaric it is. But the cemetery is terribly Chinese, don't you think? Wind and water. Lovely, really.'

And he could not, could not degrade himself by asking her

questions. Had not the right. At least, no right she would recognise.

In some disquieting way he felt that he was caught between them, and that in collusion they menaced him in some not yet specified way, menaced his life, his future, the future of his unborn sons, his ambitions, his dreams of happiness.

And disengaging his full slow stare from the intensity of Fotis's regarding him through the feathery green of the salt-trees with a faint deadly glimmer of triumph (for they never exchanged greetings), he would walk on softly, softly through the bustle of the labourers' carts and the rumbling of paraffin drums and the coiled hemp smelling like spring meadows. Walking softly, uneasily, to the ordered confusion of his own kingdom, where behind the mahogany desk, piled with orders, samples, invoices, he would suddenly be shaken with voluptuous pleasure at the thought of a whip.

19

Kathy was living with a terrifying sense of exposure, and since her tranquillity was the only garment she could muster up to cover her nakedness she wore it, and hoped that it would pass for decency.

Fotis played at discretion elaborately, with an eager pleasure, like a child playing outlaws, and tranquilly she abided by his rules, was stealthy, gently ironic, and undeceived.

They made their assignations in the morning market, behind pyramids of tangerines or over trays of silver fish all wet and glittering, where there were wreaths of dried vineleaves and figs to whisper through, ropes of purple onions and ivory garlic to use as screens, Kathy picking over the new little flaky-skinned potatoes, Fotis disdainfully rejecting a muddy lettuce, never looking at each other, but brushing lightly in passing for the sharp electric shock of contact, sleeve against sleeve, hand against hand, with all the coifed and bargaining women speculative on the cut and cost of Kathy's skirt or blazer, the contents of her shopping basket, the colour of her nail-polish.

'This afternoon?'

'Difficult.'

'Yes, Ketty. Yes.'

'I'll try.'

'Not try. Yes.' Nonchalantly crumbling dried rigani between his fingers and sniffing at it while Kathy's potatoes were weighed and transferred to her basket. Sidestepping behind the festoons of onions. 'Back of the cemetery. Go in the church first and out the side door. I wait there.'

'But . . .'

Then the contact. Brush of fingers lingering around a bouquet of wild celery. Ah . . .

'Say yes, Ketty. Yes.'

'Yes.'

Not that she ever thought they would get away with it. The town was too bare, and she herself still an object of intense interest to the population. Women ran out of their doorways when she passed. She was invited into houses. Groups of children followed her, and it was difficult to shake them off, difficult and sometimes ludicrous to be back-tracking and dodging down side alleys with an assumption of casualness that was at the mercy of any look or word.

Besides, she was aware that the last time, lying in the dried-out river bed among the asphodel and the pale prickling grasses, a goatboy had seen them. He had been kneeling, peering down through the stalks brittly parted in his hands, and his eyes had been wild and yellow and intent as those of his goats, and he had whickered, drawing his lips back from his teeth in excitement. And hadn't there been others who must have gone their ways conjecturing? A nun on a donkey, plodding the path to the monastery on High Lady, who had passed while they stood at the entrance to an abandoned sheepfold, picking burrs from each other's jerseys. And the girl with the pointed Minoan face and the long sideways-glancing Minoan eyes—a shipbuilder's daughter probably—who, holding like a shield an empty food basket, had demurely made way for them on the trail leading to the repair slips on the far side of the harbour bluff.

And then Aliki. Always Aliki. From the first she realised that Aliki observed her goings and comings in the quiet siesta hours while Milly slept. That when she slipped quietly through the garden and out of the grilled gate Aliki was always at the kitchen window, impassive, hooded, never making a sign of any sort. But she trusted Aliki, she did not know why.

There was a day when she returned to the house late and breathless, terrified that Milly might have awakened or Demetrius returned before she could change her clothes. (There had been a flinty ledge above the sea, and he had slithered down the cliffside with his arms filled and spilling over with uprooted fascomolo bushes to spread for her bed. The crushed wild smell of the little grey felty leaves. And the sea sounding so close. And a fishing boat she never saw but only heard passing beneath—the slow slap and drip of oars and the creak of the rope bindings on the thole-pins, and an old man's voice and a boy's hushed abruptly, and Fotis's arms, hard, pinning her down.)

In the bedroom she hurriedly took off her clothes stained with the wild herb colour and impregnated with the wild herb smell and stuffed them into the back of the closet. But the next morning, mad to smell that fascomolo smell again, she had gone to the closet and the clothes had vanished. The day after that the skirt was hanging clean and pressed on its hanger and the jersey was folded with her other woollens in a drawer of her bedroom chest. She did not thank Aliki, nor did Aliki mention it. But who pinned the blue bead to her pillow?

Inevitably there were times when she failed him, times when Milly wished to visit or go shopping or take a walk, times when somebody arrived unexpectedly (the female relatives came and went at all hours of the day, and Milly's little dressmaker ran in and out with half-finished garments for fitting, and Demetrius was for ever sending messages up from the port to warn that there would be guests for dinner), and Kathy accepted these times with the same tranquillity.

'For if we do not ask for more than is given what we have is our own.'

'But I go *crazy*, Ketty! Waiting! Waiting!' White-lipped and raging, his hands trembling on her face. 'Hours! *Hours* I'm waiting! Jesus! I can't stand it this way! I'm dying if I'm not seeing you, Ketty.'

'You can stand it. If I can stand it you can.'

She was queerly superstitious about it, and pocketed Milly's new mood of relaxation and frequent laughter like a credit to be drawn on the next time she would have to lie. She felt more tenderness towards Milly than at any time since she had known her, and was scrupulous to a fault in helping her with the household and all the extra entertaining that the season brought. She even thought up extra things for them to do. Stamatis cleared the orange crop from one of the trees and they made marmalade, pots and pots of it, for Milly to display triumphantly to Demetrius. Or they pressed smocking transfers on to Swiss lawn, and, sitting in basket chairs where the porch fanlight poured stained-glass colours over them, she taught Milly (looking like a Chartres window) how to take up the dots. It suited her beautifully and would, Kathy hoped, please Demetrius. That was part of her superstition too.

Inevitably they talked about love, as two women sewing together will always do. Women, Kathy considered, would either sew love into garments or else unpick it with wrathful little snips. There was something about the very impedimenta of sewing that made it inevitable—the needle with its running thread, the scissors bright and wickedly sharp to cut the thread in a second. Even the movement of the hand, graceful and subdued. It was wonderful to see how it soothed Milly, and how easily and naturally she smiled and sighed and poured out her confidences. While Kathy went nosing on after her own thoughts, fingers firmly pulling the running threads tight and knotting them and beginning to strand the embroidery cottons.

'The first time Irwin ever brought you down to the country . . . do you remember? I even remember what you were wearing . . . I can see it so clearly . . .'

'That Jaeger suit with the fringed scarf. I know. And the white cashmere. What you didn't know is that I blew two weeks' pay on that lot!' So anxious to be correct for the English countryside, correct for Irwin's parents. And not secretarial. Years later how she had felt for Demetrius in much the same situation.

'And Win took you out to the barn?'

'He did indeed.' Knowing that something was going to happen. The smell of the barn. Straw and dust. Gardening tools. Old bicycles. Bridles and bits. A broken dolls' pram. Irwin unfamiliar in Bedford cords and a jacket with leather patches. Looming. And then the expected kiss, and his moustache not prickling after all, but soft rather—surprising that, and more surprising his tongue

123

in her mouth and his urgent hands. It had been so easy to believe that this was It, the Wonderful Thing, because that was what he was saying over and over and over, Irwin Bassett, so handsome and controlled and calm, quite frantic in the barn with his hands all over her . . .

'Well,' said Milly, and giggled. 'I watched.'

'You sneaky little thing! At *ten*!'

'Well, I didn't mean to, and then I couldn't go away. And when you'd both gone back to London and Mummy and Daddy were talking about you and whether Win was serious and all that—you know that pompous way they always go on . . . after all, you were only his secretary, but on the other hand your accent wasn't as frightful as they had expected . . . and do you think perhaps she is a little *fast*?—so then I said Win had better marry you because you'd probably be having a baby . . .'

'My God! What a little beast you were. Well, at least that now explains the frigid reception the next time.'

Milly said, still giggly: 'I used to go hot and cold all over each time I passed the barn. Even the word became taboo. You know the way Mummy and Daddy are. Honestly. And then do you know the very first time Demetrius came home, all those years after, as soon as the inspection was over, what do you think I said to him?'

' "Would you like to see the *barn*?" ' Kathy grinned at her. 'And was it up to expectations?'

Milly turned up a rapturous stained-glass face. 'Lordy!' she said. 'Wasn't it just! Only . . .' she looked at the scrap of Swiss lawn in a helpless way, '. . . well, it's just that it doesn't go *on* being like that, does it? I mean before you know where you are you've lost your figure and are as sick as a blessed pig and he's suddenly master of the house and you aren't permitted to do a single thing that's *fun*. And every second word is duty or responsibility . . .'

Kathy said contemptuously: 'If they only knew that we don't want to be wives and mothers at all. We're best as lovers. The rest is play-acting. Childishness. Playing at keeping house. Men,' she said, 'are such beginners at love.' Except you. Except you, she thought, and was burnt with longing for his pillaged face and his hair as fine as a child's and his ribs as frail as a reed basket.

'Why, *Kathy*! I never knew you felt like that!' Milly looked at her in astonishment. And some distaste also. Kathy was very queer sometimes. The things she *said*.

And Kathy was filled with pity and tenderness for her, and for Irwin also, to whom her pity and tenderness overflowed, and she wrote at length, in loving kindness. There was such a lot of love to go round.

Sometimes, it was true, there was a little squeak of surprise or dismay from a certain level of her consciousness. Not guilt. The sight of that figure leaning quietly against some rock or wall outside the town—the black cap tipped, the high boots crossed, the waiting face inclined expectantly—made guilt impossible. But surprise. Definitely surprise. She went to the glass sometimes to see if her face was changing.

'*Is* my face changing?' she asked him. That was the fifth time; the last finger of one hand counted off and they shared that much past together and no one could touch it or take it away from them. Once for the old city, once for the river-bed, once for the ledge above the sea, once for the sheepfold, and the hand completed and accomplished now among the rocks above the ship repair yard. Perhaps this was what Aunt Polymnia had foreseen, holding her hand to the open door and blowing on her mouth?

It was a majestic place, for the rocks were tall and starkly sculptured, deep apricot in colour, and festooned with great, grey, spiny plates of prickly pear that made a screen through which they could look down on the slipways and winches and capstans and sheds. There were nineteen diving boats slipped on the chocks above the tarry pebbles—the Casopédes' eight among them— and four big supply schooners charred soot-black where they had been burning the old paint off with bonfires of thornbrush. The workmen slept in wedges of shade under the pepper-trees,

125

flat and stiff on their backs like little lead soldiers. There was no sound but the brush-brush-brush of the slow sea stroking the pebbles, no movement but the sea's movement and the movement of the earth on which they lay turning away from the sun. The sun gold and the turning earth gold. All gold, all still, all bare, disclosed. For a long time they were still, his mouth on her throat.

Then he raised his head and touched her eyes and the corners of her mouth and held her cheeks in his narrow hands. He did not know whether she had changed. Sometimes, indeed, he did not know what she looked like at all, and there were days and nights when he had to construct her image quite laboriously. If Fotis had ever tried to visualise his ideal woman probably she would have been someone like Milly, golden blonde, rosy, soft, tender to the touch. Not this sharp-angled face he held between his hands. Not this thin body that was austere and hard as a man's and fierce and direct in the taking and giving that he could no longer separate. He was suddenly afraid, and to hide it he rolled away from her and plucked a stalk of already dry grass and stuck it in his mouth.

'You going back to Australia some time, Ketty?'

'*Are* you going back to Australia?'

'He shrugged off the correction impatiently. 'Yes, Ketty. Yes.'

'I don't know,' she said peacefully. Meaning . . . no. Meaning this is all we have. Now and here. All still, all bare, all gold, disclosed. We are accomplished utterly. Don't ask for more. Don't think it possible. She knew all this, lying still on the turning earth, but she closed her own eyes against the interrogation of his, and said: 'Some day. Perhaps.'

'Yes,' he said, and pulled her eyelids up with the tips of his fingers, quite sharply, and held them open. 'Yes. You and me together, Ketty.'

'You are hurting me,' she said through her tears.

'Yes. Say yes, Ketty.'

'Yes,' she said agreeably. Meaning no. He could have killed her.

'I love you,' she said, and it was a new thing that no woman had ever said to a man before. The shape of the words on her mouth had the freshness of creation. She was amazed at the dazzling new-minted truth. The flesh made word. She had never understood anything before.

But Fotis was angry and unappeased and he jerked away from her and sat up straight among the stones and grasses. His face was as harsh and as bare as the bare mountainside.

'I have a husband,' she said.

'I'm being your husband, Ketty. Me,' he said. 'Me!'

'I have children.'

'I make you more children.'

Ah . . . that. And suppose he had already? Suppose there was already growing in her womb another of those wizened gnomes that would be marked from the day of its birth with that dreadful look of resignation all his children had? As if they were born with a realisation of their incapacity to fulfil his brilliant, wilful longings. You'll get no immortality out of *them*, she thought savagely. Only in me. Only in me. Now. Here.

'And Irini? What about Irini? What about your own children?'

'But, Ketty . . .' he said in surprise. 'Irini's not wanting to go to Australia. Or Irini or the children. Why *they* wanting to go? I send money. Plenty money. Women are never going. Only men. Women are liking more better to stay in their houses. Just taking plenty money every month . . .'

She said, 'I shall never understand Greek marital arrangements as long as I live.'

He was sombre and hurt. 'You thinking I'm a liar. You ask Irini. I tell you, Ketty, she's not *wanting* to go. Ask her. You come up to the house and ask her.'

'Oh, my dear . . .' Thinking sadly that now they were ready to wound each other. Because they were asking for more than was given. Australia, Australia, she thought impatiently. What did all that matter here and now? Trying to imagine him there. Doing what? Digging ditches? Laying railway tracks? Felling trees? Setting fence posts? Parched and lonely in the red dust, humiliated, beating against the barriers of race and

127

incomprehension and prejudice. An unskilled labourer, inarticulate and walled up in his pride. Or drifting at last to the cities, to work in a factory, or serve behind the counter in some suburban fish-and-chip shop? You'll die there, she thought. You'll die for the bare bright mountain and the boats slipped on the pebbles and the smell of the sea. You'll die for the bells at *espéres* and a kite streaming up in the morning air and a shepherd playing a *tsabuna* in a slope of thyme. You'll die for the sharp black olives and the taste of resin on your tongue and the bread that has blood and salt in it. Yes, and you'll die for the things you fear most, the copper helmet and the hot planks and the yellow rubber, for the fear is at least your own fear and part of your uniqueness. And in the end you will die like Dinga the Aborigine, wasting away, refusing to eat, drying up under the dry lantana leaves, with your fine bones stuck up like knobs in the dry flesh. I am doing what I can to send you to your death, and since this what you ask of me I will do it.

'Yes,' he said, watching her now, feeling the hard strength of her, the power and goodness of her. Loving her, he bent and touched her delicately with his hands until her face grew transparent and the smooth skin of her eyelids puckered and her nostrils pinched.

Far beneath them one of the labourers stirred and stretched and went down to the sea. The sound of a match striking was distinct. The hissing of urination. The other workmen began to sit up, or turn sleepily again in their wedges of shade. A saw began to rasp and screech.

Kathy tried to sit up. 'It's late,' she said. 'I must go . . . No, my heart . . . don't . . . not now . . . there isn't time . . .'

'Yes,' he said, and curved his palms around her shoulders and pressed gently down, sweetly, gently, tenderly pressing her down into the hurting stones.

20

He had never been in love before. Anything, everything, was possible. And if, away from her, he could sometimes not remember what she looked like it did not matter very much. He knew the essence of her. Had gone straight to it. She was marvellous to him, she was a dark and powerful joy that throbbed in him, she was the blood in his veins that coursed hot and quick now, she was a taste on his tongue more intoxicating than wine, warmer than new milk, she was a smell in his nostrils more wholesome than fresh bread, sharper than tangerines, she was a feeling in his hands more satisfying than the most delicate carving. There had never been anything like her. Only under the sea sometimes in those first years of manhood he had walked like a god in the limitless blue.

And since reason is no passport into the territory of love, Fotis lost what logic he had . . . Anything, everything was possible. His bloodless face lost its aloof expression of suffering beyond remedy and took on a quality of mad expectation. He lived for the morning market and each new plan of assignation, and between these times he sat for hours in the doorway of the little house, smoking cigarettes and devising further, more complicated, plans, or dreaming brilliant and quite shapeless daydreams.

Now when he wandered through the streets and lanes of the port, filling in time until he should see her again, through the clang of the forges and the bustle of the workshops and the labourers grunting between the shafts of their burdened carts, through drying sponges, new rope, coils of air-hoses, he no longer saw that men looked at him curiously and drew back to make a way for him to pass. Although he always saw Demetrius, slow, heavy, significant, portentous as a figure in a dream, and would almost have spoken, trembled on the verge of speech, but no words came. Only the intensity of the full, slow, black stare stayed with him afterwards and he shook with an indefinable excitement, shivering in the spring sunshine beneath the feathery salt-trees.

'Ai-ee . . . Ai-*ee*!' Irini wailed under the herbs hanging from old Polymnia's rafters. 'He does not speak. He does not eat. He does not even get drunk any more. He is sick . . . *Ai-eeee* . . .'

The crone cackled, mumbling her gums as she stirred camomile tea over a tiny charcoal grate. 'They often get sick at this time of the year. The captains are beginning to sign them on again. That makes many a man sick. Has he signed yet?'

'No. He only laughs when I ask and says he is going to Australia. And there is no more money until he signs and no more credit at the grocer. Polyxena's man has signed already, and Theodora's, with Captain Andreas on the *Sevasti*, and they are eating meat and their children have shoes put by for Easter. Australia! All this mad talk about Australia! It doesn't put beans in the pot. *Ai-eeee* . . . and another one coming . . .'

Polymnia tasted her tea, pouring it into a big white china cup, and sat down on a stool, grunting and wheezing. She did not offer any to her visitor. 'Perhaps,' she said slyly, 'it is true. The lady is rich. Why shouldn't she send him to Australia if it suits her?'

'Better she gave him a little money to feed his family,' Irini said with unusual bitterness. 'He has enough mad ideas in his head already.'

'Why don't you ask her, then? Men are sometimes ashamed to ask, and the rich never think that the poor must eat . . .' She laughed a little, mysteriously, slurping her tea in great noisy draughts and watching Irini over the rims of her glasses.

And Irini was all glittering excitement suddenly, mouth open, eyes round and black and shining with a sort of rapacity. 'Eeeeh! But how? I would die of shame to ask the lady for money . . . although it is true that she brought the children oranges and sweets and some medicine for the baby. Which I did not waste, because the baby was better by then. But the kindness was there. Yes, that is true enough . . .'

'Those who don't ask get the bottom of the bucket,' said Polymnia, and went off into a paroxysm of laughter, hooting and snuffling and wheezing until water squeezed out of her eyes and her glasses misted over. 'You're a poor thing, Irini. You always were and you always will be.'

Irini sat with her legs apart and her hands with their ragged nails folded over the out-thrust plastic apron and giggled a little too, in unease and embarrassment, a placatory giggle. 'Ah . . . you know things, good Polymnia . . .'

'I know what I know,' agreed the old one, and snuffled into a moody silence, which lasted until Irini, with lowered eyes and fingers picking nervously at her apron, ventured in a timid and fearful voice:

'Good Polymnia, will you tell me then? Is it true that he has the Eye on him?' And her eyes flew open in terror at her own words and she crossed herself quickly and spat three times over her shoulder.

'Hah!' Polymnia snorted, and yawned enormously, making a huge purplish hole in her face. 'So you have thought of that at last.' But she seemed bored by the idea, and sank her chin into her headscarf and sucked at her gums in a contemplative way. At last she said rather peevishly: 'Make the sign of the cross over him. Take three drops of oil from the ikon lamp and with your finger drip them into a glass of water. If the oil spreads he has the Eye on him.'

Wriggling now, Irini ventured even further. 'And the lady? What about the lady?'

Aunt Polymnia studied her with contempt. 'Who do you think you are to understand the lady? The lady is foreign and rich. She will do as she pleases without your permission. Who knows what that will be? Or whether it will be good or bad in the end?'

'But you saw her hand . . .' Irini said, shrill, eyes popping.

'I saw what I saw. And it is none of your business. Oh, go away now!' she snapped, peevish, or bored, or exasperated. Or something else entirely perhaps. She might even have been as

131

wise as her reputation would have her. 'Off with you! Wasting my time! You're a poor thing, Irini. You always were and you always will be.'

And with this much Irini, poor thing, had to be content . . .

Although, through the shimmering mists of his daydreams, the diver was aware of her furtive operations with lamp and oil and water, the surreptitiousness of crosses. Aware, and even interested, in a way.

'Does the oil spread?' he once asked her, in a decent, civil voice, and Irini shrieked at this stranger's voice across her shoulder, and dropped the glass before she could see whether the oil had spread or not, and shrank back with her arms flung up to shield her face. But instead of the expected blow he only stared at her in a puzzled sort of way, and brushed out of the house carelessly with his cap tipped forward and his thumbs hooked through the belt with the snake buckle.

What had he to do with the woman whimpering under the ikons? Or the children who swarmed in his house and at night on the bedshelf suffocated him with the pressure of their breathing? He had thought once as other men thought— that many children testified to a man's virility. It seemed to him now that they testified only to the years of his thoughtless, despairing surrender to the one consolation that was free to a man and always available. In his spirit he cast them off, as he had cast off the lead weights and the copper armour of his servitude to the sea, and soared untrammelled. Anything, everything, was possible. When he was in Australia he would send them money. A great deal of money, on the first day of every month, so that they would eat well and wear shoes and have nothing with which to reproach him.

But the fact was that at the moment he had no money at all apart from one fifty-drachma note which Irini kept hidden in the rice tin and the few loose coins he carried in his pocket. Very few divers had more. By this time their last season's wages had been spent and drunk and gambled away, and their families would all be living on credit until the men signed on for the coming summer's cruise and received their advances from the captains.

The captains sat these days in the coffee-houses, grave, dignified, wearing clean shirts and cummerbunds and well-polished shoes and formally sipping mastika or ouzo, quiet men of middle age with huge grizzled moustaches and good eyes accustomed to assessing men. The packs of cards and the *tavli* boards had been put away now, and the captains just sat there, unhurried, sipping their little colourless liqueurs, waiting.

Fotis, too, sat in the coffee-houses, neither furtive nor defiant as he had been all winter long, but sitting there quite openly, watching with his twilight eyes. Occasionally a man would rise from a group of companions, settle his cap or hitch his woollen cummerbund, and drift—as if accidentally—towards one of the tables where the quiet captains sat. And the captain would gravely order a drink and the diver would sit, and they would talk casually and politely about their families and how the winter had been passed, or what food was to be had in the market, or the quality of the new keg of mastika down from Chios.

'I'm not such a damned fool!' Fotis said aloud. It sounded poignant. He did not know it, but he was like an unfrocked priest smelling incense.

Petros and Stamatis gathered about him in their envy. And the wild young boys did, too, one of them his own nephew, a boasting lad of his elder (and long since drowned) brother, and this one would buy ouzo with a sort of maniacal hilarity, pressing his lucky uncle to drink, to drink. The lady from Australia was going to get him a permit. All the town knew it.

The men drifting so accidentally to the captains' tables knew it too, and looked at him wonderingly, as one who had already freed himself from that struggle against death on barbarian shores and in desolate seas to which they were again contracting themselves. And when at last, after the preliminary and carefully neutral conversations, they made the laborious marks that engaged them once more to endure the terrible pressures of the ocean and all its dangers, they would look at him again—at the expectant white face that was no longer quite familiar, no longer part of their ranks, passed beyond them, out of their community and understanding. His luck, that had turned on him last season, had turned again. It was a mysterious thing. They might even have asked him to drink with them were it not for his strange expression. He made them uneasy. More uneasy than ever. So that they were constrained while he sat there and did not drink quite as wildly as they normally did after the signing.

21

So the preparations went on. It was the time of weddings and betrothals and baptisms, of feasting and drinking and dancing. The contracted divers, with their advances in their pockets and their credit good at the grocery stores, mitigated their subdued and never-spoken-of horror in a passionate abandonment of revelry. In the little cubes of houses riveted to the cliffsides the music went on all through the night now, and the shepherds came down from the mountains to play their goatskin bagpipes in the taverns. In the evening lanes and alleys the groups of masked figures multiplied—women dressed as men, men padded lewdly to look like women: they wore baskets over their heads, or old sacks with eyeholes cut out of them, and around their waists they strung gourds, or fish skeletons, or the bright feathered carcasses of tiny birds. One night a figure ran the whole length of the waterfront dressed in a lace curtain and an old German helmet. There was so little time left to sing and dance, to marry or to engage hopefully to marry, to baptise the babies born out of last spring's marrying. The boats would be away by Easter.

And Fotis, rejecting it all, would yet find himself pausing outside a bakehouse savoury with the smell of fresh ships' biscuit, or his feet would lead him again towards the shipyards and the familiar rasp and screech of the big saws and the *thunggg* of tensed warplines and the crack of the shipwrights' mallets, and the squeak of dry tackle reeving through new blocks, and the smell of paint and creosote and wood-shavings and pitch and cotton-waste and marline, and the lean boats winching up on the pebbles.

'I'm not such a fool,' he said to himself. Sometimes he groaned aloud, but for what he could not have said.

There were also the nights. He wandered a great deal by

night, his hieratic staring face lit in passing by the Tilly lamps that hissed white in revelling houses where the dancing figures span like dervishes and the women's voices soared. 'Oh sea, sea, why have you blackened our mountains?' they sang. 'Oh cruel sea, be as honey, be as sugar, for my love is sailing . . .' And sometimes it was a naked screaming baby held high over the baptismal font that had been lugged up the mountainside from one of the churches, and sometimes it was a bride and groom sitting stiff and wooden under the garlands, and sometimes it was a newly betrothed couple, strangers to each other, as likely as not, exchanging the binding golden bands. It was all the same: the great seaboots stamped to the wild, wild bagpipes, the shriek of the clarinet, the scrape and screech of the violin, the twanging of the zither, and the singing women twirled and twirled, the grandmothers crowded along the bedshelf, peering lasciviously and cackling at their own knowledge, and the children fell asleep, bloated, among picked-over platters of fish and meat scraps, or unhappily vomited up their stolen wine.

As he passed silent and staring through the black and blaze of this nightly revelry, time played curious tricks on him. Through open shutters he glimpsed in a smoky blue room his own young man's face, looking out at him tired and pale from under the wedding crown, and beside him, painted red and white and still as death, was Kathy's face with the ritual white veil pouring around it like smoke. And in a house with a bamboo ceiling she came through the farther door between the oleographs of Genovefa, modestly coifed and surrounded by women, and approached the godfathers standing with the priest at the font and kissed their hands and surrendered to them the shawled son: she was weeping a little from excitement and joy. Or again, he saw himself flinging fifty-drachma bills to the musicians, laughing, urging his guests to help themselves more freely to the food and to the wine, which she served, laughing too, the high set of her head proud and beautiful in a silk headscarf embroidered with a hundred golden coins.

He had never been in love before. Anything, everything, was

possible. Even possible, on these nights of wandering, to reweave all the years of his manhood so that she was inextricably part of the pattern, the shining thread of it. Retrospectively he joined her to him from his green and sappy youth, planted his seed in her, joyed with her and for her in the mystery of birth, the strength and beauty of the sons they made together, the house where friends thronged and there was always singing and laughing in the proper season for such things, or the mature and responsible talk of men proven in their courage, to which she would listen, seated a little aside in respect, those ardent chestnut eyes warm and filled with peace. It was almost as if he could at this very moment give in to her years of pleading, broach the savings of all the good seasons since their marriage, and at last buy the boat (named long since for her, *Saint Katerina*) and take his place with the captains in the coffee houses, gravely and responsibly to choose the first of his diving team.

He was undoubtedly a little mad. But he was thirty-eight years old and had never been in love before.

Irini took the eldest daughter Maria and scoured the mountainside beyond the Chapel of St George for dandelions and edible grasses, and with tears and promises persuaded the grocer to extend a little further credit, enough for flour and beans and oil and a little tomato paste. This at a time when the whole town was feasting. Clearly, it could not go on.

22

The produce boats from the neighbouring islands—on which the town, growing nothing, depended for fresh fruit and vegetables—berthed at a pier beside the public market at the farther end of the waterfront. There were twelve ugly arches here, Italian built, of cracked concrete, in the architectural style of Mussolini's ambitions, in the 'thirties, when he would have had Rhodes the centre of an Italian empire of the Aegean. In one of them Irini waited, with the swarthy little Theodóra and Poppy holding her skirt and the toddler Doxouli balanced on her hip. She could see all the way up the waterfront, and the interior of the market as well. Occasionally she chivvied the children with automatic irritation, but mostly she just stood patiently, shifting her weight from one foot to the other, even smiling a little at nothing in particular, for the waterfront was bustling with busyness, the sea shone milky opal, and the painted produce caïques were unloading basket after basket: snowy cauliflowers, cabbages like tight green roses, little squash no longer than one's finger, stiff bouquets of artichokes, phallic aubergines: the smell of lemons was so sharp that the little girls made involuntary wry mouths every now and then. Among this oriental gorgeousness Irini stood in her concrete niche and waited, her furrowed face dark and weathered around that incredible (and possibly meaningless) metal smile, her pregnant belly pushed out hard, her stained hands placid on the straddling baby. She might have been a heathen idol.

She saw Kathy's pink shirt and ruddy hair at some distance; sharp, bright line of cheek and jaw cutting high above the darting cigarette boys, the bent backs of the labourers, the coffee-tables black and buzzing with men like swarms of flies; she looked swift and sure as a figurehead flying, making for the market like a prow dead on course.

138

Irini smiled vaguely and lowered her eyes, shifted the weight from one foot to the other in an uneasy shuffle: she was wearing grey felt slippers and her two big toes had pushed through, making symmetrical fringed holes.

'Irini!' cried the clear voice above her, and the two women looked at each other in embarrassment and confusion. Kathy flamed as pink as her shirt and then just as abruptly turned dead white: it appeared that she might easily faint. Irini leaned her weight forward and sideways a bit, balancing the baby, and bobbed her head in an apologetic sort of way. Her expression was curious. Devouring. She looks *lecherous*, thought Kathy, who was in a state of shock.

But she managed to say, in halting Greek: 'How are you, Irini? Are you well? And the children?' It sounded insane to her. She smiled dazzlingly at the two little girls. They giggled and hid their faces in their mother's skirt.

Irini inclined her head mysteriously. Then quite suddenly she pushed the children forward roughly and pointed rapidly at their mouths, at the scabby mouth of the baby, and at her own, jabbing with two fingers, still with her black eyes fixed on Kathy's in that curious, lecherous way.

'They are hungry,' she mouthed, as if she were talking to a deaf person. 'Hungry.' And went through the pantomime again, angrily this time. Then she seemed to be overcome with embarrassment and turned her head and lowered her eyes. The apologetic, almost servile, flash of steel came and went. She bent and jerked furiously at the round-eyed children.

'Oh God!' cried Kathy excitedly. 'Why didn't you *tell* me? . . . I am such a fool . . . Irini . . . please . . .' But she said it in English, and catching only the excited tone of it Irini became more embarrassed than ever and began to draw back, touching her hand to her forehead in the Turkish way.

Kathy fumbled frantically with her wallet. 'Look,' she said, 'please . . . oh, *do* take it . . . please take it!' It was a bill for a thousand drachmas. She thrust it out in front of her, failed madly to connect with Irini's hand, and stood there shaking wildly as the banknote fell between them. One of the little girls looked up at her solemnly and bent and picked it up and reached up to her mother's twisting, plucking hand. The baby squirmed violently and began to cry.

'Tell me . . . if you want money . . . tell me . . . please . . .' She struggled in an agony with the language, while her heart flew up into her throat and sank like a dead bird. I am going to be sick, she thought, for Irini's face had reassumed that devouring, lecherous expression: her hand with the crumpled bill in it was making a slavish gesture, knuckles to forehead, palm pressed to her heart.

'Oh . . . *no!*' Kathy cried in outrage, but the little girls had already been shoved towards her and had grabbed her hand in the starfish paws and brushed their wet silky mouths on it. 'Good God Al*mighty!*' she said, and snatched her hand away and turned on her heel and walked swiftly through the market and down the waterfront. Shame choked her like nausea.

She did not even see the diver coming towards her under the salt-trees, walking silently, walking with his special lonely, slouching grace, making for the market and the indispensable moment of contact with her.

'Ketty?' he said at her elbow in his dreaming sing-song voice, and moved with an elaborate casualness to mask her from the crowded coffee-tables.

But she only looked at him crazily, as mad as he, and went on without a word, almost running up the lane past the tavern of the New World, past the clanging workshops where the copper helmets glowered like Martians, through festoons of cheap shoes and bolts of gaudy cloth. She did not slow down until she had reached the square where the ancient automobiles were stationed. There was a sad little green grocery on the corner of the square, and she remembered that her basket was empty. She chose things at random—wilted celery, a cauliflower that was beginning to blacken with mildew, a withered bunch of slimy spring onions. A woman as wilted as her produce fawned upon her, the rich foreign lady, extolling the freshness and goodness of her wares and lamenting the injustice of her poverty. Her husband had been crippled sponge-diving. She demonstrated a lurching hobble. Why did the lady not shop here more often? Except for the fact that she had no teeth at all, she looked like an older Irini. Kathy felt as if her head might burst.

The kitchen, as usual, was filled with people, among them the woman who had brought the eggs and the boy with the hand-me-down moustache. Aliki pushed him forward.

'He is a good boy,' she said. 'He would earn much money in Australia. He would help his mother and his sisters. Better this one,' said Aliki intently, 'than the other.'

'But, Aliki, I *can't*. Don't you understand? I can't, can't, can't!'

Aliki took the basket and fingered the vegetables in disgust while the boy stood politely, rather embarrassed, with his hands hanging loosely, and his mother smiled ingratiatingly.

'I am sorry.' Kathy lifted her hands in a helpless gesture, and Aliki shrugged, her face set in its stony basilisk look. These women, Kathy thought. These island women. They were as mysterious to her as gryphons. Did Irini *know*, then? And if she knew did she *care*? Was Aliki threatening her?

She was terribly shaken. She closed the kitchen door behind her and went down the hall to the drawing-room and poured herself a full tumbler of whisky. Neat.

'Kath-*eee*!' cried Milly, all amazed blue eyes. 'Holy cow!'

'Hullo, lovey.' The whisky steadied her a bit. She had drunk a lot of whisky in the year before the accident, hoping . . . hoping what? . . . that all the clever well-known people she entertained might suddenly become as meaningful as they apparently believed themselves to be? Or hoping to blur her knowledge of Irwin's deep humiliation and mistrust of her and to acquiesce in the outward play of tender, protective love? And it had all ended up in a buckled automobile and the *miracle* (for everybody said, and Irwin more fervently than anybody else, with tears in his eyes, that it was an absolute *miracle*) of her being alive at all.

She put her hand up to her head in the old familiar cautious gesture.

'Is it hurting?' asked Milly anxiously. But with some relief also, as explaining the tumbler of whisky. Kathy had a wild, rakish look that Milly found disturbing. And in a funny, surprising little flash of recognition Milly realised that she had always found her sister-in-law disturbing. Right from the time she had spied on Kathy and Irwin in the barn. Kathy had always been incredibly glamorous to her, but also disturbing. That rakish look that she had sometimes, that she had now . . . there was something dangerous about it. Exciting, glamorous, but also dangerous. Her own parents had sensed it: they had thought Kathy *fast*. A vague, nebulous thought about Demetrius hovered, not quite a suspicion—no, of course not a suspicion—but something needing to be pushed away quickly, before it clarified. For all that her tender young face was suddenly glazed and helpless, and her shoulders drooped.

'It's all right,' said Kathy vaguely. 'Not to worry. But I think I might lie down for a bit.'

In her room she put her face in her hands and let the shuddering take her. She felt annihilated. They had been *hungry*! That woman. Those children. But she had known that all along, hadn't she? She had urged their hunger on Demetrius in vehement defence of her interest in the diver. Those little ragged girls kissing her hand! The shame was deep and wounding. Why, oh why, had he not told her? No, of course he wouldn't. Couldn't. But she had known that too. From the very beginning. And the plight of the woman and the children had been perfectly obvious. Only, since she had loved him, she had not wanted to think about his woman and his children. That was it, really. She had just simply cancelled them out in her mind so that she could sink into the dark and powerful joy that had possessed her since she had heard his voice and felt his hands in the chapel.

She saw that now. Also she saw that the shame of her morning's encounter would have to be accepted. A down payment—with even heavier instalments, perhaps, to follow. Nothing for nothing, she thought rather hysterically, and bloody little for sixpence! And the price would not be paid in any noble coin. Grubby tender, rather, of furtiveness and deceit, notes of small denomination, soiled, nasty to handle. Can you? she asked herself. Will you pay that much? And in that way? But it was already too late to question the contract. To stop loving him was beyond her. They had already passed through the impossibility of the surface situation into another, denser, element of understanding. Logic would not work here. Only feeling. For he was desperate enough to need, and reckless enough to accept, the very most she could give. She could not, could not abandon him.

'But it won't be for long,' she said grievously, and her voice had an aching sound in the pretty guest-room. It was just as though she was excusing herself to Irwin in his leather frame. Unnecessarily, of course, because Irwin's face so obviously preferred not to know.

23

Fotis stood on the corner until her fleeing figure had disappeared beyond the tavern. It did not occur to him to follow her. Only an infinite distress welled up in him and he felt very cold suddenly in the bright spring sunshine. He should move; do something. He didn't know where to move to, what to do. But he turned irresolutely among the coffee tables, and seeing his blind, white, blundering face a woman who had been threading through the tables with a Soul Cake took her little silver spoon and offered him some. He made the sign of the cross automatically and closed his mouth on the stuff. His mouth full of boiled wheat and spices. Full of dead souls. His throat refused to swallow and he retched and spat the food out on to the pavement. The shocked woman set up a strident clamour of indignation.

'Filthy dog! Blasphemer!' She called to witness the black-capped men at the tables, who had been watching with a sombre interest, but they averted their heads and resumed uneasy conversations. The woman went on screaming. Two strolling duty policemen paused, caught by the hint of a drama, and one of them moved a step or two towards Fotis, then shrugged, and moved back again. The eyes that looked at him and through him were the most unhappy the policeman had ever seen: he twirled his keychain elaborately as he rejoined his partner and they strolled on with very straight backs and very straight shoulders. A drunk spitting on the pavement was not worth making a fuss about. The town was filled with drunks. A savage island. The policeman, who came from a mountain village in Arcadia, hated and feared it.

On the far side of the waterfront, beside the diving-boats and the opal sea, Irini and the children passed, loaded with marketing. Fotis watched them as if he did not see them at all, but when they had passed the Twenty-fifth of March statue he tipped his cap down over his forehead and turned up the lane that led away from the waterfront. He could still taste the wheat and sugar and cinnamon in his mouth and his stomach heaved slightly. But he made his way across the town, through the back alleys, and climbed up over the ramp behind St Nikólas that buttressed the lower galleries of Epano. The doors of the church were open and a dozen Soul Cakes, one as wide as a cartwheel, glittered frostily among the stiffness of priests and candles.

Irini and the children had reached the house before him. There were brown-paper carrier-bags all over the deal table, and the children were scrabbling for spilt silver cachous. Fotis stood in the doorway, still filled with that awful distress, until the children saw him and nudged one another and drew back, and Irini, turning, made a frightened movement as if to sweep away her purchases. Then she laughed, her face crumpling into a childish gaiety above the treasures of meat and oil and fruit and vegetables and candles and silver sweets. Her hand made a triumphant circling movement over her breast.

'Fotis! Look now! I can make the Soul Cake, after all! A good one, with sugar and silver flowers and candles. And there is enough money for shoes so that the children can come to St Stephanos with me . . . and meat to eat when we come home. Ah, she is a good lady . . . I always knew she was a good kind lady . . . did she not bring oranges and medicine when the baby was sick?' And for a second she looked at him in shy amazement. 'Perhaps,' she said, 'she will truly send you to Australia!'

'Perhaps,' Fotis said in a polite dead voice, and went out of the house again.

He wandered all the rest of the morning, an aloof figure in the frantic employments of Soul Saturday, the hook of his nose contemptuous beneath the cap, but with his shoulders hunched meagrely. He paused, as he had paused so many times in these last weeks, by every workshop he chanced to pass, each clipping-room, ship chandler's, bakehouse. He paused, too, by the doorways of churches, looking in at Soul Cakes and candles and the curl

145

of incense smoke and the priests' hair-knots tight and shiny grey like peeled onions, at the silver amulets dangling beneath the ikons, the model of a ship, at kneeling figures.

At noon he drank an ouzo at a little square in the centre of the town, where a Persian lilac grew. He came here occasionally because it was one of the few places that served Cretan *raki* and often there had been need for a drink as strong as that, and through the wide-open doors of the tavern he could see the framed pictures around the walls—the heroes of the War of Independence, fierce, strong-faced men with huge curling moustaches and hair falling in ringlets to their waists, wearing bold rich costumes and with a splendour of ornaments and weapons. From where he sat under the gnarled branch of an old cedar he could identify almost all the heroes—Canaris, Kolokotronis, Botsaris, Thiakos, Karaskaikas, and the woman Boubalina.

There was an ancient well in the middle of the square, and around it the usual chatter of women with their kerosene tins and earthenware jars, and there was one old man drowsing in the sun at one of the shabby iron tables, and five small boys were squatting in the gutter over some bits of bark and torn cardboard and lumps of charcoal: evidently they were making Carnival masks for the evening.

It was very peaceful there with only the ping of the bucket and the slap and gurgle of the water: the women's voices were muted and the children too absorbed to talk: the old man made small whiffling noises, more soothing than disturbing.

Fotis was overcome with lassitude, and yawned behind his freshly lit cigarette. A prodigious yawn. He was racked by yawning. It occurred to him that there would be nothing more pleasant on earth than to go to sleep over the sun-warmed table. To have the right to sleep in the sun like the old man whose puckered lavender eyelids drooped peacefully, slack jaw munching and mumbling over clean old hands folded on clean faded shirt while a thimbleful of cognac winked topaz-brilliant in front of him for when he should choose to stir and wake enough to drink it. He had a full, proud moustache, like the moustaches of the heroes of the lithographs, but of a silky fawn colour, and an old black diver's cap settled firm on his forehead, and his two legs, stretched out evenly under the table, ended in huge felt slippers and there was no stick hooked over the back of his chair.

Passionately Fotis wished that he might be that rare old man who had survived with two sound legs and need to do nothing ever again but whicker and sniffle in the sun and bore his grandchildren with tales of the exploits of his youth.

There were few old divers with two good legs. If you thought about it there were few old divers at all. His own father had not lived to be old. Nor Irini's. He had uncles living, but badly twisted. And of all the divers who had been middle-aged when he had been a boat-boy, or when he had first, with leaping heart and quickly stifled foreboding, submitted himself to the copper armour of manhood, who was left? Old Christodoulos, limping around on his two sticks, bawling the shipping schedules. Stephanos Lathianos, coughing up his lungs in a cigarette factory. Mad old Saklarades, undoing his shirt buttons with hands like shaking brown leaves to show the marks of the shark's teeth. There were a few, and of the few some were fortunate enough to have sons and daughters willing to look after them. A man needed many sons to insure himself against the helplessness of a crippled old age. His own father had had four sons, and of the four only one other had survived the starvation of the German occupation to keep his appointment with a cut air-hose and a hundred seconds of strangulation in that heaven-blue of the Cyrenaica beds, the blue of the dome of St Stephanos, but without the angels flying. If the women made Soul Cakes every day of the year there would still not be enough boiled wheat and spices to feed all those dead mouths.

His blood beat up behind his eyes with an angry throbbing, so that the sunlit little square pulsed and blurred in a red mist. What else could they have done? Any of them? Himself? What choice had ever been given? He had been dedicated to the sea from the moment he was born. The fact that he had been born a male had been sufficient consecration. When he was seven years old his father had taken him out on the Lenten trial run of the *Twelve Apostles*, to which he was contracted for the coming summer, and had stripped him naked on the deck and put a stone in his hands and shown him how to hold it, and he had looked once at the circle of interested faces watching him and he had taken a great single agonising breath and jumped. What else could he have done? There was never a time he could remember when he had not been amphibious. All the long burning summers of boyhood, when the adult males had gone with the boats to Africa, he had spent with his brothers and all the other divers' sons in or under the sea, vying with one another as to who could dive deepest, stay longest, until their ears and eyes were bursting with blood and their skins turned soggy and crumpled in spite of the fat with which they greased one another, and they had sprawled gasping on the hot still rocks like so many dying fish. What else could they have done? It had been play then, all those long summers of trial and preparation, the ecstatic burning summers of childhood. But serious play. Religious almost. Queer little naked priestlings—undernourished, scrofulous, scarred, with sobbing pigeon breasts and nostrils streaming blood.

And his own sons? Suddenly they weighed upon him as the chest-weights weighed, leaden heavy. In giving them life he had condemned them also, as his father had condemned him, as his grandfather had condemned his father, as his great-grandfather had condemned his grandfather. It went back for ever, beyond men's memories. Generation after generation, blind, witless, smirking under the wedding crown but following without protest the pipes and strings that screeched ahead to the imprisoning walls, the roof that shut out the sky, the arranged darkness with bedsheets glimmering in it and the lascivious old women cackling as they turned the key in the lock. He could have screamed in outrage to find himself thus fettered by the long chain of disregarded years. A trap. A trap! It was all a trap! He had submitted himself to the wedding crown as he had submitted to the diving helmet, because he was a man, and the time had come for that particular part of the inflexible ceremonial to which he had been committed by being born. He had done exactly as the other men had done. What else had been possible?

But to his newly awakened and still groping perceptions it seemed that all the time he had been dimly aware that he had another life, a parallel life as it were, that walked with him like a cast shadow and lay down beside him when he slept, a life that he could have lived under other circumstances, a life which he could live even now if he could only wrench himself free from the bitter plausibility of this one. In his recent deranged night wanderings this other life had seemed to reveal itself to him. She was the reality of it. Holy Jesus, why had she delayed so long to reveal to him the existence of his other life? The thought of her dawdling away the years on the other side of the world filled him with fury. When *he* had needed her, to live, to be, to complete himself, to understand . . . and she had not been there with him. She had cheated him of all those years of his real life.

He needed her now. His chest ached with the effort of breathing. His head ached with the effort of thinking. His being ached with a hungry yearning. Even the roots of his teeth ached tenderly in his aching gums. He was one great ache of wanting.

Across the square five little figures with grotesque faces of bark and cardboard crept giggling towards the table where the old diver dozed in the sun and leaped up all around him with fiendish shrieks. The old man let out a trumpet of dismay, blubbering his mouth against the fine silky fawn moustache and clutching at the air with his hands. The women at the well honked and hooted in the folds of their headscarves, and after a bewildered moment the old man laughed too, the deprecating laughter of the aged, and simulated cuffs and fury before he dispensed *caramellas* from his pocket.

Fotis watched for a moment in amazement, then abruptly put down a two-drachma piece on the table and walked away through the laughter and out of the square. It was imperative that he should find her. Unthinkable that he should not. Thoughts, words, memories, were boiling up behind the crumbling dam of his defences, and the pressure was intolerable. Holy Jesus! Holy Mother of God! he thought. Let her take this from me.

Both Fotis and Kathy walked miles that afternoon, circling out and beyond the town along dust roads, goat trails, cliff paths, pausing in hope or panic at sheepfolds, behind boulders or clumps of prickly pear and aloe, retracing their ways again with steps that were irresolute or stumbling in haste. Puffs of nervous blue smoke signposted their halting places. They left the echoes of savage heart beats—surely the other would hear and recognise? Through the still sweet hours of the spring afternoon their two incredulous questing faces took on a strange similarity, so that perhaps the few persons who could have directed either of them to the path of the other—a shepherd motionless on a golden rock, the driver of a Citroën rattling along the valley with a grandmother and a load of turkeys, two young girls gathering dandelions for boiling above St Stephanos, a gang of bullet-headed boys lusting for blood around the slaughterhouse—thought it was the same figure who passed or lingered in such unlikely places that afternoon. Or perhaps the erratic movements of the rich foreign lady were too utterly mystifying to be within the comprehension of simple people. As for the diver, he had the Evil Eye on him, or so it was rumoured, and in such cases it was better not to risk any taint of contact.

24

Several more buyers came in on the afternoon steamer, one an
elderly man with the proud name of Leonidas, who had been
a family friend ever since Demetrius could remember—a jolly
hairy old fellow with pendulous purple dewlaps and an air of
invincible jauntiness. He had travelled widely in Europe and
America, and was even a poet in a modest way. Demetrius was
immensely glad to see him, finding his urbanity reassuring. They
looked at sponges and bargained pleasurably, and afterwards they
drank sherry in the office and talked of Paris and London and
Demetrius sent a boy with a note to the house to tell Milly there
would be a guest.

Walking home through the surging bells of *espéres*, the old
gentleman, who was after all very short and fat beside his young
host, said slyly: 'And the little bride? How does she do?'

'Well enough,' said Demetrius moodily, and added, 'she is
pregnant.'

'So? Good freedom to her. May she be fruitful, noble boy;
may your sons and your sons' sons have a hundred years.'

Demetrius gave an involuntary sigh at the conventional
compliments. The formal phraseology was so deeply familiar,
really so very beautiful to him, and he felt a warm sense of
kindredship with his guest, a sense of race that completely
excluded his relations with his troublesome foreign women. For
a second he most painfully wished that he had married an island
girl.

'But it's changing, all this,' he said with sombre conviction.
'It would be madness for me to travel in the same old ruts.'

His guest evidently followed his train of thought, and took
his arm as they threaded through the clanging lanes.

'So. So. It will see out my time. But you are right. Not yours.

151

Go your own way, boy. You do well. But sometimes it is a little difficult, eh? Even alarming. Never mind. New blood is good in this old race.'

'Lazarus and Paul have no confidence. They want everything to go on as before. They are afraid of new ventures.' And Kathy condemns me as a monster battening on crippled bodies, he did not add, but only said broodingly into the silence that rushed back after the bells: 'The wife of my wife's brother is staying with me. You will see.'

'I heard it. That is pleasant for the little one. To have one of her own about her at this time, one of her blood and her tongue. Eventually one's own tongue is the only vehicle for confidence.'

'It is pleasant just now for me to be using mine,' said Demetrius, and put his hand on the old man's shoulder and smiled down at him affectionately. The uneasy premonition of some shapeless disaster that had been haunting him lately dissolved. Perhaps it was just this heady weather that was upsetting him, and the pressure of work. Perhaps nothing more than that. 'Good Leonidas,' he said.

They crossed the square and turned in the grilled gate just as the sun slipped behind High Lady. The white villa flushed delicately and the windows in their louvred green shutters flashed suddenly gold. Milly in the front doorway looked as succulent as a peach. She was big now. Demetrius felt a hot gush of pride. Yes, yes. It was good. Sons and sons' sons.

In the drawing-room he stroked her a little, finding in her submissiveness some new quality of appeal that was particularly pleasing: he showed her off in little domestic ways, like a rare pet patiently trained, and basked in the approval of the old family friend. She poured the drinks, fetched a clean handkerchief for him, took the tray of savouries from Aliki and offered them herself, lit the cigarettes.

'And where is the sister-in-law of whom I have heard so much, Madame Millee?' asked Leonidas.

'I don't know,' she said, setting down ashtrays. 'Walking

152

somewhere, I expect. Kathy has itchy feet or something. One would think she should know every individual stone on the island by this time, but she's always rambling off again.' She frowned. 'She had a bad headache this morning. Perhaps she is walking it off.' *Now* what have I said? she wondered helplessly, for the veins at Demetrius's temples swelled and his nostrils grew dark and he suddenly ground his half-smoked cigarette into the ashtray. Old Leonidas watched them slyly in one of the gilt mirrors.

Kathy did not come in until they started dinner. They heard her cross the hall with her firm, hard stride and go upstairs, and in a little while she came down again, scrubbed and brushed, wearing a cream wool shirt-dress with silver buttons. The men rose, and she acknowledged the introductions evenly and slipped into her place.

'I am so sorry to be late,' she said. 'I walked too far. One forgets that there is no twilight here. Just day and night.'

'Yes, yes,' said old Leonidas cheerfully. 'That is right. One forgets that.' And went into a story of his first experience of an English twilight.

Demetrius poured wine. It was a good retzina, from a freshly tapped barrel. Kathy drank hers quickly, and the glass chattered momentarily against her teeth. Demetrius refilled her glass without comment. Only he still had that dark stain around his nostrils, and the shadow of his beard made his face look heavier, more jowlish.

'Shall I call Aliki to bring you the soup, Kathy?' said Milly. 'Although I wouldn't bother if I were you. It's not awfully good.'

'Then I must apologise for that, too,' said Kathy, still in a perfectly even voice. 'I bought the celery. Don't blame Aliki. No, just give me some of the *moussaka*, lovey, and I'll skip the soup.'

The dinner dragged on, with Demetrius brooding, Milly jittery, Kathy agate-hard and precise, Aliki stumping in and out as if she bristled with grievances, and Leonidas intrigued. Milly drank only water, but Demetrius and Kathy drank wine, glass for glass, and old Leonidas wondered, but paced them gallantly.

153

'This is felicity indeed,' he murmured when dinner was over at last and Milly led him to a chair by the stove and poured whisky and soda and brought him the cigar box. His English was heavily accented and charmingly precise. He presented it to the two women in stiff little bouquets of words, to which the accompaniment of a formal bow would have been quite appropriate: the bow was indicated, sketched in, as it were, by the gallant glances of his jolly little black eyes, which darted about under the huge hairy eyebrows like lively insects. He was very puzzled.

The little English wife would do very well. A pretty morsel. Malleable. Fruitful. The boy had done well there. New blood. They needed new blood. It was the sister-in-law he found intriguing. She had a smouldering quality that both attracted and disquieted him. He had always preferred the mettlesome ones himself. Troublesome, but more exciting eventually. He rubbed wistfully at his dewlaps, and again turned his attention to the sister-in-law. He was conscious that she was suffering, but the form of her suffering was obscure to him. All her movements, the very tone of her voice, were painfully restrained and under control, but there was a quivering of—of what? . . . mistrust? . . . rebellion? . . . fear?—of something beneath the surface, and the sidelong shying glances of her chestnut eyes were shamed in some way. The old man smelt a situation, latent if not already existing. What was puzzling was that the situation apparently was not the obvious one, although, again, there were moments that evening when some word or look from his young host seemed so very obvious that he himself was amazed at the little bride's obliviousness.

'You will remain in Greece long, Madame Katherine?' he asked, and there was a curious pause in which he noticed that the little wife's face went quite blank and glazed and his young friend Demetrius turned so that he appeared to crouch lightly forward towards the sofa, fixing the sister-in-law with a hot fathomless stare. As for her, erect as though encased in armour, a flicker of stark terror seemed to ripple through her and her

154

top lip lifted away from her teeth. He had the impression of an animal in a trap, not daring to breathe. Then they were both murmuring, their words folding together: '. . . as long as we can keep her' . . . '*months* yet . . .'

'Until Milly's baby is born and my husband comes to collect me,' she said evenly. 'I am so lucky. There is the Greek Easter yet. And then, of course, the boats going away.' She went on, smiling, talking rapidly. 'The ceremonial on this island is fascinating to me. I have never seen anything like it. All those lovely white-and-silver cakes today, and the candles and the chanting. I must have been in a dozen churches. And people dressing up so strangely and running about the town without any self-consciousness at all. It's like being in . . .' She hesitated, then looked at him directly, frankly, with sudden interest as though he might understand, '. . . in another *world*,' she said.

'It is another world, Madame Katherine. An older world than yours.'

'More *potent*,' she said eagerly. 'I feel that so strongly.'

'And anachronistical, eh? Can you relate this island to Telstar, madame, or Mariner Two? To astronauts and cosmonauts?'

Her eyes grew wide with pain. She lifted her hands briefly and let them fall again. 'Human risks. Human courage.'

'But of a peculiar order.' They were speaking very quietly to each other, with an extraordinary intentness. The fat and hairy old man no longer looked jolly. But he looked older. Racially ancient. And weary. 'A courage that is non-aspirational. Only enduring. The courage of an inherited despair,' he said. 'I think you understand?'

'Kathy has become an incorrigible romantic about sponge-diving,' Demetrius cut in with an edge of real bitterness. 'She doesn't need encouragement, Leonidas.'

'So?' The old man glanced at him quickly and showed his little brown teeth between the thick wrinkled lips. 'Surely it is the privilege of the young and beautiful to be a little romantical. It is of high suitability. But not too much sadness. Yes, you are right, my friend. So come now, Madame Katherine. At this season it is the time of Carnival. You will observe how happy this island can be. You will make Carnival, Madame Millee?'

'Well, there's to be a dance at Paul's on Sunday night. And I expect we shall go out to the threshing floor on Clean Monday. Shan't we, Demetrius? Kathy ought to see that.'

'Threshing floor?' she said.

'Oh yes. Didn't you know? Everybody in the town simply packs up and goes out to the village on Clean Monday—that's the beginning of Lent, you see, and the last day for feasting— and they all dance on the old threshing floor. It's very gay, actually,' said Milly on a faint rising note of surprise. 'I mean to say, they sing a lot, and they all bring food—unleavened bread and olives and things, special sorts of food for Lent and masses of wine— and it's sort of one great huge picnic out under the trees, and visits from family to family, and it goes on all day long and goodness knows how long through the night . . . We will go, Demetrius, won't we?'

'Of course,' murmured Demetrius in his suavest voice. 'It would be pleasant to have that picnic, after all, eh?'

Puzzlement grew on the old man, watching them. There was a situation. Definitely there was a situation. But the shape of it still eluded him. He accepted another whisky-and-soda with a quick little nod. So did Kathy, looking hard and clear and chiselled again, and emptied her glass in about three good swallows. The sponge-buyer tried a different tack.

'You have perhaps explored the old Byzantine city above the village, madame? It is of considerable interest if you-'

'Yes,' she said quickly. 'Yes, I have. Once,' she said. 'It rained.'

'The people here have many strange stories about that ruination. Treasure tales. Highly romantical.'

'Yes,' she said again, and now her lips were parted and her eyes deeply shining. 'I have heard.'

Demetrius laughed. 'My dear Kathy, these people are treasure mad. I should have warned you. Did you believe what they told you? Tiaras and all? Crowns? Jewelled collars? And chests stuffed with gold? And white-robed women appearing in dreams?'

156

'I found a little bit of glass,' she said, and pressed down on her wedding ring. Her finger still hurt when she did that.

'Oh, there are fragments, of course.' Demetrius shrugged with his head and his hand as well as his shoulders. 'Pottery too. I remember when I was a child that my Uncle Christodoulos had a whole collection of bits he had found at various times. Even a few intact plates. He was something of an amateur archaeologist. Do you remember that collection, Leonidas?'

'Well. It was of much interest. Christodoulos had plans to make a small museum. Then the war came . . . ah well, God rest him. What became of those things, Demetrius? He loved them, those small fragments.'

'I don't know. I think Paul has them somewhere in the big house. Or Lazarus. Do you know, Milly?'

'It could be Paul,' said Milly, anxious to please. 'Or Lazarus.'

'Do find out, will you?' He looked towards the sofa and a curious little smile rose up out of the blue of his jaw and lingered around his cheekbones somewhere. 'Kathy might like to see them some time.'

'I'd love to see them,' she said in the cool voice of one accepting a challenge, and went on in mockery: 'But it's not good enough, your fragments, Demetrius. Oh no! I want glittery things. Collars studded with rubies and lapis lazuli. Royal diadems. Hammered gold and gold enamelling. That's what I want. I want that bird on that bough singing to those lords and ladies of Byzantium. Don't try to fob me off with a few old shards. Didn't any of your forefathers ever dig up anything that *shone*?'

And Demetrius, with a certainty that swept him like a physical dizziness, said: 'Ah, so you heard that one? Of course,' he said.

'*Which* one?' cried Milly plaintively. 'Demetrius? Kathy? Oh, *tell* me, one of you . . .'

'And were you so gullible as to believe it, Kathy? Grandfather in his nightshirt holding the lantern and old Amelia digging where the white-garbed woman had instructed? And Great-grandmother bribing the Italian commandant to let the sponge crates through without examination? It's a very favourite story of mine. I, too,

157

believed it implicitly. When I was eight.'

'I believe it implicitly now,' Kathy said, with a glittery note of laughter breaking through. 'It's just what I wanted. Of course the treasure was hidden in the sponges.'

'Of course. How else to smuggle it out? And the crates were shipped to London where the various pieces were sold privately, excepting for one necklace which my great-grandmother wore until the day she died. It was buried with her, tucked inside her shroud.' He was acting badly, with the dizziness behind his eyes, so that he said the word *shroud* in a hammy, sepulchral voice, straining for ease, or laughter, or a moment to rationalise the fear that assailed him. Kathy must have heard the story from the diver. Must have. Who else? But, then, she talked to so many people in the town. Her friendliness was commented upon, greatly appreciated.

Milly said, astonished, 'But you never *told* me!'

'My dear child,' he said politely, 'why should I tell you such rubbish? Only a simpleton could believe it. Or circulate it, either, for that matter.'

But Kathy kept on laughing and clapping her hands together. '*Non*sense, Demetrius. It doesn't necessarily mean it is untrue just because it has been made up. Milly and I intend to believe it. We *want* to believe it. Don't we, Milly? We want tiaras and rings and necklaces. Don't you want a tiara, Milly?'

Milly giggled. 'Oh, but yes. I want a tiara too. Kathy and I both want tiaras, Demetrius.' She began to laugh helplessly. In relief, although she did not analyse it.

'And *snake* bracelets!' gasped Kathy, demonstrating on her arm.

'And *ear*rings!' Milly jumped up and began a mannequin strut, but collapsed sobbing after she had taken six steps. 'And Great-grandmother's *neck*lace . . .'

'. . . out of her *sh-r-ou-ou-d*!' Kathy concluded hysterically. Tears streamed down their contorted faces. They shrieked and gasped with laughter.

Still as a shadow in the dark garden, Fotis peered into the

lighted room. It was blurred by the heat-mist on the window-panes, and distorted by the flaws in the glass, but it was still the most beautiful room Fotis had ever seen in his life. His despair took on a stark tinge of hatred. She was utterly beyond him. She belonged in rooms like this. The rest was lies. Lies, all lies. She had been amusing herself with him, a bit of titillation for a rich bitch who wasn't getting any! Or perhaps she was getting it from that fat young slug as well! And the eloquence of those encounters that had seemed so miraculous to him . . . yes, yes, holy even . . . he had *worshipped* . . . and this had been nothing more than copulation! His mind framed a foul word and flung it at her laughter weaving with Milly's among the warmth, the cigar smoke, the expensive comfort of deep chairs, polished tables, winking glass, thick carpets, the rainbow drops of the chandelier trembling, the mirrors that he thought must be framed in real gold . . . For these things he had crawled along the floor of the sea . . . for these things his pores had sweated blood . . . there were a hundred wooden crosses at the high cemetery that had paid for these things . . . And she sat among them and laughed with those fat swine in their soft warm clothes that he had bought and paid for in a thousand nightmares. Those fat swine who had the right to sit with her, to laugh with her in front of the whole world.

He might have turned then, in the impotence of his hatred, and left the garden with a curse on that rich room and all its occupants, but he heard, at that moment, a shuffle of footsteps on the other side of the garden wall and muffled laughter and the click of the latch on the gate. He drew back into the shelter of the banana-trees as a group of mummers rushed up the path in a wild little eddy and swirled through the front door and into the lighted room.

There were sacks over their heads, or baskets, and their bodies were padded into fantastic humps and mounds. Four were dressed in women's clothes. One was wrapped in sheepskins, one hobbled on a knotty staff, one wore a necklace of fish skeletons, very delicate and feathery. They carried gourds and tin cans and they swept whirling into each separate corner of the room to prance and leap and rattle the gourds and bang the cans with sticks. All were voiceless, all without identity.

'Oh! . . . Oh! . . .' cried Kathy, enchanted, and clapped her hands, and old Leonidas showed all his little brown teeth in laughter.

'*There*, madame!' He had the air of a successful conjurer. 'Observe,' he said. 'They dispel the evil spirits from each corner of the room. They are careful not to disclose by their faces or their voices who they are, lest the spirits of the dead who are at large should recognise them. We must respect this anonymity. Yet we must sing and dance with them to the prosperity of this house. Come, come, Demetrius, my young friend. Come, madame . . . yes, yes, we will show you the steps . . . Madame Millee . . .?' But Milly, who was still possessed by that irrational hilarity, was incapable of rising from the sofa. She sprawled there, clutching a cushion, and with her mouth square open she howled like a young witch.

To Kathy it seemed that they were all being moved by quite incalculable forces, for Demetrius, having finally surrendered to the contagion of their laughter, opened his throat and surprisingly began to sing. Kathy herself was tugged forcibly into the forming circle, between the fish skeletons and the sheepskins, and dipping and lunging they all began to dance around the laughing Milly, with old Leonidas leading by the length of a stretched white handkerchief and Demetrius's voice deep and pure through the gasps and grunts muffled by baskets and sacks and the seedy rattle of the gourds and the clanging of the cans.

To Fotis it was curious but inevitable, transposed only from the white-hissing rooms on the cliffside where also he had stood in the night and watched through windows, and distorted into nightmare as much by his own desolation as by the flawed glass which in one spinning gyration would turn each of the dancing figures from a dwarf to a giant and then to a hunchback. It appeared that his exclusion was

160

to be total. If he could have done so by willing it he would simply have stopped living there and then.

The dancing circle became wilder, more abandoned, as one grotesque after another in turn took up the leadership at the end of the handkerchief, each apparently bent on shaking the walls down or rocking the chandelier from its hook. They leapt and lunged, went backwards in curious balancing feats, slapped their boots with both feet off the ground, and all the time the rhythm was precise and the circle revolved, hesitated, retreated one step and two, and spun triumphantly on. Demetrius dropped out and clapped for Aliki to bring glasses and wine for the dancers, and Aliki in her turn was pulled into the circle: she took up the song, high and harsh, and her petticoats whipped out around her legs. Then Kathy, with her face flushed hectic pink above the creamy wool shirt-dress with the little winking silver buttons, span out of the dance suddenly and whirled towards the window like a spinning top, her arms crossed over her bosom and each hand resting lightly on her shoulder.

He saw her coming as a winking, spinning blur that shot up into immense elongation as he stepped forward lightly from the dark shelter of the trees.

'Air! Air! Air!' she cried, and undid the window catch and pulled it back and flung herself gasping over the sill to take in at one gulp the biting freshness of the night, the ragged shapes of trees and shrubs, the smell of the earth, one star plummeting in glory, and Fotis's cold and desolate mouth full on her own.

25

'There is no shame in this for you. Only shame for me that I neglected it before. It is my shame that Irini had to ask me. But between you and me there must be no shame.'

But there was shame for him. His mouth was stern, with a cramp of pain to it, and his eyes were washed out to the colour of twilight, bleak under the black cap. The envelope lay between them on the scabby surface of the iron table, untouched, and they faced each other rather tiredly, no longer particularly conscious of the audience of women and children who had come jostling around them the moment Kathy had stepped out of the old taxi.

It was in the blue village, and she had particularly chosen it for this rendezvous because she wanted this matter settled between them, and knew it would not be settled without at least a table's width between them, and as it was impossible for her to sit publicly with him at the port she had thought of the village. It was a good table, as tables went, near a blossoming plum-tree and the conical-capped well, and they were enclosed in all the other blues, bright and dark and pale and transparent. Even with the pungent steaming smell of donkey droppings it was a little like sitting in the sky, and the donkeys had blue bead necklaces.

'Do this for me,' she insisted. 'I have never asked you to do anything for me before. Take it and put it away somewhere and use it for them as they need it. I don't ask you to use it for yourself. Use it just for them. It is all in notes of small denomination, so that you don't have to go to the bank to cash it.' That's right, she thought, let it be as crude as possible. Better.

'O.K., Ketty,' he said softly. 'O.K.' He took the envelope and put it in his pocket without another word, and she knew that she had robbed him.

That is all very well, she thought angrily, but *you* have to pay too for this pinpoint of time that is all we are allowed.

'Let's drink some wine,' she said. 'We have never drunk wine together.'

So he called for it in a voice still sombre and hurt, and it came in a tall carafe, the palest clearest gold in the sun, with two ribbed glasses and a plate of olives and bone-white goat cheese. The women came or went or lingered around the well, and in the seat of the old battered Citroën the monkey-faced driver watched impassively. A little girl brought a handful of blue hyacinths and shyly laid them by Kathy's glass. Fotis poured the wine so that the level was exactly to the rim of the fluted ribs, halfway up the glasses, and then took his and poured it on to the pavement and refilled his glass.

'Why did you do that?' she asked.

He grinned at her with the old derisive, shaky grin. 'Don't know. Every feller does that with the first glass. Good luck if you do that.' So she poured hers to the ground and he refilled the glass for her too, and they sat rather sadly on their blue chairs in the blue sky and emptied that carafe and then another, trying to find their way back through the wine to the magic country they had occupied only yesterday. They drank themselves into a state of blurry pensiveness, like the first stages of convalescence after fever, and out of that into a bleak clarity where they saw each other drawn precisely on the surrounding blue like portraits of a man and of a woman. Fotis saw a skinny foreign woman, too tall and no longer quite young, with the marks of sickness on her sharp face and a lot of silver sprinkled through her hair. And Kathy saw a slight and pallid Greek, thin from a lifetime's undernourishment, pasty from dissipation, wearing arrogance like the one last raggy garment of his patrimony that served only to emphasise the other inheritance of despair beneath. And each of them knew certainly that he loved the other, and that love takes no count of suitability or reason or the punctual appointments of persons in space and time, and each of them

163

felt a humility greater than defeat.

We can't win, thought Kathy. The most we can do is score a bit. And Fotis covered her hand with his own and they laughed at each other in recognition.

'Ketty,' he said, indicating the women at the well and the driver of the Citroën, who was now sitting at the next table sipping at a coffee and still watching them with expressionless monkey eyes. 'These fellers here is going to be talking.'

'I know,' she said. 'I don't think it matters now. They've been talking anyway.'

'Does *he* know?'

'Demetrius?'

'Last night. At the window. I was crazy, Ketty. Crazy.'

'He didn't see,' she said. 'At least I don't think he saw. You were gone so quickly, and I closed the window immediately.' She frowned, considering. 'But I think he knows. Or if he doesn't know he suspects. And if he suspects he will find out.'

He drew a wobbly dolphin in the sparkling wine puddle on the table, with a leering rust spot for an eye. 'What will you do, Ketty?'

'I don't know,' she said harshly, but his face was so troubled and drawn that she touched him to give him reassurance. 'Don't worry about it. When the time comes I shall know what to do.'

She left him in the blue village and went back to the port in the old Citroën. Every time she looked up at the driving mirror she saw the monkey-face of the driver grimacing in the most extraordinary way, and they had turned into the square before she realised that he was ogling her.

26

The driver, Anastasis, told the other drivers—Costas, Panyotis, Takis, and Stavros—with some little embellishments—for although he had been in no doubt whatever about the mood prevailing at that table near the blossoming plum-tree, he needed detail to convince. Such as leg-rubbing under the table and hand-holding on top of it. And Takis, a little put out that such a thing had never occurred to him on that rainy day when *he* had driven the foreign lady and the diver back from the village, was now oratorically wise after the event. It had only been his sense of honour, his *philotimo*, that had prevented him from speaking before, for were they not all in a sense the hosts of the foreign woman? Since he had scarcely looked into the driving mirror at all that day (there had been a stew of lamb and onions for supper and he had been hurrying to it) it was easy for him to imagine what was going on in the back seat, what *must* have been going on, and he described it in some detail, thereby silencing Anastasis, whose story was tame by comparison.

But Stavros, who was of an older generation, and had been with foreigners in the Western Desert and at Rimini, was more thoughtful. 'Yet she is a good lady, with a word and a smile for everyone, and the courtesy to remember each name and give it. I believe it is only out of her goodness she is sending this diver to Australia. I think you are seeing what you desire to see, and not what is there. For why should such a lady choose one like that if it was love she wanted? There are many brave men, captains, of strength and courage, and *pallikária*, she could choose among.'

'They have fire between the legs, foreign women,' said Anastasis, nettled at being doubted. 'Perhaps she could not wait to choose.' And he embellished his story even further when he told his wife on the bedshelf (after the children were sleeping), because Takis, having put aside his *philotimo*, would undoubtedly be telling too, and Anastasis was not going to have Takis appear the sharper. When he had finished the story Anastasis's wife had a little fire too, and it was as exciting as the early days, and afterwards she remembered a thing that had puzzled her in the market, a thing that she had not thought about consciously but that now seemed to spring quite clear in the reflection of her husband's story. So eagerly in the dark she whispered her observations also, and they lay for a long time awake, imagining and wondering, and she thought how she would surprise the women at the well next morning when they began their praise of the friendliness and the goodness of the red-haired foreign woman.

By public well and bakehouse and market-stall and work-shop, by coffee-house and barber-shop and tavern, through house servants, labourers, shipwrights, taxi-drivers, and pedlars, the scandalous story filtered through the town, receiving many flourishes and additions in its progress, and even some surprisingly factual confirmations. (Only the sponge-divers turned away when they heard it and lowered their eyes from one another and said nothing.)

By the end of the week various exciting versions had penetrated even the high stone walls of the bourgeoisie, stirring up such thrills and tremors that those who had been invited to the Casopédes' Carnival dance on the Sunday night could scarcely wait, and those who hadn't said they wouldn't go even if they were begged on bended knees to do so.

27

By strict family protocol the dance should have been held in the white villa, since Demetrius was not only the head of the family business but married and a householder in his own right. However, it was the tradition that family parties were always held in the heavy Othonian mansion that had been his place of birth and was now occupied by Uncle Paul and his family. It was the biggest house on the island, and would come to Demetrius and Milly in due course. He had brought her there as a bride while the villa was being completed, and they both detested the place.

Perversely, Kathy loved it. It was a house which, she thought, had suffered a dignified deflowerment, and in any case the violation had been patrician in character and so far back in time that a certain glamour had grown around it. Originally it must, admittedly, have been excessive, in that the German architect who had designed it at the time he came to Greece with the young Prince Otho of Bavaria had incorporated in it the whirling admiration of his discovery of classic Greece as well as his own Bavarian baroque, and his heady ideas of reinterpreting Italian Early Renaissance, but the house had survived his excesses in decoration and adornment and gradually developed a kind of ageing aristocratic purity simply because of its basic harmonies, so he had probably been a good architect after all! There must have been times when the dissolution of floridity had been noisy— when one of the main flat pilasters had cracked away and fallen, for instance—but it was for the most part just something that went on happening, and would go on happening, very slowly and silently. Rain and stain and new coats of whitewash and cement patches were reducing it to a simpler austerity. It had almost grown beautiful.

In any case, it was a splendid house for a party, and aside from its suitability there was another reason for the family's tacit agreement that Milly should not be troubled by arrangements for the dance: nobody considered her capable of conducting such a function, and they were probably right. But any prospect of gaiety pleased her, and the beautiful old native costume she would wear—and had already tried on—certainly disguised her pregnancy better than any of her clever maternity clothes. She loaned Kathy a costume, too—she had a trunk full of them, handed down from Demetrius's mother and grandmother and even great-grandmother.

It was a simple costume, and simply beautiful. There was a striped silk garment like a kimono, worn over many petticoats of silk with hand-made lace and embroidery. One side of the skirt of the kimono was folded back to display the petticoats and tucked in a triangle under a wide sash like an *obi*, tied high at the back. From the loose sleeves lace undersleeves fell to the wrist, and the headscarf was lace also, sewn over taffeta. Milly's kimono was in stripes of blue and grey, and Kathy's darker, black on red. Aliki sewed an extra frill to Kathy's petticoat to make it long enough, and Milly brought from her jewel-box curious old necklaces of gold coins.

'Here, darling, we'll split them. Three for you and three for me.' She slipped them over Kathy's head while Aliki finished arranging the stiff folds of the headscarf and the elaborate knot of the sash, and Kathy looked at her own strange face in the glass, blanched to an ivory tenderness by the ivory lace that confined it, and she lifted one long hand in its foam of embroidery and touched the barbaric blaze of gold upon her breast and she thought: This is the way I was meant to look. This is the way I would have dressed for him on feast days and the days of farewell, standing with the women on the wharf, but standing proudly and not weeping even with the black scarf in my hand, and even when the songs were finished and the boats were only sun-spots far out on the sea and I took off the lace headscarf and tied the black in its place, even then I would not weep because of

168

his pride in me . . . and then she met Aliki's eyes in the mirror and Aliki's eyes had that same devouring, lecherous look that Irini's had had in the market; a long, cold, premonitory shudder rolled through Kathy and her face in the glass nodded foolishly back at her like a paralytic's.

'We are very beautiful, Milly,' she said unsteadily. 'I never realised what beautiful women we are.'

'It is a super rig, isn't it?' Milly pirouetted. 'Although, frankly, I could do without Junior padding it out! But do let's get cracking, darling. I promised Demetrius we'd not be more than half an hour after him, and he has been in *such* a filthy mood all this week . . .' And Milly's eyes, too, met Kathy's in the glass, and faltered, and looked away uneasily. 'Come on, then,' she said. 'All the old crows are itching to see us decked out like this.'

Aliki, who was to help with the serving, attended them across the square to Uncle Paul's house. Most of the houses around were brightly lit, and there were masked figures running everywhere, without any apparent method or objective, and there was music jetting through all the town. The old rank garden was hung with paper lanterns, and over charcoal pits Stamatis and another cripple turned whole sheep on spits. All the doors on the ground floor had been folded back to make a gigantic chessboard of black-and-white marble squares, on which the chosen, licensed by tradition, abandoned themselves to the set moves of Carnival. Many of the younger women wore the native island costume, and for this were permitted to make up their faces also, crudely red and white with black charcoal spots to stimulate moles. Even the glandular children were painted and decked with paper roses and jewellery: the boys wore white pleated fustanellas and pom-pom shoes and red tasselled caps, or baggy trousers of Turkish cut, and blew on hooters, threw paper streamers and handfuls of confetti, shrieked at the tops of their lungs, or pelted up and down the vast expanse of chequered marble with the express intention of bowling over the dancers.

The men did not wear costume. But in their pointed glossy shoes and formal suitings they were gallant and very gay. They

169

danced tirelessly with the painted young women, and attended the seated moustached matrons with little thimble glasses of cherry brandy and strega and crème de menthe and compliments that were consciously daring. Over the black-and-white squares the black-and-white serving women skimmed, crisp in fresh headscarves and aprons, offering trays of meatballs and cheesecakes and stuffed vine leaves, bowls of *zig-zag*, tarts and sweets and pies and pastries. The marble-topped buffets were laden with ranked carafes of wine, bottles of gin and whisky and ouzo and beer: crates more were stacked in reserve in the kitchen passage.

By one of these buffets Demetrius stood like a man caught in the dark mesh of a dream. He had had three whiskies already and was now drinking his fourth. It was good whisky—he had sent it over himself earlier in the day, with the L.P.s and the pick-up—but at the moment the taste of it was less important to him than the fumes that were rising to his head and releasing the terrifying clamp of his thoughts. His eyes never left the dark silk and crimson sash of his grandmother's dress, and the calm ivory face above it that composed itself in the sculpture of ivory lace as purely as the tender kernel of a nut. I am going mad, he thought, thinking in Greek, holding to his language like the last straws of sanity. I must be going mad because seeing her now I cannot believe it in spite of the evidence. He had a distinct sensation of his very existence being undermined in some mysterious manner, of his moral supports falling away one by one. In disbelief he watched her serene progress with Milly across the marble squares, seeing also the seethe and eddy of the currents that whirled around her, the laughter that vilified, the politeness that traduced, the calumny of hands. Milly veered towards him in a pale squeaking of brittle old silk, petticoats foaming, but seeing his face her forehead pleated uneasily and she half waved and made a little mouth, and hurried again after Kathy, who was trailing her laces through an electric crackle of speculation towards Uncle Paul and Aunt Sophia and the reception committee at the foot of the great staircase. The aunts and cousins reached for her and passed her around like a rare doll, stroking her cheeks and her clothes with little yelps of excitement, as though touch might verify her dishonour. The men swarmed, moustaches quivering, hands hot to hold, thighs hot to press. And she smiled at each one of them in turn, and said her stilted little Greek phrases, and was captured and triumphantly borne off by Captain Raftopoulos, the chief of police, whose smirk changed to an expression of careful dignity as he met Demetrius's full, slow, soiled stare. Milly was engulfed by the aunts and the cousins, patting and petting and rearranging her. Demetrius poured another whisky.

He knew that he was getting drunk. Too drunk to attend to the courtesies of the occasion. The painted girls looked longingly in vain. He did not ask them to dance. They consoled themselves with chocolates in the shapes of roses and daisies and the attentions of the civil servants and the bank-tellers and the schoolteachers, who were now twitching with eagerness to cha-cha-cha. Oh, how anxious they were to prove their sophistication, and how pointedly they steered their partners within range of Kathy's vision that she might appreciate their demonstrations. Even the children were affected by the heightened air of excitement: they hurled the tight rolls of their paper streamers with screeching malice, and blew showers of confetti through hideously blaring horns. The pace of drinking speeded up perceptibly: beer disappeared by the caseful and the Turkish-style toilet squats were in such demand that most of the men settled for the garden, where beyond the lanterns there were dark shrubberies and trees. The smell of the roasting sheep was rich and hot, and many corseted ladies, following Kathy's progress from partner to partner, were yet greedily conscious of the sudden flow of gastric juices and dabbed at their dark-downed lips with little lace handkerchiefs.

The old house pressed in on Demetrius like a reproach. From beneath the painted ceilings, the plaster cornices with their proliferation of acanthus leaves, grape clusters, and Byzantine eagles, the generations of family stared down at him censoriously. He felt their disapprobation strongly and suffered under it. He

171

drank more whisky and watched the dark silk and crimson sash go past again. She was smiling a scrupulous smile, but there were white lines about her nostrils and her cheekbones gleamed damply; her partner, who was the headmaster of the primary school, was holding her with all the body surface he could bring to bear. Her smile touched Demetrius in passing, wavered in involuntary relief, and tightened again: she was too proud to appeal.

His cousin Thespina, Paul's youngest daughter, with her strong modest face disguised by paint and charcoal spots, was giggling and waving to him to attract his attention to the Twist she was attempting with the chief clerk at the National Bank. And he wished suddenly, with a dense and powerful atavism, for the wail of the pipes and the clarinet and the lute, and the squeak of the fiddles, and the circle weaving in the old dances, the *tsámikos*, the *kalamatianós*, the butcher's dance, the *syrtos*, the whirling full-blooded dances of Crete and Rhodes, their own island dances, the round dances that he remembered when only the women would dance, hands on hips, heads turned coquettishly, waists swaying, and all the little black feet stamping in imperious command.

'Demetrius?' Milly's voice at his side, frightened, and Milly's English face turned up to him like a little dead flower of a face, crumpled uncertainly in the lace of her headdress. 'Oh, what *is* it? What *is* it, Demetrius?' There were scraps of confetti caught in the lace.

He looked at her slowly with his slow, stained eyes, focusing on the grey-and-blue ribbings of the silk, the gold of his mother's necklaces, the embroidered whorls as delicate as tide-patterns on the sea's floor. A dusky flush rose up from his thick throat and suffused his face.

'Greek is your language now,' he said with soft contempt. 'It is time you began to use it.'

Watching her retreat, with her clumsy pregnant woman's walk and her hand lifted trembling to her mouth, he was overcome by sadness. Well, he would have his sons from her. That much

172

he would have. The whisky was a sadness in his head and in his stomach. An intolerable sadness. And across the chessboard the Red Queen moved lightly to challenge. He had known she would.

'Don't you think it's a little ungenerous to take it out on Milly?' So quiet, contemplative even, taking the whisky he slopped for her, head bent, examining the point of her black slipper emerging from the laces. 'Let's twist again like we did last summer . . .' screamed the record with built-in nostalgia, and the sophisticated obeyed, shrieking their self-consciousness.

He said, with all the steadiness he could maintain: 'Look, that is Thespina. And Calliope over there. There will have to be dowries for them too. And the son of Lazarus must be educated suitably. My cousin Themolina is pregnant. If it is a son that will mean another education. If it is a daughter another dowry and marriage settlement. Dowries and settlements and land and houses and education and investments that the generations may go on and prosper. Don't you understand even yet? That not even asking for it or desiring it, yet it has been given to me to provide the dowries and settlements and land and houses and educations and investments. To squeeze them out of sponges . . .'

'And human lives, incidentally,' she said, still contemplating the tip of her shoe, her face musing, tender and tired above the gold coins and the white and crimson and black, but by him unassailable.

He whispered to her, close to her, shaking, gulping at his drink: 'You are mad. You are deluded. You cannot go on with this. No one understands—no one excepting myself will even try to understand your intoxication with this insane philanthropy. You cannot expect them to understand. For there are barriers in this society too. Just or unjust. But as strong as the barriers of which you once warned me. Do you know what they are saying about you? Here? Tonight?'

'It can't be helped,' she said tiredly, and smiled at him from a very long distance, through a blur of coloured rain. 'I must go to Milly now. I wish . . .' she said, or he thought she said,

173

for her voice too was coming from a very long distance, 'I wish we might have been friends, Demetrius.'

At some time he found himself in the garden, in a hot sickening smell of roasting meat and smoke and charcoal. The Chinese lanterns swelled and swayed and rushed away into pinpoints of jumping light. His Uncle Paul, huge and jolly, was carving at a sheep. The serving women in their glimmering white coifs clustered like gulls around a trestle-table piled with plates and forks and tumblers filled with paper napkins and the great doors of the house were open on a sluice of music and laughter pouring out into the garden. Bodies pouring out to stuff themselves with hot reeking flesh that they might be purified tomorrow. Music twisting down from the sky in many writhing colours. A child with a face smeary with paint thrusting a plate into his hand. The nauseating fat stench of the meat. Then there was no plate and no child and he was sitting among dark and rather glittering leaves, wanting a drink very, very badly . . .

'Don't worry, Milly,' the Red Queen said. 'He's a bit high, that's all. This cold air will sober him up. Leave him here to cool off and you come and eat. Now, *don't*, lovey . . . here, mop up with this. The way I see it, it's absolutely in order to get drunk tonight. An old island tradition, they tell me. Almost obligatory, if I am to judge by some of my partners tonight!'

The crimson sash and the blue receding, swishing away under the lighted dilations of the paper lanterns and disappearing into a blowfly swarm of men. There was a door beyond the darkly glittering leaves, and beyond the door an immense chequerboard of black-and-white squares tilting uncertainly, but the buffet was stable, as it should have been considering its size and weight, and he poured himself another drink under the disapproving eyes of his ancestors, whom he found it impossible to conciliate. They would not understand either, being of a rigid persuasion in matters of morality. It was sad beyond belief that nobody would even try to understand but himself, who could not, would not, believe in spite of the evidence because such a thing was inconceivable. Given a little time he knew he would bring her to reason, or even force her to reason, if necessary, in the old way, his father's and his grandfather's way, and he agreed that it was his duty to do so as her lawful protector in the absence of her husband, her lawful protector by authority and tradition established . . .

A whip, he thought, with a shudder of pleasure, and then the grotesques were hopping and leaping in through the door, also by tradition licensed, eyeless, headless, sexless, voiceless, bizarre beyond nightmare, padded and humped, spawned out of the Carnival music that wailed over the cliffs and cubes of the town, for this one night licensed by tradition to feast and drink anonymously and to frolic in whatever house they chose . . . and then everybody was dancing again and now it was the old music and the old dances, the circles weaving on the black and white, spinning, wilder and wilder and wilder, grotesques, serving women, moustached matrons, painted girls, smeary children, drunken gallants, spinning and spinning . . . yes, and the crimson sash and dark silk spinning too on the arm of a figure exactly of her stature, thin and light even in sheepskins and black hood . . .

The whisky was a slow-burning pain of apprehension in the pit of Demetrius's stomach. He felt a sudden terrible fear of her, and disgust, as though he was harbouring something pestilential. Radiant in his grandmother's silks and laces, she was spinning spinning on the arm of that figure unmistakable in spite of disguise, the two of them spinning out of the circle, spinning across the marble squares, spinning out through the cracked entrance columns, into the shelter of the darkly glittering leaves.

Aliki's nod was like a prearranged signal. Without protest or comment, he followed her along the kitchen passage where the crates of empty bottles were stacked, his feet heavy, difficult to lift and place, not reluctant but lifeless rather, and Aliki led him through the pantry door and out into the garden where he did not really need to go at all because he knew quite well what it was she intended him to see.

28

At some hour in the morning Kathy awoke, knowing that Demetrius was in the room. The thin new rind of moon that had lighted them home from the party had long since set, leaving no gleam of radiance nor afterglow, and she had not left her night lamp burning. She remembered afterwards thinking in that straining minute: This is the darkest night that ever was. Nothing at all was revealed to her intently peering eyes but sparks and coloured ribbons like Carnival leftovers, yet she sensed his soft bulk somewhere between the bed and the door, a solid where there should only have been the empty black air, a warmth where there should have been only the night chill, and after a moment she could hear his breathing, very quick and shallow, held in.

'Yes?' she said, and sat up. 'What is it?' But she whispered in spite of herself, and her heart began to thud in agitation as she got the smell of him—Demetrius's own heavy, sweet, insistent male smell tainted and soured with the smell of whisky.

'I could yell,' she said evenly, in a normal conversational pitch.

'But you won't,' he said. His disembodied voice seemed more strongly accented, and furred with drink, which gave it a strange overtone of sadness, of some deep and terrible regret.

She considered that. He was right, of course. She would not yell. That's clever of him, she acknowledged, on a funny little surge of exhilaration, and quietly drew up her knees and began to slide her legs over the side of the bed. But before her feet touched the floor a wedge of darkness lurched and there was a rushing of warmth and air and his groping hands skimmed her head and reached and found her. His hands were quite cold: he must have been standing in the room already for some time.

It was a queer wrestling match, fought silently, sightlessly, and with ferocity, as if that black room had been preordained as the site for mortal combat long, long ago—he could have built the gimcrack villa for that very purpose—and the appointed hour had struck. But it was of necessity a clumsy business, fought blind like that and under a ban of silence. Neither of them dared to roll or bump and they struggled so close that sometimes their teeth grated together. His hot soft bulk was overpowering, smothering in sheer weight of flesh, and twist and strain as she might, with all her advantage of lightness and quickness, she could not pull up against him and stand on her feet when her quickness and lightness might tell. Her eyes seemed to be exploding with the effort to see, and the backs of her knees, pushed against the bed frame, hurt cruelly. She had never known that there could be such strength in his cushioned hands, which had found her wrists and held them fast. Slowly, panting now, he forced her arms up and over her head and wrenched them back and used his weight to push her down. The bedclothes had tangled around one of her legs and one of his, tying them together. Her nightgown had worked up around her waist, and a hard disc of button—she thought of the blue paisley leaves and could have laughed if she had not been smothering—pressed into her flaming cheek. Her arms, almost torn out of their sockets, were still held stretched behind her head. And at that moment she did not truly know if his intention was to rape her or kill her, nor did it seem to matter very much. She withdrew all resistance to the sobbing mass of flesh pinning her down and went quite limp and let him do what he wanted, which after a moment of suspicion, and still awkwardly trying to pin her arms, he did, quickly and brutally, as if that, after all, was only a formal acknowledgement of victory and not the point of the struggle at all.

Afterwards, still lying on her, he said in his sad, drunk voice: 'If I had realised it was only hot pants bothering you I could have accommodated you long ago. I thought it was idealism.'

'Get out,' she said tranquilly into the hot cave of sweat and

177

soft flannel that was probably his armpit. He moved then, as wearily as an old man, or a gladiator after combat, and she looked at the dim shape of his head above her before she realised that she was seeing it, and that the oblong of window framing it was grey, and that she could make out the objects in the room, even the heavy silk fall of the lovely costume over the chair, even the unmistakable figure of Milly in the doorway with her hands over her mouth, swaying backwards and forwards as if she were drunk too.

'I've packed,' she said, pouring coffee from the silver pot on the sideboard. She held the cup in both hands, perhaps to steady them. She was not wearing the now familiar monkish brown robe, but skirt and shirt and blazer, and she had come into the dining-room carrying a leather satchel, which she had placed on the still unoccupied chair beside her own—Milly's chair.

Aliki and the two little nieces were still rushing about in a whirl of house purification; the scrubbing and the scouring had been going on since dawn, which seemed to have been quite a long time ago now, even the dawn of some other day entirely.

Demetrius (whom Tomás had shaved twice over for Clean Monday, according to custom) did not move, nor even look at her, until the little girls, with a haste almost unseemly, had whisked away all the breakfast things except the cup she still held, and Tomás had obsequiously wished them the formal good wishes for the beginning of Lent and bowed himself out. She put down the cup then and opened the satchel and took out an Ethnos packet and lit a cigarette and waited. In spite of the twice-shaved cheeks and the newly clipped black and silver of his hair, crisp as steel-wool against the frosty muslin of the curtains, he had a swarthy look, and his eyes, finally meeting hers, were soiled still, and even now incredulous.

'There is a steamer at half past two,' he said.

'But I don't intend to leave the island.' Her down-slanting face was very tired and quiet, and veiled by a waver of cigarette smoke.

'You must! Don't you see? How can you stay here now?'

His dusky colour deepened into the grapey look of his older male relatives. Aliki burst in with a bucket and a handful of sponges and began sloshing water over the floor: the little girls tucked their skirts into the legs of their knickers and began to mop furiously. Kathy automatically put her feet up on the rungs of the chair.

'I imagine there are rooms to rent in the port,' she said.

'No!' he said. 'For God's sake!' The little girls crawled around him, leaving an irregular dry island. One of them furtively forefingered off a spot of soap flung accidentally on to the toecap of one of his glossy shoes, around which little rainbow bubbles exploded and vanished.

'Would Milly see me, do you think?'

'No.'

She flicked an ash absently, and then, becoming aware of the activity around her feet, stood up and walked across to the window and leaned on the sill and nipped off a basil leaf and sniffed at it. 'No,' she said. 'Perhaps better not yet.'

He made a little dismissive movement with his hand.

'You don't have to worry about Milly. I will deal with her. But you must go.' He glanced at her. 'Away from here altogether.'

'I can't, Demetrius. That's the truth of it. I can't.' Out in the garden Stamatis limped from the well and sluiced water down the garden path. There was the smell of wet boards in her nostrils, and wet stones and wet earth, and even the basil leaf in her fingers was damp from watering. Monday was obviously going to be as clean as they could possibly make it. But Demetrius did not move from his chair on the only dry patch of floor in the room, and finally Aliki and the girls moved the table back into place, arranged the remaining chairs, flicked dusters, and whirled out again, elaborately oblivious.

'You can make it all right with Milly,' she said. 'Say you were drunk. She knows that, anyway. Say I tempted you. It is the usual thing in these cases, I understand. She will believe you because she has to.' She picked up the satchel. 'I will leave my bags and let you know where to send them. And tell Milly I will see her or not, as she pleases.'

He said in a strangling voice: 'You are insane! I have to *insist* that you leave . . .'

'You can't,' she said tiredly. 'You know that,' and swung the satchel strap over her shoulder and walked out of the room and down the wet hallway with her firm hard stride, and he heard the door open and then close quietly behind her.

It was barely nine o'clock, but the exodus from the port had begun already. In the square every old tourer and sedan was packed and people were still trying to crowd in. They sat on each other's laps or stood on running-boards or straddled the bonnets, men drunk already or perhaps still, women with holiday faces, children in clean clothes: there were kites and baskets and bundles and musical instruments and wicker wine flasks. From the waterfront the living bloodstream of the town poured in one direction, inland, gushed into the square and trickled out along the valley road to the blue village. Those who could not find a place in the cars and preferred not to wait for the next trip set off walking, many of the aged rode donkeys, even the labourers' handcarts were in service, two singing men to each shaft and the carts spilling over with baskets and children.

Outside every bakehouse there were trays of flat elliptical loaves of unleavened bread, outside every grocery store bins of pickles and olives, oblong blocks of pressed sesame-seeds, salted sardines, and pink fish roe in round tins, and soused green peppers. There were still women in clean shapeless cotton dresses and laundered headscarves filling their baskets, while their menfolk emerged from taverns with wicker flagons or filled bottles stoppered with a twist of brown paper, but some of the shops had already closed and where they were still open there was an obvious impatience to terminate the business. Kathy went past to the waterfront, where cigarette boys and peanut-vendors and shoeblacks were crying their wares and their talents, but moving inland from the sea as they plied their traffic. The barber shops were closed, or closing to a brisk harsh sweeping away of hair-clippings and crumpled shaving paper. She walked along beside the salt-trees, walking with a long firm stride that neither hurried nor loitered, and turned round the crumbling town hall (locked and shuttered this morning) to the arches of the public market.

The market was emptying. The stall-holders were covering up their fruit and vegetables with sacks and tarpaulins, the fishmongers shovelling pounded ice into the flat boxes, the old potato woman stacking her baskets. Somewhere a hose hissed, gurgled, and died away to a slow, lazy dripping. All along the arches there was a clanging of metal, as the long, corrugated roller screens clanked down and were fastened by the padlocks through the pavement rings. A young butcher took off his long striped apron and twisted a coloured silk shawl round his neck and put a carnation behind his ear and walked off singing.

Kathy went out along the deserted mole and sat on a bollard. The water was oily and dirty here by the market, with a pointillist stippling of floating fruit, but even in the scum of garbage and vegetable peelings the diving-boats looked gay and spotless in new paint and white canvas weathercloths, with their diving ladders lashed up and the mesh propeller cages looking like outsize kitchen-strainers on the decks. On most craft the reeving-blocks had been carved in the shape of fish or mermaids or dolphins and vividly painted.

The sun was already warm on her hair and face, and after a while she took off her blazer and slid down and leaned her back against the weathered bollard and let the sun and the iodine sea-reek seep into her. There were some gulls resting plump and sleepy-looking out near the breakwater, not even quarrelling this morning, but just rocking peacefully on their own reflections, as if they were taking a holiday too.

Sleepily, she looked back at the emptying town. There were only scattered figures now, hurrying away, the door of a shop closing, shutters folding blankly against the dark squares of windows. Now I am alone, she thought, and the 'o' of the word was a perfectly blank circle that slowly expanded, pushing out on its periphery a scum of words, faces, whispers, thoughts, desires, perplexities, decisions, pushing them out and out and out until even the sound of Milly sobbing blurred indistinctly into a dim and remote whirling as of astral dust and infinity was not cold at all but blessedly warm in the beautiful centre of nothing whatever . . .

. . . The skin of her cheekbones felt tight-stretched and hot and she opened her eyes in the centre of nothing to see Fotis's face suspended quiet and meditative somewhere above her, and the circle rushed into contraction like a tunnel mouth receding from a hurtling express train and she was sitting on the mole with her back slumped against a bollard and Fotis was leaning upon it looking down at her. He was wearing a clean white shirt with the cuffs folded back, a black silk cummerbund wound tightly around his narrow waist over the black pants, there was a scarlet geranium tucked behind his ear and a lazy leakage of smoke from his nostrils.

He handed the cigarette down to her without comment and she drew hard on it and handed it up again, and then he slid swiftly round the bollard and dropped down beside her, squatting easily but balanced lightly forward. Water reflections were caught slipping and sliding under the peak of his cap, and through them the oblique eyes, not grey now, but transparently sea-coloured, examined her carefully. Then he held the cigarette to her mouth again, moving his fingers very gently against her cheek, watching her.

'O.K. Tell me now.'

She touched the sleeve of his shirt and the scarlet geranium. 'How good of you to be so beautiful for me. You are so good to me.'

'O.K. O.K. But you tell me now, Ketty.' Very quiet and deliberate, but the sea-washed eyes with the faintest, deadliest glint in them. 'Tell,' he said.

She straightened her back against the bollard and drew up her knees and clasped her arms around them and looked past him down the mole to the waterfront, where nothing moved except some hens scratching about under the salt-trees and a brown dog chasing its own tail. She blinked a little at the surprising abandonment, the emptiness, the padlocked market, the shuttered shops and public buildings, the houses climbing up the cliffs all closed and blind. It was like a town deserted because of war or pestilence. 'Are we the only ones left?' she asked, and

183

vexatiously she felt tears springing. 'How can I find a room if there is nobody left to ask about one?'

His hand gripped her chin and he jerked her head round to meet his eyes again, and holding her like that he said without any inflection at all: 'If he has been touching you . . . If he has been hurting you . . . one hair . . .'

'No,' she said quickly. 'No, of *course* not.' Trying to laugh and dissemble. A tear dribbled down her hot cheek and childishly she licked it off her lip. For the first time she understood, and with a feeling of astonishment, that Demetrius and Fotis were really of the same race. While she was still floundering in a civilised convention of behaviour and reaction, their minds turned to physical violence as a natural and inevitable consequence of a breach of morality. What Demetrius had really wanted to do was to beat her, and this Fotis understood.

'One hair . . .' he repeated. 'I would kill him, Ketty.' And she saw that this also was a statement of fact, which Demetrius, reciprocally, would understand quite as well as Fotis.

'No, no, no, my darling. It's nothing like that at all. It's just that . . . well, we knew he would find out some time, didn't we? . . . so it isn't anything we didn't expect. He guessed it was you at the dance last night, so of course it is rather awkward now for me to go on staying in the house and . . . well, I just thought the easiest solution all round would be to try to rent a room down here in the port . . .'

He watched her carefully through this, and then, his face troubled, he said: 'I had to come last night. I'm *dying* if I'm not seeing you one day. You know that, Ketty.'

'It's all right. I'm glad. I would have died too if you hadn't come. But now we have to . . . to try to find a room. Because I can't go back there.'

He stood up and leaned on the bollard and examined the town speculatively. Then he laughed, with that quick broken flash of teeth. 'O.K. Come on now.'

It was very strange to walk openly with him, and stranger that the town was so empty. As though we are the last people left in the world, she thought. But in the interior tangle of the back streets and lanes there was a little activity, and even a couple of taverns that were open. One of them was in a small square that she did not remember ever having passed through before. There was a covered well, and a Persian lilac still bare and hung haphazardly with clusters of big brown berries, and the tavern that faced the well was very small and dark, with a ceiling of buckled brown paper from which three coils of sticky fly-paper were suspended and bulging stucco walls washed patchily peacock-green as a background to a series of lithographic prints of the heroes of the War of Independence, each decorated with a laurel wreath containing the dates, 1821-9. Demetrius had instructed her about the heroes and she could name them all, even without studying the Greek characters of their names. The proprietor of the tavern was a thick-set brown and tawny man, pouched and heavy, with a bulb nose like one of the later Rembrandt self-portraits—his face as he moved harvested shadows and highlights as if they had been prepared in oils and were waiting on a palette to be applied in the right places— and he brought them a beaker of wine and a plate of the soused green peppers with a courtesy that had no inquisitiveness in it, and retired again to his newspaper at a deal table set beneath a long shelf of bottles that were very old and dusty and bore, she was surprised to see, some very famous labels.

Fotis said quietly, in explanation: 'This Themistocles is one good man. Was very rich feller once. Everybody was coming here. See those bottles, Ketty? They used to say they were coming from every place in the world. Costing ... I don't know ... one glass out of one of those bottles costing maybe more than one barrel of retzina.'

'What happened?' she whispered. He handed her her glass and she poured the wine on to the stone floor, and the proprietor lifted his rugged head and nodded gravely and approvingly. Fotis did the same and refilled the glasses and touched hers with his own and they drank.

Then he lifted the glass significantly and made a back-jerking

185

movement of his head towards the corner and with it a concealed circling of one hand. 'Locks himself in here. Sometimes one week. Sometimes one month. Drinking plenty, not eating for one month, just drinking and drinking. But one good man, Ketty. Not like other fellers in this town, always . . . always . . .'—he frowned, searching for the word— '. . . you know, talk, talk, talk, all the time like old women.'

'Yes,' she said, thinking how extraordinary it was that under the circumstances she should be so relaxed and happy. Yes, and *safe*, that was it, as though they were truly hidden in this dark cool little room and nobody would ever be able to find them again and there was no need to hurry about anything because the Rembrandt man would bring them beakers of wine and plates of green peppers all day or forever if they chose, and perhaps when the time came to lock himself in for his drinking bout he would lock them in with him and the fierce heroes on the walls, and they would all drink together for a week or a month. And it was so good and beautiful to be able to look at Fotis quite openly, lingering over his hand on the glass and the white cuff turned back over the turn of his slender wrist and the way his shirt bloused balletically out of the swathed cummerbund and the scarlet geranium singing against peacock-green and the rakish tilt to his cap and the rakish slant to his cheekbones, and mentally she put a walnut frame round this portrait her mind had drawn, and she hung it there on the green wall with Karaskaikas and Botsaris and Miaoulis and Thiakos and Kolokotronis and the others.

After the second beaker of wine he said, 'Sit here a minute,' and he went over to the deal table in the corner and talked quietly for a while to the Rembrandt man, who glanced across at her once or twice consideringly, and occasionally nodded his heavy, time stained head.

Then Fotis came back and said: 'You go with him, Ketty. I wait here.'

And she followed the man through the barrels to the back of the tavern and up a steep flight of wooden stairs painted yellow, and beyond a tiny landing there was a room painted peacock-blue instead of peacock-green, with a bamboo ceiling and a bedshelf covered with rag rugs of faded brilliance. The floor was bare planks, scrubbed white and splintery, there were round Turkish tables hooked to the walls and four rush-seated chairs and a carved wooden stool, and a tiny kerosene burner on brown tiles under a white plaster hood which had a frill of flowered cretonne. The two windows looked out on the square with the well and the Persian lilac's branches almost scratched the window-panes, and there was a door in the opposite wall which the Rembrandt man opened courteously to show her a flight of stone stairs that led down to an alley area fronted by a wall without windows. In a shed at the foot of the stairs there was a Turkish-style toilet squat, thickly whitewashed and smelling of creosote, with a ribbed jar of water that was milky with disinfectant and neatly cut squares of newspaper and a tin dipper. It was very clean and the Rembrandt man was obviously very proud of it, and Kathy complimented him and he gave a quick little grateful bow, and then they went upstairs again and through the room and down the yellow ladder and back into the tavern.

There was a litter of broken matchsticks on the table in front of Fotis's hands, and he said diffidently: 'It isn't like the sort of place you always been living in, Ketty, but it's clean and this Themistocles is one very good man. You know. Not talking all the time . . .'

'I think it is the most beautiful room I've ever seen in my life,' she said. 'It's . . . it's . . . just the job!' And then the Rembrandt man joined them and they all sat down together to drink a beaker of wine on the bargain, and after a while everything became weightless; possibly, she thought, because the town had so conveniently emptied itself that day, and she wondered if it could be at all probable that she, Kathy Bassett, was to live in a peacock-blue room with a bamboo ceiling, but it must have been because she was in it and there was the sound of heavy iron bars going up downstairs.

'He's locking himself in now,' Fotis said into her hair. 'He's one good man, Ketty. He won't be worrying you, or talking or anything. Just drinking down there . . .'

Then she was sitting on the bedshelf on a mattress covered with rugs and Fotis was arranging a kilo measure of wine, and glasses, and a plate of olives and cheese and peppers, and a broken loaf of unleavened bread, and two oranges. When all this was arranged to his satisfaction he went to the windows and closed the shutters so that the room was suddenly dark and she could only make him out by his white shirt.

'Why did you do that?' she asked dreamily, not as though it mattered, but because his actions were so deliberate. Perhaps it was part of the plan that she should live from now on in the dark.

The white shirt advanced luminously and Fotis sat down beside her on the mattress and pulled the round table closer and poured wine and lit cigarettes. In the gloom his grey eyes looked almost phosphorescent, and his just-discernible face wore a closed, secret expression.

'Don't laugh, Ketty.'

'No. I won't laugh.'

'See, when one man and one woman get married here they are going together to their house and . . . and, well, it's all closed up like this, see. Windows closed, door closed, everything like this. Just some wine left out, and something to eat. Ketty . . . *Ketty!*' he said, and there was so much anguish in his voice and his groping hands that she almost cried out. 'Ketty, I want it to be like this is *our* house . . . like it was truly ours and we was married . . . and no feller could ever be coming between us ever again.'

30

Themistocles kept his tavern locked not for a week or for a month but for three days, and Fotis came and went by the alley, and for those three days Kathy did not leave her room except to go to the toilet at the foot of the stairs, and once or twice in each day to tiptoe down to the shuttered tavern where, under the cobwebbed ghosts of Mumm and Bollinger and Haig and Courvoisier and Lafite and d'Yquem, her landlord sprawled on a deal table. He progressed from retzina to ouzo to cognac to raki, and sometimes when she went down he was silently toasting the whiskered heroes and sometimes he was sleeping and sometimes he was sobbing into his folded arms, and he never uttered a word, but he never seemed to mind her presence whatever he was doing, so she would put a plate of food down in front of him and if the embers still glowed in the three-legged tin she would take the long-handled copper pot from its hook and measure out water and coffee and sugar, and blow up a few lumps of charcoal to brightness and make the coffee hot and sweet as Fotis had showed her to do the first time, and set that down in front of him too. It was, she felt, the least she could do.

On the way out she would take the plate and coffee-cup from her last visit and wash them at the scullery underneath the yellow stairs and dip a jug of water from the ribbed jar for herself to take upstairs again. She used the water to wash herself and her underclothes every night in an earthenware dish set on the window ledge, and that, for three days, was the extent of her toilet.

Fotis brought provisions—bread and cheese and fish-roe and olives and fruit and *halvah*—and they picnicked at one of the round Turkish tables, sitting cross legged on the floor. When they wanted wine they went down to the tavern and got it, leaving the proper price in drachmas on the counter beside the wicker flask.

She did not send to the villa for her bags, and for those three days it was almost possible to believe that the world was entirely peacock-coloured, green or blue, and its only inhabitants themselves and the excellent landlord. Yet she was attracted to the windows in spite of herself, and, standing back, cautiously static where she could not be seen, she would look down into the little square and watch the women coming and going around the well, and the children playing, and the activity in the surrounding houses, and whenever anybody, by chance or design, looked up at her own windows, she would be seized with a cramp of inexplicable woe. Several times men came to the door of the tavern, and seeing it bolted and the windows shuttered they laughed and went away again. Twice a policeman strolled into the square, and once he stopped and talked with the women by the well for some time, and as he sauntered away, twirling a key-chain, he too looked up casually. Or was it casually? A ripple of stark unreasoning terror went through her.

On the fourth morning she awakened to the sound of a new activity downstairs, and when she had dressed and tiptoed down the yellow ladder she found the doors and windows of the tavern open to the day and her landlord, freshly shaven and wearing a clean white shirt, scrubbing down the table-tops. He greeted her with grave courtesy, as if the last three days had never been at all, and again she was seized by that cramp of woe, of some bitter and irrecoverable loss, although on the face of it there was no reason why she should be in hiding, and in fact had gone into hiding quite fortuitously, nor was there any reason either why she should feel like a fugitive unmasked just because the tavern was open for business again. None the less, she did, and upstairs in the blue room she found herself snivelling because her shirt was grubby and she had no clean one in which to appear.

'Well, then, you damned fool,' she admonished herself aloud, 'do something about it!' So she took paper and an envelope from her satchel and wrote a clear spare note to Demetrius and went out into the square to find a child who would deliver it for her. The women at the well looked curious, certainly, but they returned her greeting eagerly—too eagerly?—and the children plucked around as excitedly as ever, squabbling for the privilege of being her messenger.

Then she walked deliberately down to the waterfront, deliberately giving a pleasant good morning to the faces that were familiar. In a hardware store she bought a basket, and with the same deliberation took her usual course to the market where she shopped at her customary stalls, neither seeking nor avoiding the eyes of the women, and after that she went to the post office where she explained in her clear simple Greek that in future she would collect her mail every day, and was there any now for her? And the clerk explained effusively (coming out from behind the counter to do so) that of course it had been sent up to the house because of course he didn't—hadn't . . . and his eyes were bulging and his moustaches positively quivering, so that again she suddenly found herself outside her defences, and with a terrifyingly raw sense of exposure. Once on the waterfront again, she resisted a mad impulse to bolt for it and went back through the lanes at the same deliberate pace as before and into the square and through the front door of the tavern where a policeman with a blue-and-silver duty armband was sitting quietly and twirling a key-chain.

But it *can't* be against the law, she thought wildly. Even here there couldn't be a law against it. Or could there? Perhaps they put women in the stocks for immorality, or stoned them, or shaved their heads . . . but then hers had been shaved once already, and they might accept that as a sort of payment in advance . . .

Captain Raftopoulos, the duty policeman said, wished to see her at the police station at her convenience, and he said it politely and went away flicking the thin silver chain, and then she was sitting down and Themistocles was pouring a colourless liquid into a tiny glass and putting it into her hand. It exploded inside her throat and went down in flames.

191

'Raki,' he said courteously. 'From Crete.' He inclined his massive head seriously and topped up the glass again.

It seemed to act like molten solder to her collection of unhinged joints, so that after this second glass she was able to stand up almost as well as ever, and even to walk. Which she did, and immediately, before the effect could wear off.

The police station, under a blue-and-white-striped flagpole and a crown picked out in electric bulbs, was another of the concrete Italian buildings, squatting scabrously on the square behind St Stephanos. Captain Raftopoulos kept her waiting fourteen minutes, twenty seconds by the clock in the melancholy chocolate brown ante-room, which also seemed a passageway for a great many policemen who all carried dossier folders or sheafs of paper, and looked, she thought, extremely vicious. She found her mouth setting into a foolish placatory grin, but the solder was still holding and when eventually she was summoned she walked into Captain Raftopoulos's office as though it was no trouble at all.

'Ah, I regret,' he said, bowing her to a chair. 'With excessiveness. The trouble.' He fondled a printed form with one hand and his clipped moustache with the other. He smirked. He was gallant. 'Your residence permit, madame.'

'My *what*?' she said.

'A formality,' said Captain Raftopoulos hastily. 'If you have in your possession the . . . the pass-a-port?'

'Yes,' she said, and rummaged in the satchel for it. But her fingers seemed to have come loose again, and she wished she had had a third raki to fix them properly. Captain Raftopoulos examined her passport as if it were the Dead Sea Scrolls. He was fascinated. His eyebrows flew up in astonishment. His mouth pursed into a wet pink bow, and a slow little hiss emanated from it. 'But, see, it is *already* three months since you entered Greece, madame.' His eyes were wet too, and slippery: they slid over her face and down the front of her shirt.

'I . . . I'm afraid I do not understand.'

'Your application for the residence, it is overdue,' he said primly. 'It is not applied for. But perhaps . . .' He made a little cough. 'Your so admirable brother by marriage did not inform of the necessity?'

'No,' she said, scarcely breathing.

And then Captain Raftopoulos giggled. 'Ah, but there *is* necessity, madame. Under the law of aliens. After three months a permit of residence is obliged. Of necessity.'

'I see,' she said. 'I am sorry. I didn't know. What must I do?'

He spread the printed form on the desk, lovingly, and took a pen from his tunic pocket. Again his eyes slid down the front of her shirt. 'Your name?' he said.

31

'Ketty, Ketty, it's nothing, see? Just the same for everyone. Every feller's got to have a paper.'

'It was the way he acted. It—'

'It's nothing, Ketty.'

'Well, it looks like something to me.' She soaked a wad of cottonwool in the blue alcohol that Themistocles had provided and held it against the bruised grazed patch on Fotis's cheekbone. 'It will sting a minute. I don't expect,' she said, 'that you would care to tell me the truth.'

'I told you, Ketty.'

'You told me you had been in a fight. You didn't tell me why. No, be still while I clean this properly.'

He gave her a rather tight little grin. His eyes were neutral, sombre, and hurt. 'That feller Petros is just liking to be fighting, that's all.'

'He works at the sponge factory, doesn't he? That big, surly man? Big black moustache? Used to be a diver?'

'Sure. O.K. O.K., Ketty, it's all right now.' He pulled her hand away and kissed the palm of it hungrily. 'Ketty,' he said.

'And he was the one who fetched my bags that day, wasn't he? Themistocles said it was somebody from the warehouse.'

'Sure. Now don't you be worrying. No feller in this town is going to be saying anything. Not one word.'

'What *are* they saying, my darling? It's been a week now. Time enough for somebody to be saying something.'

He took her face in his hands and looked at her with a certain grim little air of enjoyment. 'Nobody's going to be saying anything. They know what they'll be getting if they do.'

Kathy sighed and corked the alcohol bottle and put it on the window ledge beside the pile of letters. The top one was addressed in round, neat, sepia writing. She had not opened any of them.

'Do you know what I want?' she said. 'I want a drink. I think I want a number of drinks.'

There were four men in the tavern, divers, but she made herself go in, and she crossed the room and sat at the table under the heroes and waited for Fotis to go around the alley and come into the square from the opposite direction. One of the divers met her eye and said good evening. Then the others said good evening, rather shyly. She felt so grateful she could have cried, and indeed did blink a little mistily as Themistocles brought her wine and a saucer of grilled octopus tentacles and arranged the beaker and the glass and the saucer with his customary care. He always brought only the one glass, and when Fotis would appear in the doorway ten minutes later he would wait with a delicacy that touched her deeply until they had gone through the fiction of greeting and she had invited Fotis to share her table. Only then would he bring the second glass.

Waiting, she nibbled at the rubbery tentacles of the octopus and tried again to summon the sense of irony that was little enough protection to her anxious and vulnerable heart, but better than nothing. Kathy Bassett, stop playing The Scarlet Letter, she admonished herself. It doesn't suit you. Why not the role of eccentric foreigner instead? The whims of foreigners were incalculable, and whose business was it, after all, if a foreign woman had a family squabble with incompatible relatives and marched out in high dudgeon? Ah, but the police captain . . . The slimy, horrible police captain. Hold on, she told herself, hold on now. That permit business probably *was* a formality. Aliens in any country were obliged to have papers and permits. And you are the kind of woman who always gets wobbly knees and a guilty expression just going through the Customs. Oh, but so *slimy!* Tapping with his pen and unbuttoning her shirt with his eyes. *What is the Christian name of your father?* It is Alexander George and I am waiting for a letter from him. Oh God! Why doesn't he write? *What is your business in Greece?* My business is to hold on with what dignity I can muster until that letter arrives. My business is to love one man with all my strength and to send him away from me to the other side of the world where he will die of humiliation and loss . . .

'Good evening,' he said in the doorway, standing there in the oblong of spring gloaming looking at her—always as if he was seeing her for the first time—a thin taut figure in blue jersey and high boots with a livid blaze on one high cheekbone like an eruption of the raging dream that his bones and breath could never quite contain.

32

Then it was another week, and now the shepherds were coming down from the mountains, swarthy men in wide flat hats tied with thongs beneath their chins and soft knee-high boots of goatskin, and the waterfront was a frothing pasture of Easter lambs that were crinkled and still awkward on thin legs, and for identification by the butchers who had bought them, all their fleeces were dyed rose-pink and turquoise-blue and chrome-yellow and carmine and olive-green and viridian. The flocks spread and scattered from the waterfront and up the rocky slopes and mountain gullies, and everywhere there were blobs and clots of grazing colour, and they were attended by children weaving garlands of wildflowers for their necks or making twisting, leading ropes of coloured wool with brilliant pompoms to hang between the lambs' eyes, and the bright air lilted with the tinkling of bells and the plaint of wooden pipes and the voices of children singing.

The nights were fiery, Vulcanic, with great holocausts of pinebrush and charcoal burning on every vacant allotment beneath the huge oil-drums in which the salted beef was stewing to be hung and dried for the long months of seafaring ahead, and around the makeshift vats Bosch-like figures in seaboots circled, stirring at the odorous messes with thick billets of wood, drinking and singing as they worked. By day the women were out in the streets with long-handled brushes and pails of limewash, coating walls and houses and steps and even the cobbles of the streets. Boats were returning to their moorings from the shipyard every day, rank after rank of them spangled in new paint, each rivalling the other in some different juxtaposition of tints or colours, with new flags snapping at mastheads and new white ropes reeved through the coloured blocks and deadeyes in the shapes of fish

197

and birds and sea-sirens and new white weathercloths stiffly lashed above the bulwarks. The labourers sweated with the loading of them—the sacks of round ships' biscuit and flour and macaroni and rice and the drums of petrol and oil and water: and the divers (who allowed nobody but themselves to handle the actual working equipment) went backwards and forwards from the warehouses and the workshops burdened with coils of new air-hose and copper helmets and chestweights and thick boots and patched diving suits.

And every day the town watched, with an interest greatly heightened by all the other seasonal activity, for the appearance of the red-haired Australian woman, who emerged each day on to the waterfront exactly half an hour after the mail steamer from Piraeus had called and threaded her way through the bustle to the market and from the market to the post office, where she waited at the wire window without appearing to notice nudges or grins or exaggerated politeness either, and took her letters, if there were any, with the same courteous word of thanks and put them in her basket and vanished into the lanes again. And that was all the town saw of her or knew of her, although speculation was rife, and the curious or salacious or malicious who decided to use the tavern of Themistocles for their Lenten drinking (and there were quite a few) came away dissatisfied and thwarted, because the door was closed on the peacock-green walls and the whiskered heroes, although Themistocles himself had been seen at the public well on several occasions and was certainly not on one of his usual drinking jags. The diver Fotis had abandoned his usual haunts since that spectacular brush with Petros, but from time to time he was seen entering and leaving his own house, and his children had a cerise-dyed lamb grazing by St George's Chapel, and his wife was certainly making no fuss or accusation, or not that anybody knew about (although the sceptics pointed out that every one of her children was wearing shoes, and that she had paid cash at the grocery store, so perhaps her apparent obliviousness was not quite as stupid as it seemed).

It was not until the Friday of that second week in Lent that

Kathy changed her routine. She was seen to leave the post office and to walk right down the mole in front of the market, and out by the boat moorings where she stayed for some time reading a letter. Twice she folded it and put it in her basket, and twice she stood for a long time staring at the diving-boats, and twice she took the letter out of the basket and read it again, and then she began to come back down the mole again, stepping over the crates and stores and cables, and occasionally she would stop to look more closely at one particular boat as if it interested her more than the others. On this day she did not turn up into the lanes as usual, but walked straight on down the waterfront towards the Casopédes warehouse, and although her back was erect and her head as high as ever, her face wore the most extraordinarily absent and hallucinated expression.

33

'So.' Demetrius's breath expired on a strange little hissing sigh. He closed the office door carefully and stood with his back against it. It was funny, she thought, noting the Irish tweed and the Viyella shirt and the polished shoes and the heavy sad face with that touch of sweetness to the mouth, that she should have this little kick of surprise that he looked so exactly like himself. She had expected that he would have changed in some visible and outward way.

'You don't look very well,' he said softly. 'Not very well at all.'

She made an absent, brushing movement with her hand. 'It doesn't matter.' She set the basket down and stood behind one of the leather chairs, with her hands resting on its back and her head bent. 'How is Milly?' she asked abruptly.

'You didn't come here to talk about Milly.'

'No,' she said. 'But it seems only decent to inquire.'

'Then Milly is perfectly all right. You must take my word for it because it is most unlikely that you will be able to see for yourself.'

'I'm sorry,' she said. 'Poor Milly.'

He let out a puff of laughter. 'Don't worry. She has not written any denunciations to your husband, by the way. I dictated the letter myself. The climate is not agreeing with you, Kathy, and since medical facilities here are rather on the primitive side your loving sister-in-law cannot, in the circumstances, permit you to sacrifice your health and run the risk of a nervous breakdown. She has urged her brother to insist on your immediate return.'

Again she made that absent, brushing movement in front of her downcast face. Demetrius examined her with a dark stare.

'Actually I am delighted by your visit. I was beginning to

wonder,' he said. 'I heard that you had made an application for a residence permit.'

'Yes,' she said, and looked up at him. 'Was that your doing?'

'Not exactly. It is quite normal procedure, and I should have attended to it myself in the ordinary way. Will you have a cigarette?' He came across to where she stood behind the chair like a defendant at the bar and offered her his case and lit the cigarette for her. He smelled, as always, of expensive lotions. 'But as things stand, Kathy, I am afraid the ordinary way is out of the question. I think you will find that your application will be refused. Why don't you sit down?'

'Thank you.' She sat politely, like a little girl mindful of her deportment in company. 'Reason? she asked.

'The Aliens Bureau is not obliged to furnish reasons. Your dossier is confidential.'

'Queer,' she said. 'Permits. Dossiers. All that sort of thing. I've never been an alien before. Anywhere.'

'I have,' Demetrius said bleakly, and she looked up on a quick flash of sympathy that was like a salutation.

'Yes,' she said. 'Yes, that's true.' Then she smoothed an eyebrow thoughtfully. 'How long have I got, do you think?'

'Possibly a week. Perhaps a little longer. Bureaucracy. Official channels are as devious here as anywhere else. But your application will be returned from Athens very soon, you will be informed that it has been refused, and after that you will be given three days in which to wind up your . . . *affairs*,' he said savagely. He went to the window and stood there with his back to her. A little girl in a ragged dress staggered past, buckling under the weight of a bright yellow lamb. 'Surely you won't submit to that indignity, will you? Go now. Go before such a thing can happen. God Almighty, Kathy, haven't you any pride?'

'Probably not,' she said. Against the brown faded background of a desert coast the moustached men with folded arms stared out fiercely from behind the weathercloth. She looked from them to the lithograph where the army of divers crawled around on the sea-bed beneath the armada of boats, and from the lithograph to the shark's jaws, and from the shark's jaws to Demetrius's back in the sleek-fitting just-brawny-enough Irish tweed. '*Pride!*' she said on a queer little laugh. 'I came here, Demetrius, to ask a favour.'

He turned from the window then. 'Yes?' His voice carefully neutral.

'I had a letter from my father today,' she said. 'And my father does not see his way clear to sponsor a Greek migrant.' ('Dago' was the word her father had used.) 'Like you,' she said carefully, 'my father believes that these matters should be left to the official organisations that have been set up to deal with them. And for his part he does not believe in or approve of all this migration, anyway. He quotes crime statistics. He says that Greeks won't stay on the land; they all rush off to the cities or the sea.' (The only thing they're good for, her father had said, is running a fish-and-chip shop or selling ice-cream or keeping a greengrocery, or a fishing-boat.) 'He is of pure British stock himself, you see, Demetrius, and that, of course makes a difference. I suppose there are problems and prejudices everywhere, if one is an alien,' she said.

He watched her and said nothing.

'He also considers me to be an impulsive creature and is not prepared to commit himself to expense and enormous responsibility on what may prove to be no more than a romantic whim on my part. I am sure you will agree with him.'

Demetrius smiled with placid sweetness.

'So,' she said, and sat very still, with her face turned directly to him, waiting with a sort of indomitable patience while the seconds ticked into a mounting silence and Demetrius rubbed his fingertips gently over his smooth cheek and looked at her from ancient, impenetrable eyes.

'You have diving-boats,' she said harshly at last.

'I *see,*' he said. His fingers continued to move gently over his cheek as if exploring for some secret spot of tenderness. 'An alternative way out?' he said.

She was motionless and silent, watching him.

'But it is our inviolable policy to refrain from interference in the choosing of diving teams. That is the business of the captains. They are very careful about it, too,' he said. 'Only the best are signed on. Quite naturally, Kathy. Other men's lives may depend on one moment of . . . of cowardice, let us say.'

'He has dived from your boats before. You said so. Therefore he must be one of the best.'

'He may have *been* one of the best.'

'Then he can be again.'

'Can he, Kathy?' Demetrius said slowly, staring at her. 'There is also the psychological factor. Superstition, if you like. The sea is an incorrigible breeder of superstition. No captain will willingly take bad luck aboard. Even the suspicion of bad luck. Your—er—your friend—has a bad smell about him, Kathy. A very bad smell.'

Her face, still turned directly to him, was dead white under the jagged red cap of hair that covered her ears now, and her eyes were like two big burnt holes. 'He will conquer that,' she said. 'I swear it to you. He will conquer even the smell of fear because of me. Because I will be with him waking and sleeping, I will crawl with him along the bottom of the sea, I will be the air that he breathes, I will be his lungs and his eyes and the pump of his heart. I promise you this, Demetrius.'

A slow dark flush rose up from Demetrius's collar. 'In my experience a man who has funked once is a bad risk. He almost never survives another season. There is no second chance in that business. And frankly I doubt whether even the sort of spiritual assistance you offer would be of much practical value in a tight spot.'

'Do it for me, Demetrius. No . . . no, don't do it for me. Do it for the thing itself. Give back just one thing for all you Casopédes have taken, you and your father and your grandfather and that old pirate over there whom you once said had scale. Have scale too. Give back a grain of human dignity. Give one man at least the chance of retrieving the right to live with himself.'

'Even if he has to die to do it?'

'Yes,' she said. 'Even then.'

Demetrius looked incredulously at her still upturned face with the huge burnt eyes, her pestilential face that even now was unassailable, and when he spoke his voice was as thin and forlorn as a cry on the wind.

'Why couldn't it have been me, Kathy?' he said. 'Why *couldn't* it have been me?'

34

In the fourth week of Lent the blessing of the boats began and every day groups of priests in embroidered robes hitched up their skirts and clambered from boat to boat, where on the after deckhouses the divers had improvised altars with tablecloths and handfuls of fresh flowers. Divers' sons, improbably scrubbed, and rigged out as altar boys, carried the tasselled banner of St Stephanos, with the saint painted thin and ascetic on cream silk, and the miraculous ikon encased in hammered gold and hung with scores of amulets—little silver cut-out boats and diving helmets and figures of divers and scraps of sponges and sharks' teeth and dried octopus tentacles.

Each diving team lined up in turn on the scrubbed deckplanks of its own boat, dressed in clean shirts and trousers, bareheaded, solemn, holding their black peaked caps to their breasts, while a priest with an enamelled basin and a sprig of mountain herbs clambered over the equipment with his robe hooked up around his hips, sprinkling with holy water everything in sight. The men were blessed and the sea around them, and the rudders and tillers and windlass-wheels and diving ladders and anchor-bitts and drums and kegs of food, the engines were blessed and ropes, the air-lines and the rubber diving suits, the anchors and the cooking-pots and the stanchions and the scuppers, the gaffs and masts and booms, and when it was all done what holy water was left was emptied into an upturned diving helmet.

On any day by the time the last boats were blessed the first were making their departures.

Kathy watched them, day after day, from the arches outside the market. She felt free to do this because everybody was too caught up in personal emotion, she thought, to even notice her. Personal sadness, she had thought at first, and then had realised that this was perhaps not the word, because although the women wailed and shrieked and beat their breasts and clung sobbing to their men, she wondered how much of it was real and how much a purely formal expression of grief, like ritually removing the white headscarf and tying on the black. So much of their lives was ritual. She thought that they must feel secure in that, knowing the responses, that is, to any given situation—a time to laugh and a time to weep, a time to grieve and a time to refrain from grieving. There was a lot, she felt, to be said for it. The pattern simple and clear from birth-bed to death-bed and nothing to do but scrupulously to follow it. So the women who were weeping today would be laughing tomorrow, packing up their children and their rugs and cooking-tins and setting off for the orange groves and the banks of myrtle to picnic for the whole of the summer, free of their houses, free of their troublesome, gambling, drinking, fighting menfolk, free of further pregnancies for a whole seven months. (It was Fotis who had told her about it, about how it was all those summers of childhood, telling her in great detail, and with that smile on his mouth that was tempered these days by a profound gentleness, as if all the rage and the violence and the desperation and the desire had at last consumed themselves in their own fierceness.)

She wished achingly that she could walk out along the mole and be part of it. In a tangle of baskets and bundles and wine-flasks she recognised the heavy shoulders of a diver who had greeted her one evening in Themistocles's tavern: he was bowed and laughing beneath a swarm of wriggling children. The boy with the hand-me-down moustache looked out embarrassed over his mother's bent and sobbing head. And in one of the dinghies plying ferry from the mole a ferociously swarthy moustached man raised his fist and bellowed like a bull.

But the chanting was in the air and the priests were busy among them with holy water and sprigs of rosemary, and she knew it would not be proper for her to appear among them. The divers, she knew, would be as grave and as diffidently courteous as ever, but the priests and the women would regard

her presence among them as an insult—or worse, as bad luck—
and since it was their day and their right she stayed as still and
as anonymous as she could within the rank fish-smelling shadows
of the arches and tried to make her heart accept that woeful
constriction that was no longer inexplicable, but fearfully defined.
For acceptance, she told herself, was only a matter of rehearsal.
If she watched the boats go every day she would die a little
bit in advance every time and there would be that much less
dying for her to do when the last time came, when exhausts
were slow-thudding from the Casopédes flotilla and the diving-
boat *Agios Nikólas* would be drawn on a short warp, and he
would be there on the crowded mole with the drops of holy water
glistening on his face . . .

Between the two appalling cliffs with their riveted tiers of
blue and white and ochre cubes, eight diving-boats—four blue
with a lime-green trim, three crimson with orange-and-yellow
strakes, and one all-white—ploughed their sharp white furrows
into the yielding sea. The two big two-masted mother ships stayed
out beyond the breakwater, sitting wide and heavy-burdened in
the water like huge sated sea-birds: the diving-boats skimmed
and circled the harbour, slim, brilliant, leanly leaping in
anticipation, and the dinghies were rowing out with the men
standing in them, balanced with their legs astride and their arms
clasped around each other, singing, singing—Christ! perhaps he
would sing too?—as though, after all, this moment they had feared
through all the long winter held some esoteric joy for them that
was only now remembered. Then the church bells began to peal
and crash and the women to shriek and faint, and one by one
the lean curved bows swept in and past on a foam of white—
*John the Pathfinder, Saint George, Poseidon, Gorgon, The Twelve
Apostles, Persephone, Spring of Life, Metamorphosis*—the rigging
strained and the decks canted crazily with the weight of the men
hanging in the shrouds and stays, and on the mole the priests'
mouths opening and closing on a soundless chanting.

She turned into the market then—her eyes bleary, half blind,
into the cool and the dark and the muted colours throbbing through

207

the rock of bells and thud of engines, and square between a mound of early tomatoes and the tilted crates of marrows there was Irini with the limp cotton dress hooked up in front, where her belly stuck out, holding the baby in one arm and with the other hand fidgeting at a wreath of dried vine-leaves. Fecundity garlanded, Kathy thought, and wondered that she had been such barren soil to that same burning seed. But gardens needed placidity to grow, and they had never had that. No temperate zone. Irini provided a climate more equable than she ever could.

She would have moved away and slipped out through the farther arches into the lane beyond (everybody in the market was hushed, looking slyly, expectantly, from her to Irini and back again) but that Irini turned then and saw her. Across the vegetables her eyes in that old young woman's face were blackly craving with the old devouring, lecherous expression. The same soiled white headscarf was draped loosely about her face, and Kathy wondered whether she would exchange it for a black one when Fotis left or whether, the pattern having been disturbed, she would not know how to go on. She could not imagine Irini improvising.

Very carefully, searching for the right tense, she said: 'I shall be going away, Irini. Far away.' But if Irini understood or not she had no way of telling. She stood there hunched forward and sideways a bit with the weight of the silent baby and twirled the vine-leaves nervously around her wrist. It was such a public place, after all, and clearly she did not know what to do. This situation had not been marked out in the pattern at all: no ritual had been prescribed with which to establish either an emotion or an attitude. If I was a woman of her own race, Kathy thought, I expect she would have assumed the appropriate attitude and forced the appropriate emotion without a hesitation. Avenging fury, probably, with hysteria for the onlookers and a knife or vitriol for the proper sense of drama. But how could she cope with this? For I am alien, and of a different class, and in any case strange. Irini was like an actress come on stage to find, most mystifyingly, that the familiar play had been switched for one completely unknown, and none of her lines fitted the situation.

She glanced around the market with such a woebegone expression, hoping, perhaps, to find a prompter among the watching faces who would furnish the cue, and then she looked at Kathy in a pleading way and bobbed her head and smiled apologetically, although her eyes were focused not quite on the foreign woman but just a little to one side of her.

So, because there seemed to be nothing else she could do, Kathy smiled at her in return and hoped she understood and left the market. The women pretending to shop drew back as she passed and one of them spat. It was the first time any of them had gone that far and Kathy was deeply shocked, deeply wounded, and thought sadly that even such a thing as that, repeated often enough, might also be accepted. Yet she was trembling as she passed out into the bell-beaten evening.

There were still tablecloths flapping and fuming in farewell from the houses on the cliffs, although the boats were only bright freckles now against the Anatolian mountains, and when she blinked her eyes they were gone.

There was no way to get from the market to the lane which led back to Themistocles's tavern except by passing along the waterfront for about a hundred yards. That hundred yards had become a terrible ordeal, the more so this evening because it was already the time for promenade, and there were so many extra people about because of the boats leaving. The women in their black scarves were still grouped about, wailing a bit every now and then—an intermittent wailing, though, as if they only remembered occasionally through their chatting what was expected of them. There seemed to be only one who was putting any heart into it. She was in the centre of a group and her headscarf had come off and she was lashing her hair backwards and forwards, so that it seemed as if it was the hair that was screaming. Perhaps, Kathy thought, she was a bride.

She walked as quickly and unobtrusively as she could, sticking to the pavement behind the salt-trees with their tassels and fringes of drying squid and octopus among the hen droppings, and the coffee-tables crowded with men and the amber beads flicking.

The bells had stopped and the silence rolled back, frightening somehow, with only the women's wailing voices threaded by that one shrill, sobbing scream. She wondered how the woman's breath could hold out that long, and whether the lungs of the women as well as the men had been adapted over the generations by the exigencies of the diving profession: did nature, in evolution, distinguish between male and female foetuses in these matters? (And his ribs as frail as a reed basket . . . too frail, surely, for those deep and silent places of the ocean? *Dear God, help me to bear it.*)

Her own lungs were not behaving very well, rasping and tight, and cold, too, as if encased in a subcutaneous film of ice, but she managed to walk quite steadily, and with her head high (an assumption of dignity was so apt to look like defiance in the circumstances, but it was the best she could do: the alternative was to slink, which was not to be thought of), through the blur of faces and the eyes she could only feel, past the bakehouse, a tavern, a barber's shop, a coffee-house, past the trees feathering past one by one (so slowly), when she saw, down by the Twenty-fifth of March statue, and pacing the waterfront towards her, two grey police uniforms.

She panicked then, even knowing that panic was stupid. But then there had been the boats leaving, and running into Irini like that, and the woman spitting at her. And she knew that the two policemen were coming to her. So she ran. She ran to the corner, and bolted up the lane, gasping, sobbing like a mad woman, wild, past caring who saw or what they thought, because she knew then that no rehearsals were going to make her bear it easier, no little deaths help her endure the final death, and she knew only a gluttony for the little bit of life that was left, and if they came to take her away she would fight them and be dragged screaming.

There was a cigarette boy in her path, grinning. Why? she thought, and dodged to the right, and he sidestepped to the left, and she swerved and he swerved, and she remembered doing just that in a London street one day, hurrying from Oxford Circus to lunch with Irwin at L'Etoile, and perhaps the boy was grinning because the situation was ludicrous and he felt foolish too, and then the boy bent down and picked up something while she was still running but not getting anywhere, and the expression on his face had changed completely, although he was still grinning. She scarcely felt the stone when it hit her.

MERMAID SINGING
CHARMIAN CLIFT

In the 1950s Charmian Clift and her husband George Johnston decided to escape the cold and routine of London for the warmth and spontaneity of life on a Greek island.

Far from the tourist trail, Kalymnos was bare, poor and by no means paradise. Yet as the months went by, Clift and her family became part of the small community. Writing with her usual charm and wit, Clift captures the essence of island life with great fondness and insight.

'If you were enchanted with other books of Charmian Clift . . . you will want to read this one too, for it complements and expands the others in her own individual style. Her wit and understanding pepper each episode . . . and make *Mermaid Singing* one of her very best books.'
NINA VALENTINE, *COURIER MAIL*

'Clift is a writer of great beauty with a lyric style of narrative that flows easily and swiftly with a literary force . . .'
VIVE LA VIE

PEEL ME A LOTUS
CHARMIAN CLIFT

In 1954, writers Charmian Clift and George Johnston took their family to live on a small Greek island. *Peel Me a Lotus* is an evocative and warmhearted chronicle of daily life during their island year, with all its high points and plenty of its less-than-romantic moments too. As in all her writing, Charmian Clift has captured the people around her with clarity and humour, whether it be the motley collection of 'foreigners' with their eccentricities, or the curious locals and the objects of their curiosity — her own family.

Peel Me a Lotus is about escapism, about people who have dreamed of islands, and about what happens to them when their dreams come true.

IMAGES IN ASPIC
CHARMIAN CLIFT

In 1964, after fourteen years abroad, Charmian Clift began writing a weekly newspaper column in the women's pages of the *Sydney Morning Herald*. *Images in Aspic* is a selection of these pieces, edited by Clift's husband, George Johnston. It includes Clift's observations on a wide range of subjects, from her first reactions on coming home to reflections on teenagers, the advent of the computer, the view from her window and the Australian addiction to clichés.

As with all Charmian Clift's writing, *Images in Aspic* is written with concern for style, elegance and the choice of the exact word. It will bring back fond memories for Clift devotees and introduce new readers to one of Australia's finest writers.

THE WORLD OF CHARMIAN CLIFT
CHARMIAN CLIFT

Between 1947 and 1964 Charmian Clift won critical acclaim as a novelist and travel writer, with books such as *The Sponge Divers* (written in collaboration with her husband George Johnston), *Mermaid Singing* and *Peel Me A Lotus*. In 1964 her writing took a different turn — she started writing a weekly newspaper column, and her gift of observation, along with her qualities of compassion, honesty and wit, quickly established a wide and devoted following.

Introduced by Rodney Hall, *The World of Charmian Clift* brings together seventy-one of Charmian Clift's outstanding essays, most of which were selected by her before her tragic death in 1969. The majority come from her last two years of writing for the Melbourne *Herald* and the *Sydney Morning Herald*, where her weekly audience numbered a million or more readers.

TROUBLE IN LOTUS LAND
CHARMIAN CLIFT

In late 1964 Charmian Clift was asked to write a weekly column for the *Sydney Morning Herald* Women's Section. Her brief was to give readers 'real writing' and controversial opinions. Of the 240 or so essays that she contributed over the next four and a half years, 107 were collected in the anthologies *Images in Aspic* and *The World of Charmian Clift*.

Edited and introduced by Nadia Wheatley, *Trouble in Lotus Land* is the companion volume to those anthologies and brings together for the first time in book form the remaining essays from 1964 to 1967. Although the quality of these pieces is as outstanding as always, this volume includes Clift's more topical and contentious observations while also opening a window on the turbulent passions of the 1960s.

Trouble in Lotus Land is both informative and a delight to read, and presents some of the lost work of one of Australia's finest and most popular prose writers.

THE SPONGE DIVERS
CHARMIAN CLIFT AND GEORGE JOHNSTON

In the eastern Mediterranean stands the rocky Greek island of Kalymnos, ten miles long by five wide. For some three thousand years its ships have put out to sea. In recent generations the men of Kalymnos have been sponge divers, then somewhere a chemist learned to make synthetic sponge, perhaps not so good as a natural sponge but cheaper. The continuity of three thousand years is broken, a way of life is ending.

The Sponge Divers is the story of people facing this great break in the life of the island, some blindly, some weakly, some with purpose and determination. It is primarily about two of the strong ones: Manoli, captain of a sponging fleet and a fine diver, and Mina, the woman Manoli loves. Together they are the expression of what is timeless in the Greek isles, the eternal struggle with the sea, the hard work, the wine drinking and the zest for life.

THE FAR ROAD
GEORGE JOHNSTON

Imagine the entire population of Melbourne abandoning their homes and taking to the road in flight from the city . . .

This was how the then war correspondent George Johnston described the Sino–Japanese uprising in 1944. From personal experience came his novel, *The Far Road*, a powerful story of war in China.

Amidst a landscape of corpses, two foreign correspondents, the American Bruce Conover and the Australian David Meredith, set out on an assignment into the interior of drought-stricken China. There they find the population in a state of panic — not from the invading Japanese, but from the local officials.

Through Johnston's self-critical and sensitive protagonist, David Meredith, 'hero' of *My Brother Jack*, *Clean Straw for Nothing* and *A Cartload of Clay*, George Johnston exposes the essential self-interest, not only of the role of the war correspondent, but of journalists in general.